ONE EYE OPEN

K.G. LEWIS

To Ashton, for sharing your limitless imagination with me.

VELOX BOOKS
Published by arrangement with the author.

One Eye Open copyright © 2020
by K.G. Lewis.
All Rights Reserved.

Cover art by Mr. Michael Squid.

This book is a work of fiction. People, places, events, and situations are the product of the author's imagination. Any resemblance to actual persons, living or dead, or historical events, is purely coincidental.

No part of this book may be reproduced, stored in a retrieval system, or transmitted by any means without the written permission of the author and publisher.

CONTENTS

Small World _____ 3
Colonized _____ 11
Bohemian Rhapsody _____ 18
Table for Two _____ 30
The Battle for Bagwell Park _____ 42
A Holly Jolly Christmas _____ 54
Weird Wolf _____ 63
Best Path Forward _____ 83
Return Carts Here _____ 87
Say It Sally _____ 95
Water Treatment Plant _____ 109
119 _____ 119
Viral Video _____ 134
One Eye Open _____ 152
Holiday Acres _____ 166
The Sky Is Falling _____ 178

SMALL WORLD

My wife, son, and I ran up to the entrance of the ride right as the young attendant latched the rope to the metal pole, blocking our path.

"Sorry, folks," he said, "The ride's closed for the night."

"Don't you have time for one more group?" I pleaded, looking over at the young couple he had let through a moment before we arrived. "This is our last night here, and we didn't get a chance to ride earlier." I put my hands on my son's shoulders, hoping he would take pity on us and let us through.

The attendant looked at each of us and then sighed, "Go ahead." He nodded towards the entrance as he unlatched the rope.

"Thank you so much," I said, ushering my wife and son before me.

We hurried down the ramp until we caught up to the couple that had entered the ride before us. The young man and woman didn't seem to be in much of a hurry. They took their time walking through the winding queue, stopping every once in a while to make fun of one of the silly graphics that adorned the wall.

I cleared my throat, hoping the teenagers would take the hint to either hurry up or let us pass, but they did neither. What they did do was turn back and look at me then start whispering and giggling to themselves.

Thanks to them, our progress to the loading platform was painfully slow. By the time we were assigned a row to sit in, it was just me, my wife and son, and the couple, riding together in the last boat of the night. Everyone else that was already in line when we started making our way to the loading platform had already boarded the ride several boats ago.

That's weird, I thought. For some reason, the attendant had placed the couple in the front row and us in the last one, leaving the four rows in the middle empty. I thought they were supposed to always fill the rows one after the other in order whenever possible. At least, that was how they did it for every other ride we had gotten on in the park while we were there.

The attendant was probably just trying to be nice. That seemed like the most reasonable explanation for the seating arrangement. Since it was the last boat of the night, maybe the attendant was trying to ensure that we would get to enjoy the ride by placing us as far away from the obnoxious teenagers as possible.

"Are you ready?" I nudged my son, who was already grinning in anticipation of what was to come.

He nodded his head several times in rapid succession, which was a sure sign of his excitement.

As the boat lurched forward, I leaned over and whispered in his ear, "Here we go."

He giggled in response, eager to start his first journey through the *World is Small*, a dated boat ride through the nations of the world as depicted by animatronic children singing a catchy tune in various languages.

When the boat entered the tunnel that led into the ride, I glanced down at my son. He looked up at me. That big grin still plastered across his face. "You're gonna love this ride," I said to him, and then I started to hum along with the music.

Being on the ride brought back memories of when I was a kid. I would have been embarrassed to admit it at the time, but I've always liked it. It was one of my favorites at the park. I couldn't help but smile every time I heard those little animatronic children singing the ride's theme song in all of those different languages. It always made me feel like I was a small part of something bigger.

This is the perfect way to end our trip, I thought.

My son's eyes grew large as the boat entered the vast open space that encapsulated the ride. He dropped the grin from his face and replaced it with a look of awe. All of those animatronic children singing and dancing in the colorful clothing of the countries they represented filled him with a sense of wonder. I probably had a similar look on my face the first time I rode the ride.

I continued to hum along with the music. It was hard not to. The song had a way of infecting you with its peppy message of unity. As we progressed through the ride, I would point out my favorite scenes to my son. He would respond by pointing to the ones he liked.

The couple in the front of the boat didn't seem to be too impressed with the ride. They just sat there, looking around with bored expressions on their faces. If this was their first time on the ride, I could understand how it would feel old and cheesy to them—especially when compared to all of the newer high tech rides in the park.

I put my arm around my son, glad to see that he was enjoying the ride. "Cool, huh?" I asked him.

He nodded in response without looking at me. His eyes were too busy trying to take in everything there was to see on both sides of the boat. It was sensory overload for him, but he seemed to welcome it.

I looked over at my wife and smiled. She was looking down at our son, smiling at the enthusiastic way he pointed and gasped whenever he saw something unexpected.

A second later, the smiles were erased from our faces when the ride came to an abrupt halt, and the lights went out, plunging us into darkness. The sudden silence was unnerving. The only sounds echoing through the closed space was the water lapping against the side of the boat. Nobody moved or said anything for several minutes as we waited for the ride to restart.

"Seriously!" the young woman at the front of the boat called out. "It figures." I could hear her audibly scoff after she said that. "Of all the rides to get stuck on, we get stuck on the stupidest one in the park."

"I thought you said the Country Bear Jamboree was the stupidest," her boyfriend said, responding to her outburst.

"That's not a ride," she snapped back at him.

My son scooted as close to me as he could. I put my arm around him, reassuring him that everything would be okay. "It's probably just some technical difficulties. These old rides break down from time to time." I hoped that was what had happened. A small part of me began to fear that they had shut the ride down for the night, forgetting they still had people inside of it.

I squinted as the young man turned on the flashlight app on his phone and shined it in my face as he was looking around. "Sorry," he apologized and quickly moved the light to the side.

"One last ride." The girl folded her arms across her chest, glaring at her boyfriend in the dim light of his phone.

"It's not my fault it stopped," he replied.

Without warning, the boat suddenly lurched forward, throwing us back against our seats as we made our way along the track.

"Looks like it's starting again," I said, expecting the lights to come on and the music to start playing again, but the ride didn't resume. We were moving through the darkness. The dim illumination from the boy's phone casting long shadows over the motionless little animatronics as we passed swiftly by them.

"What's happening?" my son whispered, keeping his eyes focused on his feet.

He didn't want to look at the robotic children any longer. The darkness cast shadows over their faces, giving them a menacing appearance.

"They must have activated an emergency retrieval system to pull us back to the station. I guess they couldn't get the ride started," I answered.

"I think I got whiplash," the young man said, reaching his hand up and starting to rub his neck.

"You okay?" I leaned down and whispered into my son's ear. I knew the situation was making him nervous, but he was doing his best not to overreact to it.

He nodded.

"How about we stop on our way out and get some ice cream?" my wife suggested.

"I think that sounds like a great idea. What do you think?" I asked my son.

"Can I get hot fudge?" That was his favorite topping.

"Of course you can," my wife answered, "and whip cream if you want it."

I glanced forward as the boat was rounding a curve, but instead of following the track like I expected it to, we suddenly veered in the opposite direction. Our new path was taking us straight into a wall.

"We're gonna crash!" I heard the girl call out as she and her boyfriend raised their arms to protect themselves.

I pulled my son close and braced myself as best as I could, but there was no impact. Right before the boat would have slammed into the wall, a concealed door opened up, which allowed us to continue on our way without slowing down.

"Where are we going?" my wife asked.

"It looks like some sort of maintenance tunnel," I responded after looking at the undecorated concrete walls of the passageway.

"Why aren't there any emergency lights?" she asked.

There were emergency lights. I saw them evenly spaced down the length of the tunnel, but none of them were on. If it weren't for the boy's phone, we'd be entirely in the dark. I didn't mention this to my wife. I didn't want to scare her or my son any more than they already were.

"I want to go home," my son whispered. That was his way of letting me know he couldn't take it any longer. The darkness was finally closing in on him, making him feel claustrophobic.

"We are going to go home," I tried to comfort him. "Once we get off this ride and get you that ice cream, okay."

"Okay."

A few seconds later, the boat was pulled through another set of doors then came to an abrupt halt in the middle of a small room. The boy shined his light around, illuminating hundreds of plastic body parts that were hanging from the walls and ceiling. There were also a couple of workbenches lined with tools and several unidentifiable electronic components. We seemed to have stopped in some sort of animatronic workshop.

"This is creepy," the girl said.

"Don't look," I said to my son. Even though the body parts weren't real, I was afraid the scene might prove to be too much for him.

"What happened to them?" he asked while looking at his shoes.

"It's just where they repair the robots from the ride," I explained even though I wasn't sure that was the real purpose of the room. It looked more like an animatronic slaughterhouse if the condition of the body parts was any indication.

"Maybe we are supposed to get out." The boy stood up and looked back at me. I knew he was hoping I would agree with him, but I didn't say anything. "There has to be another way out of here."

The boy stepped out of the boat and onto the platform. His girlfriend, not wanting to be left alone, was close behind him. If they did happen to find an exit, I would gladly follow them, but until then, I was going to stay where I was.

The pair searched along the wall, moving body parts out of the way as they searched for a door. They didn't seem to be having any luck.

While my family and I were watching the couple, silently hoping they found an exit, there was a loud clatter from the opposite side of the room. Something had fallen and was rolling across the floor, getting closer to us.

The sudden noise caused us to jump and turn towards the sound.

"What the hell was that?" the boy asked, shining his light across the boat.

My son buried his head in my side, not wanting to look. I could feel him trembling.

My wife looked back at me when the object came to a stop a few feet away from her, illuminated by the boy's light. It was the head of one of the animatronic children.

"Oh my god, it blinked!" the girl cried out.

My wife and I were looking at each other when she cried out. Neither of us saw anything. I assumed the girl was in a heightened state of fear and that her mind was just playing tricks on her. It was probably a shadow or a trick of the light playing across the eyes of the animatronic head.

My wife and I looked over at the motionless head then back over at the girl.

"I swear to God, it blinked."

I don't know if she was trying to convince herself or us. She seemed like she was on the verge of having a breakdown. That was something I didn't want my son to see if I could help it.

"Why don't you try calling guest service," I suggested to the boy. "Tell them we are stuck on the ride." I would have done it, but my wife and I left our phones back in our hotel room.

"That's a good idea." The boy turned his attention to the phone as he started to look for the guest service number. "Got it," he said triumphantly then pushed a button on his phone to connect the call.

Before the call could go through, there was a whistling sound. Everything went dark as the phone flew out of the boy's hand. I could hear the screen shatter as it struck the floor several feet away.

The girl screamed.

My son started breathing quickly. I pulled him close and rested my chin on his head, using my embrace to comfort and protect him.

As we sat there huddled together, I could hear the shuffle of feet as someone ran across the far side of the room towards the boat. The first person was quickly followed by a second and then a third. They kept coming. Before long, there were too many to count.

The room suddenly felt crowded. The boat rocked as the unseen group that came into the room used the open rows of seats to cross from one side of the room to the other. My son started to sob.

"Shh," I whispered into his hair. I didn't want to draw attention to ourselves. I didn't know what was going on, but I was sure that it was in our best interest to stay where we were and to be as quiet as possible.

"What the..." The boy was unable to finish his thought as the mob reached him.

The girl's hysterical screams were muffled and then silenced completely.

All of this happened in the blink of an eye. It wasn't hard to imagine what had happened to the couple. Not when I could hear their bodies being dragged across the floor. I didn't know if they were alive or dead. I could only hope the same thing didn't happen to us.

My wife, son, and I sat silently as the mob used the boat to move back to the other side of the room, pulling their heavy burden along with them. I winced every time I heard a thud, knowing it was the sound of one of the teenagers' heads striking the bottom of the boat.

At one point, I felt like I was being watched. I knew that if I reached out with my hand, I would find someone standing on the seat right in front of me. I held my breath and didn't move until I felt the boat sway, signifying the person had walked away.

I don't how much time passed before the lights came on, but it felt like an eternity. The room didn't look as threatening when it was all lit up. I glanced around, looking for any sign of the couple. There was nothing to indicate they had ever been there.

"What the hell just happened?" my wife hissed.

I shook my head to let her know we weren't safe yet and used my eyes to point over at the sign hanging in front of the boat. I wasn't trying to get her to look at the sign. We had already seen it when we first arrived. It was a common sign seen hanging on the walls of most theme park attractions. It said: PLEASE REMAIN SEATED AT ALL TIMES.

What I was trying to get my wife to notice was the small animatronic child standing below and to the side of the sign. It wasn't there when the boat arrived. Given everything that happened, its smile seemed more of a threat than a friendly greeting.

"Oh," my wife said when she saw it.

"Are you ready to get that ice cream?" I asked my son. I was trying to pretend this was all a normal part of the ride.

He nodded his head and wiped his nose with the back of his hand.

"PLEASE REMAIN SEATED," I jumped when the announcer's voice was broadcast into the room, "YOUR RIDE VEHICLE WILL BEGIN MOVING MOMENTARILY."

The boat suddenly started moving backward, throwing the three of us forward. I had to put my hand on the seat in front of me to steady myself. As we left the workshop, I kept my eyes on my son as the doors we exited through began to close in front of us.

"Why did you do that?" I asked after seeing my son raise his hand and wave towards the workshop.

"The robot was waving at me."

I tensed when he said that, but didn't give any other indication of how much that frightened me.

Our boat returned to the ride's original path and continued on its way. The three of us just sat there staring straight ahead, waiting to return to the unloading platform. The song blasting through the speakers didn't sound joyful to me any longer. It now held a sinister undertone I never recognized before.

As the boat entered the exit tunnel filled with all of the numerous signs saying "goodbye" in various languages, I allowed myself to relax. I hadn't realized how long I had been clenching my fists until then. But my relief was short-lived. At the end of the tunnel was an animatronic child, the same child that was in the workshop. It was waving its hand from side to side and holding a sign that read: THE WORLD IS SMALL underneath which was SEE YOU REAL SOON.

My son was pleased when the familiar robot came into view and returned the wave. I was not happy to see it.

I had sat through that ride too many times to count, and there was never an animatronic in the exit tunnel, just the signs. I couldn't help but think of its presence there and the sign it was holding as a threat—a threat to keep our mouths shut.

COLONIZED

"How did he die?" I paused before signing the document, "If you don't mind me asking." They were required by law to inform me of the death of a previous tenant, but they didn't have to tell me how they died.

"Suicide," the complex manager responded.

"How?" The word flew out of my mouth before I could stop it.

The manager fixed me with her eyes for a few moments before responding, "I'm not at liberty to discuss that." It was clear that my question had struck a nerve.

Not wanting to irritate her any further, I signed the rental agreement and slid the paper back towards her along with a check for the deposit. The apartment was too cheap to pass up. I wasn't worried that it might be haunted or anything. I didn't believe in ghosts. I only asked about the previous tenant out of morbid curiosity.

I moved in two days later. That was when I first noticed the strange ant walking along the seam of the counter. As a pest control specialist, I thought I knew every species of ant in the state, but I didn't recognize this one. It was small, even by ant standards, and was a vivid red color, like blood.

I watched as it ran over to the window and escaped outside through a tiny crack in the frame. Even though I was an exterminator, I still had a lot of respect for insects. Just because it was my job to kill them didn't mean I liked it. I knew how important they were to the ecosystem and how the loss of a few select species could mean the end of civilization as we know it. You might think I am exaggerating, but I'm not.

Ants were one of those species. Without them, the animals that relied on them for food would quickly die off. That would affect everything else in the food chain, including us humans. Also, other insect populations, like roaches and termites, would explode if they didn't have to compete with ants for food and habitat.

If I could safely and humanely remove insects from a person's home without having to use a pesticide, I would do it. But their size and numbers make that nearly impossible, especially when it comes to ants. Once they established a nest, there was no telling how big it was. Some species are known to create colonies that could stretch for miles.

I made a mental note to keep my eye open for any signs that the little ant's colony had infiltrated the apartment. I didn't want to spray if I could help it. That shit is dangerous. I already spent a good part of my day around it and would like to avoid it in my home, if possible. Thankfully, there were several other ways I could pest-proof the place before resorting to chemicals. I would start by getting the maintenance man to come out and seal off all of the cracks around the kitchen window.

One ant was not an invasion, but it was a sign that they might be looking to acquire some new real estate, someplace with easy access to food and water. I planned on making sure they chose somewhere else.

The reason I moved into that cheap rundown apartment was that I wasn't very good with money. The truth is, I had a bit of a gambling problem. Not the casino kind of gambling, my problem stemmed from betting on sports games.

I had a great system that worked for a few years, and then I got cocky. I placed a bet on what should have been a sure thing and lost big. Then I started to place bets in desperation, hoping to recoup my losses, but I just dug myself in deeper until I lost everything.

That forced me to live paycheck to paycheck with a good chunk of my income going to pay off my last failed attempt to recapture my winning streak. That is also why I moved. I was trying to delay my next payment to Antonio, the loan shark I owed a large sum of money to for my gambling debts. I was going too low for a little while. I just needed an extra couple of weeks to scrape together the required amount.

A couple of days after I called the office about getting my window repaired, the maintenance man showed up. When he walked into my apartment, he set his toolbox on the floor, opened it, and pulled out a caulking gun. "You're not going to call me every time you find a crack in your apartment, are you?" The tone of his voice conveyed how annoyed he was.

"Excuse me?" I was a little put off by his comment.

"These apartments are old. It doesn't matter how many times I seal the cracks. They always keep opening up. I just hope you aren't one of those people who are going to call me every time you have some minor problem pop up."

"It's the kitchen window," was the only thing I said in response.

He walked into the room and caulked around the entire window frame. I knew it was going to look like shit because of how quickly he finished.

"All done," he said, walking by me to let himself out of the apartment. As he was about to open the front door, he stopped and turned back, eyeing me for a moment before speaking. "You know about the old guy that killed himself in your apartment, right?"

"Yeah," I replied. I figured the maintenance guy was just trying to rattle me.

"Did you hear how he did it?"

I shook my head and glared at him. I didn't try to hide my annoyance.

"He filled the tub with pesticide, the kind that comes in those big gallon jugs you use on your lawn, and then took a bath in it. He used to complain constantly about there being ants in here, but I never found any. Dude was crazy, probably high from all that meth smoke wafting up here from the junkie downstairs."

He was referring to the young lady that lived in the apartment beneath me. I figured she might be an addict based on her pale, gaunt appearance and sunken eyes, but I have my own vices and try not to judge others for theirs.

The maintenance guy had some nerve. I decided I was going to call him every time I had a problem, no matter how small it was. If my toilet made noise, I was going to call him. If my lights flickered, I was going to call him. If my next-door neighbor farted, I was going to call him and complain about the smell.

After the maintenance guy left, I got to thinking about what he said. Why the hell would someone poison themselves like that? You'd have to be insane to sit in a tub full of poison. That made me want to scrub my bathtub, and I probably would have, if I had any cleaning supplies. Instead, I opted to rinse it with hot water a few times.

When I moved into the apartment, I used all of my vacation time so that I could lay low while I saved up enough money to pay off my gambling debt. I thought it was a good plan, but I didn't realize how resourceful Antonio was. The day after my payment was due, there was a knock on my door. There wasn't a peephole or a window I could look out of, so I wasn't able to see who it was before I answered it. I didn't expect them to find me so quickly.

"Hello Steve," Antonio said, "You weren't thinking of trying to skip out on your payment, were you?"

I wasn't afraid of Antonio. He was a scrawny little weasel of a man. The man I feared was the Neanderthal named Roland that stood mutely behind him. Roland was Antonio's enforcer.

"No," I said as Antonio pushed his way past me into my apartment. He was followed by Roland, who shut the door once he was inside. "I had to move. I wasn't making enough to cover rent at my old place and what I owe you."

"That right?" He knew I was lying, "Because it seems to me like you were trying to hide."

"I wasn't…I swear," I pleaded with Antonio. "I just needed a little extra time to get the money together. I was going to pay you."

"I want to believe you…I really do. But I feel like I just can't trust you anymore. If you needed more time, all you had to do was ask, and we could have come to some sort of arrangement." His idea of an arrangement was to add a fee to what I already owed him.

I didn't respond. If I opened my mouth to say anything, it would have just pissed Antonio off even more.

"You're lucky I'm feeling generous. I will give you until this time tomorrow night to come up with the cash," He then started to walk towards the front door. As he walked past Roland, he said, "Show him what will happen if he doesn't have it."

Roland didn't hesitate. He walked right up to me and punched me in the gut. When I clutched my stomach and bent over, he clasped his hands together and slammed them down on my back. Then, when I fell to the floor, he started kicking me.

I curled myself into a ball and let him kick me. If I were to try and run or defend myself, he would only beat me harder.

I didn't hear them leave. My ears were ringing, and my pulse was pounding in my ears. I only knew they were gone because the beating had stopped.

I managed to bring myself to my hands and knees as I struggled to stand. Before I could get my feet under me, my arm gave out, and I was flat on the floor again. Something didn't feel right. I couldn't focus my thoughts, and my heartbeat seemed off. It would be racing one second, and then it would stop for a moment. When that happened, I felt a shooting pain down my left arm.

I clutched my chest, finding it suddenly hard to breathe. *I think I'm having a heart attack! I need to call 911!*

I struggled to get up. I needed to find my phone and call an ambulance. But the pain was overwhelming, and I couldn't orient myself or remember where I put my phone.

As I lay there dying, I remember looking at the floor and seeing a tide of tiny red ants rushing towards me. They were coming out of every available crack and crevice in the floorboards. Even they knew I wasn't going to make it. They'd probably devour half my body before someone came to check on me.

The old guy who committed suicide wasn't lying. The apartment did have an ant problem.

I tried one last time to stand, but it was too much for my body. My head spun, and my vision dimmed before fading to black. The last thing I remember was the feeling of thousands of tiny feet as they marched along my arms and legs and across my face.

I awoke with a jolt, having no idea how long I was out. I was both surprised and thankful I was still alive. When I sat up and leaned against the wall, I expected to be in more pain than I was. The only lasting damage I seemed to have was a strange buzzing noise in my head. It sounded a lot like muted static. I figured that was a sign that I had a concussion.

I tucked my legs underneath me and slid up the wall until I was standing.

I should be dead. I was sure I was having a heart attack when I passed out.

I placed the index and middle fingers of my left hand to the side of my neck to check my pulse. I couldn't find it. I tried the other side of my neck. Still couldn't find it. Then I tried my wrist. No matter where I checked, I could not detect my pulse.

That was when I also realized that I hadn't taken a breath since I woke up. I stood there and counted the seconds while I waited for my lungs to demand I breathe. They never did. I had no heartbeat, and I wasn't breathing. I was dead.

I stumbled into the bathroom and stared at my reflection. I was incredibly pale, and my features were sunken in a bit. As I watched, an ant crawled out of my nose then ran across my cheek and into my ear. Usually, such a thing would have freaked me out, and I would have quickly flicked the insect off, but I had a strange feeling it belonged.

I also had a feeling that I needed to drink some water. This idea did not originate from me. It was relayed to me through minor fluctuations in the background noise buzzing inside my head. I can't really describe it any better than that.

I turned on the faucet, cupped my hands under the flow of water, and proceeded to drink until I felt full.

No longer feeling thirsty, I turned off the faucet and walked out of the bathroom. When I caught sight of the entrance to the kitchen, I suddenly felt hungry.

I walked into the kitchen and opened the cabinet doors. As I scanned the shelves, I could feel what could only be described as another presence in my mind. That is what the static was. There was something in my mind with me, and it was trying to decide what we should eat.

Peanut Butter, that is what it wanted, so I reached out and grabbed the jar.

This part might sound disgusting, but it felt natural to me. Instead of eating the peanut butter with a sandwich or on a cracker, I spooned it into my mouth, holding it on my tongue. A few seconds later, a large mass of ants descended upon it and carried it off in small pieces to feed the rest of the colony. I couldn't see them do this, but I could feel them.

This act felt perfectly natural to me. When the ants moved into my body, they must have somehow connected me to their hive mind. I knew what the colony needed when they needed it. When the impulse to do something came, I didn't hesitate to act. Everything was for the greater good of the colony.

I think I was starting to understand what had happened to the previous tenant. Being a walking ant colony was a bizarre way to live. I wasn't sure I could handle it. If the colony had tried to move into the old guy, that would explain the bizarre way he killed himself. For the time being, I was happy to be alive and was willing to see how this new arrangement would work out.

Out of curiosity, I grabbed a knife from the drawer and sliced a short but deep cut into my wrist. I was not surprised when a river of red ants poured forth from the wound, instead of blood. I watched in amazement as some of the ants used their oversized mandibles to pinch the edges of the wound together while the others secreted a dark substance over the damaged flesh.

A few minutes later, there was a knock at my door. I opened it to find my downstairs neighbor standing in front of my apartment. She was the woman the maintenance man had referred to as the junkie. She looked pale and gaunt, just like me.

Welcome to the colony, I heard her voice in my head. *I'm Abigail.*

I raised my eyebrows in surprise. *I can hear you in my head! Can you hear me? This is so weird.* I projected those thoughts and many more at her before finally realizing I had forgotten to introduce myself. *Sorry, I'm Steve.*

I heard her mental laugh as she smiled at me. *Yes, Steve, I can hear you,* she said, *We all can.*

Is everyone here part of the colony? I thought her comment was referring to everyone who lived in the apartment complex.

She couldn't keep her smile from growing as her laugh echoed through my mind again. *No, just the tenants in this building,* she clarified. *If you ever need to reach one of us, all you have to do is think about us, and we will hear you.*

It felt good to know there were others like me; that I wasn't alone. Then I started to think about the events of the previous night and the threat posed by Antonio and Roland. They would be back just like they promised, and I didn't have their money.

You don't have to worry about them, Abigail read my thoughts. *The colony provides, and the colony protects.* When she spoke, a series of images flashed through my mind. In each one of them, a person was being overrun by millions of ants.

Before I could ask her if the images she showed me were real, she cut me off and repeated what she had just told me, *The colony provides, and the colony protects.*

BOHEMIAN RHAPSODY

"He's waking up," I heard my father say.

I cracked my eyes open, trying to figure out where I was and what was going on, but the light was too bright, forcing me to close them again. When I tried to move my head, a sudden wave of vertigo left me disoriented and nauseous. I reached out to steady myself, but couldn't. My arms were bound to the chair I was sitting in, as were my legs.

"What's going on?" I asked, squinting and blinking until my eyes adjusted to the light. "Where am I?"

As my vision cleared, I saw my parents standing on the other side of the kitchen table, neither of them making a move to help me.

"Why am I tied to the chair?" I asked, looking from my father to my mother.

"It's for your own good," my mother replied. "We're going to save you from a life of sin."

"What?" I was confused. My head felt heavy, and it was hard to focus my thoughts. "Did you drug me?"

The last thing I remember was sitting at the table, eating dinner. I had brought home some take out from that chicken place my parents loved. I was trying to put them in a good mood because I was finally going to tell them that I was gay. *No, I did tell them.* I remembered everything now.

Neither one of them said a word after I declared my sexuality. My father turned to mother, letting the piece of chicken he was holding drop onto his plate. My mother got up, grabbed the pitcher of tea from the refrigerator, added what I thought was some extra sugar, and then refilled my glass.

I took a huge sip of the tea to combat the dryness that was taking over my mouth as the silence between us stretched on. There was something off about the way it tasted.

"You put something in my tea!" I couldn't recall anything after drinking it. "Why?"

"We needed you out of commission while we decided what to do with you," my father said.

"What the fuck are you talking about?" I said, struggling against the bonds that held me.

My mother leaned across the table and slapped me as hard as she could, "You will not use that language in this house."

My eyes began to water. I tried to hold the tears back, but I couldn't.

"Look at you, crying like a little girl," my father mocked me, "You always were a little sissy. I'm not surprised you're a queer."

"Why are you doing this?" I sobbed. I couldn't understand why my parents were acting like this. I knew it would be hard for them to accept that I was gay, but I didn't expect them to tie me the kitchen chair and torture me. The worst-case scenario I had planned for was them kicking me out.

"You brought this on yourself by being a homosexual," my mother said. "Lucky for you, we know how to fix that."

"I don't need to be fixed," I said. "This is who I am. If you can't accept that, I'll leave. Just untie me." I already had a bag packed and ready to go waiting for me in my closet.

All three of us turned our heads towards the front door when someone started knocking.

"HELP!" I started yelling as my father left the kitchen to see who was at the door.

My mother slapped me across the face again, "I've wanted to do that for so long," she spat out the words. "You know, you're father, and I always suspected you liked boys, but we could never prove it. Thanks to your little confession during dinner, now we don't have to."

"HELP!" I kept yelling until my voice was hoarse while my mother mocked and taunted me.

Whoever was at the door didn't seem to care that I was in distress. Between my cries for help, I could hear my father talking to whoever was at the door. He was acting like nothing was going on.

"Are you sure you don't want to join us?" I heard my father ask.

The person at the door mumbled something I couldn't understand.

"Alright, Pastor," my father said, "We'll see you on Sunday and let you know how it went. Thanks for bringing this over on such short notice."

Pastor?

My father shut the front door and walked back into the kitchen with a thick white book in his hand.

"Was that Pastor Reed?" I asked. *Why would a religious man just stand there and ignore my pleas for help?*

"It was," my father said. "He told me to tell you that he is praying for you."

What was that supposed to mean?

"Give me the book," my mother said, reaching out to take the tome from my father.

My mother set the book on the table and began flipping through the stiff yellowed pages, searching for something. The text, from what I could see of it, looked more like artwork than words. The calligraphy was beautiful, and the ink that was used made the pages shine.

"What is that?" I asked. Looking at the pages filled me with warmth.

"This is none of your business," my mother said, lifting the book off of the table so I could no longer see the pages.

An unexpected sadness overcame me when she pulled the book away.

"Here it is," my mother said to my father, pointing to a page in the book, "The Purity Rite."

The Purity Rite, what kind of book was that?

"Do we have everything we need?" My father asked, leaning in close to my mother so he could read the book.

"Let's see," my mother said, running her finger down the page. "It says we need seven white candles, a handful of rose petals, a basin of holy water, salt, and an egg."

"An egg?" my father scoffed.

"That's what it says," she replied.

"What the fuck is going on here!" I yelled, testing the strength of the ropes that were tied around my wrists and ankles, hoping to loosen them enough to pull free. Unfortunately, I wasn't strong enough. All I did was give myself a rope burn.

My parents looked at each other, then over at me.

"What did your mother tell you about that kind of language?" my father said.

"I'm sorry," I blurted out, "I just want to know what's going on." I could feel the tears wanting to pour out of my eyes again, but I held them back. "What's that book?" I looked at my mother then over at my father, "And what is the Purity Rite?"

There was a small part of me that hoped this was all some sort of sick joke, but I knew it wasn't. The crazy gleeful look in my parent's eyes told me that they were seriously committed to whatever they had planned for me.

"We might as well tell him," my mother said. "If it works, he won't remember anything anyway, and if it doesn't work, he'll be dead."

I didn't like the sound of that. I didn't care how many burns I got from rubbing against the ropes. I wasn't going to sit there and let them kill me.

"You're not getting out of those," my father said, walking around the table to stand next to me. "I made sure of that."

I stopped, trying. He was right. There was no way I was going to be able to loosen the knots he had tied.

"Shouldn't I get a say in what happens to me?" Begging and pleading was the only thing I had left. "If you let me leave, you will never see me again. I won't tell anybody about what happened tonight. It will be like I never existed. I swear to God."

"God doesn't listen to people like you," my mother said, walking around the table to stand on the opposite side of me. "But don't you worry, the Lord has provided us with the Book of Virtue so that we may cleanse your soul." My mother set the book on the table in front of me and placed her hand reverently upon it.

"That's insane," I said. I was an atheist. I didn't even believe in God, but I wasn't going to tell them that. When my parents had decided to become religious a few years ago, I thought it would just be a passing fad. I never thought they'd become fanatics.

"Remember Troy Daily?" My mother asked.

"Yeah," I said. Troy was a kid who went to my school before a skateboarding accident turned him into a vegetable and sent him to a mental hospital. It was his parents that had convinced my parents to start attending church with them. "What does he have to do with any of this?"

"It wasn't a skateboarding accident that put him in that hospital," my father said. "His parents tried to save his soul and ensure his place in heaven, but the devil's hold was too great. His mind couldn't handle the glory of God."

"Don't worry," my mother said, placing her hand on my shoulder. "You're not like him. I'm sure we can save you. Troy's folks waited too long to perform the ritual. They should have performed it years ago if you ask me. Your father and I always knew that kid was a bad egg."

"I think we've told him enough," my father said.

"Quite right," my mother agreed. "It's getting late, and we need to get started."

"Where do you want to do this?" my father asked, following my mother into the kitchen as she started gathering the necessary materials for the ritual.

"I thought we could do it right here in the kitchen," she replied.

"Are you sure that's a good idea?"

"What do you mean?" My mother stopped what she was doing to look at my father.

"What if something goes wrong, like with Troy?" he said. "You remember how close the Daily's came to being investigated by child protective services?"

"Good point," my mother replied. "Maybe we should do it in his room. That way, if anything happens, we can stage it to look like an accident before we call anyone."

I couldn't believe what I was hearing. I thought my parent's sudden religious fervor was crazy, but hearing them talk about this ritual was far more insane. I didn't believe in magic any more than I believed in God. But that gave me an idea. Maybe if I played along, I might get them to lower their guard at some point so I could escape.

"Are you going to be able to move him by yourself?" my mother asked, "I don't want you throwing out your back again."

"He's not that heavy," my father replied, grabbing the chair I was sitting in and tilting it back.

I didn't say a word as he dragged me down the hall and into my room.

"Sit tight," my father said, patting his hand against the side of the chair before walking out of the room.

He left me in the center of the room, facing the doorway. Once he walked out of sight, I began to scan my room, looking for anything I could use to help me get out of the chair. I couldn't find anything.

While I waited for my parents to return, I stared at the poster hanging over my bed. Out of all of the posters that adorned my walls, it was my favorite. It was for the band, *Queen*. It featured a phoenix with its wings spread. Below the mythical creature was a prodigious letter Q flanked by two lions. Sitting on top of the letter was a crab while two fairies sat near the bottom, looking up at it. In the center of the Q was an ornate crown. Below all of that was the word *Queen*.

Knowing what I now know about my parents, I was surprised they let me hang it on my wall. I got the poster before I even suspected I was gay and before I even knew anything about the members of the band. I'd be shocked if my parents didn't know the lead singer was gay.

I wouldn't have started listening to the band if it weren't for my parents. They would always listen to the classic rock station when we drove anywhere, and Queen songs were played frequently. I remember the first song of theirs I fell in love with after hearing it for the first time. It was *We Will Rock You*. I heard it one morning while my father was driving me to school. I remember asking him who the band was after the song ended.

He told me the name of the band and then said, "If you like that one, you'll probably love *Another One Bites the Dust*."

How could someone with so much hatred towards me for being gay be a fan of a band like Queen? Unless it wasn't gay people that was the problem. That had to be it. They didn't have a problem with gay people. They just couldn't stand the fact that I was gay. They were being selfish and couldn't bear the thought of people knowing they had created a gay child. The more I thought about it, the more I thought I was right.

I became so mired in my thoughts that I didn't hear my parents until they walked into my room.

"Put everything on the bed," my mother said to my father, pointing at the bed with one hand while cradling the book against her chest with the other.

My father walked in and dropped the box he was carrying on the bed.

"What now?" my father asked, turning to my mother as she opened the book and began reading over the instructions.

"First, we need to use the salt to draw a seven-pointed star on the floor around Lawrence," she replied.

That was the first time I heard her use my name since I woke up tied to the kitchen chair.

"A seven-pointed star? I can draw a five-pointed star pretty easily, but I've never seen one with seven points," My father said, walking over to look at the book over my mother's shoulder.

"Hold this," my mother said, thrusting the book into my father's hands. "I'll do it."

My father and I watched as my mother grabbed two salt containers from the box and began to draw a seven-pointed star around me. While she was on her hands and knees, pouring the salt, I had the overwhelming urge to spit on the back of her head, but I didn't. It would have made me feel better, but only for a moment, and that wasn't worth the slap I would get from my mother in response.

"Done," my mother said as she got to her feet and placed the empty salt containers on my dresser. "Now, we have to place a candle on each of the seven points."

"I can do that," my father said, handing the book back to my mother. "Should I go ahead and light them?" he asked after the candles were in place.

"Not yet," my mother replied. "We have to place the bowl of holy water first."

"Where does that go?" My father lifted the bowl and jug of water out of the box.

"Place it at his feet." My mother pointed to the floor in front of me.

"Are we supposed to bless the water before we put it in the bowl?" My father held the jug of water above the bowl, ready to pour it.

"I don't think it matters...oh shit, we forgot the egg."

"Language, mother," I didn't mean to say it out loud, it just sort of slipped out.

"I bet you think you're funny, don't you?" My mother slammed the book closed with one hand and took a step towards me. When I saw her raise her hand to slap me, I clenched my jaw, bracing myself for the impact.

I wasn't trying to be funny. I just didn't like being held to a different standard than my parents

"Let it go, Jean," my father said, "He's just trying to rile you up. Why don't you go to the kitchen and grab that egg, and I'll bless the water so we can finish this? He won't have such a smart mouth after tonight."

"Don't you have to be a priest to bless water?" I waited until my mother had left the room before I spoke. I wasn't trying to be a smartass. I honestly thought holy water had to be created by a priest.

"If you attended church with us, you'd know the answer to that," my father said, pouring the water into the bowl.

I guess that means you don't need to be a priest to create holy water.

I watched as my father pulled a beaded chain from his pocket. Attached to the end of it was an ornate cross. My first thought was that it was a rosary of some kind, but that didn't make sense. I was sure my parents weren't Catholic. As I thought about it, I realized I didn't even know what denomination their church was. They never mentioned it.

My father placed the cross in the water, dangling the chain over the side of the bowl. I couldn't make out the words he was saying, but they sounded Latin. When he finished speaking, he stood up, lifting the cross out of the bowl by the chain. Then he leaned over me and placed the chain around my neck. The cross was cold and wet against my shirt.

"Every little bit helps," he said, stepping away from me.

"Here's the egg," my mother said when she returned to the bedroom a few moments later. She held the egg out to my father.

"What am I supposed to do with this?" he replied, taking the egg from her hand.

"Put it in the bowl," she pointed.

He bent over the bowl and let the egg roll off of his hand and into the water.

"The last thing we need to do is light the candles," my mother said, "And then we can begin."

My father reached into the box and grabbed the lighter, using it to light the candles. He was careful not to disturb the salt pattern on the floor. After the candles were lit, he tossed the lighter back into the box and went to stand beside my mother.

"Once we say the incantation, we need to prick our fingers and place seven drops of blood in the bowl." My mother reached into the pocket of her pants and pulled out two safety pins, one of which she gave to my father.

"Seven drops total or each?" my father asked.

"Each," she replied.

"Alright, let's do this," my father said.

My mother reached out and grabbed my father's hand, squeezing it as she smiled at him.

I couldn't believe how excited they were. It was pathetic.

I sat there as they recited the words from the book, which sounded like a bunch of gibberish to me. When it was time for them to prick their fingers, my mother went first. If I could have reached the bowl with my foot, I would have knocked it over, but I couldn't. Not with my ankles tied to the chair.

"Something's happening," my father said, backing away from the bowl after adding his drops of blood to it.

I looked down at the bowl, trying to see what my father was seeing. He was right. Something was happening. The egg was absorbing the drops of blood before they could disperse in the water. *That has to be some sort of trick.*

"It's working," my mother said, staring at the bowl in awe.

I need to get out of here. I frantically tried to free myself, rocking the chair from side to side as I struggled against the rope tied to my wrists and ankles. All I managed to do was tip the chair over on its side.

My father took a step towards me, intending to lift me back up, but my mother stopped him with a hand on his arm.

"It doesn't matter now," she said, "Look." She pointed at the egg floating in the bowl. "It's really happening."

I had to lift my head off of the floor so I could see. At first, I couldn't tell what my mother was talking about, but then I saw the cracks. The egg appeared to be hatching.

That's impossible. My mind still clung to the idea that this was all just an elaborate hoax.

When the egg burst open and spilled its contents, my mother gasped, "That's not supposed to happen."

Hundreds of wriggling grey worms had suddenly filled the bowl.

I turned my head away and gagged, not because of the worms. It was the smell that came with them that made me sick to my stomach. It smelled like raw sewage.

"It was supposed to bloom," my mother said, turning to face my father. "That's what Beth said happened when they performed the ritual with Troy."

"Maybe we did something wrong," my father suggested, "Why don't we get a new bowl and try again?"

"That's not going to happen," Someone said from the hallway outside my room.

I didn't recognize the voice of the person who spoke. They had a British accent, and I didn't know anyone from England. I didn't think my parents did either.

"Who the hell are you?" my father said.

I didn't get a good look at the person until he stepped into the room, standing between my parents as he put his arms around their shoulders. He was wearing blue jeans with a white tank top. Around his waist was a studded black belt, a smaller matching band was around his right bicep. I recognized him immediately. *Freddie Mercury?* He looked exactly like he looked the day he performed at Live Aid. Well, almost everything was the same except for his eyes, which were solid black orbs.

"Who am I?" Freddie said, "Don't you recognize a *Killer Queen* when you see one." He looked down at me and smiled.

"Get your hands off of me," my mother yelled, trying to pull away from Freddie, but he just pulled her in closer.

"Oh, how I love *Fat Bottomed Girls*," Freddie said, letting my mother go so he could slap her on the ass.

My mother whirled around, intending to smack him, but she suddenly found herself frozen in place after Freddie snapped his fingers.

My father lunged at Freddie, "What did you do to her?"

"*Don't Stop Me Now*," Freddie said, sidestepping my father's attempt to grab him. Before my father could turn around, a snap of Freddie's fingers rendered him motionless.

I watched from the floor as Freddie walked to the bowl of worms and squatted in front of it. The smell didn't seem to bother him. I cringed when he placed his index finger in the center of the wriggling mass and swirled it around. I watched in amazement as the worms stopped wriggling and became stiff right before they started sprouting flowers.

"That's much better," he said, standing up.

The nasty smell was replaced by an overpowering floral scent that burned my nostrils and forced me to breathe through my mouth. *How did he do that, and what did he do to my parents?*

Freddie cocked his head to the side so that it was on the same level as mine, "It's *A Kind of Magic*," he said, reading my mind. Then he winked at me. "What say we get you off the floor?"

He made a quick gesture with his hand, and the chair I was sitting in returned to its upright position. It happened so quickly that I felt a little dizzy afterward.

"I don't think we need those anymore." Another gesture from his hands and the ropes binding my wrists and ankles fell to the floor.

"Thanks," I said, rubbing my wrists.

"My pleasure," he replied.

"Is this real?" I finally asked after a few moments of awkward silence. "Are you really..?"

"Am I really Freddie Mercury? Is that what you're asking?"

I nodded.

"No, I'm not," Freddie sighed, "When people summon me with these rituals, I have to take a form that's relevant to the situation. For example, when the Daily's summoned me, I took the form of Amanda Potter."

I knew who Amanda Potter was. She used to go to school with Troy and me, but she committed suicide several months before Troy's alleged accident.

"Why her?" I asked.

"Because Troy was the reason she killed herself. He raped her and left her pregnant and then turned the school against her."

I had heard the rumors circulating about her, but I didn't know Troy was the one responsible for them.

"He got what was coming to him," Freddie said, smiling, "He's *Radio Ga Ga* now." He pointed his finger at the side of his head and twirled his finger to indicate that Troy was crazy.

"I thought the ritual was to save people. That's what my parents thought."

I looked over at them to see that they were both looking over at Freddie and me. The rest of their bodies were frozen, but they could still move their eyes.

"That's what most people think, but they're wrong. The Purity rite doesn't purify anything. It's a judgment, a measure of one's purity in the eyes of God. All who take part in the ritual are judged. Your parents tried to *Play the Game* without knowing the rules, and now it's time for the *Hammer to Fall*."

"What does that mean?"

"It means they've been judged unfavorably, and I must pass sentence on them," As Freddie spoke, he walked around them, running his hand along my father's back before moving over to my mother and doing the same thing. "They aren't good people. They have twisted that *Crazy Little Thing Called Love* into something perverse and unrecognizable. They were never going to accept you. This probably won't come as a surprise to you, but your father was hoping the ritual would kill you."

"That doesn't surprise me," I said, standing up. The sudden change in elevation after sitting for so long made me lightheaded. "What about me? Have I been judged?" I asked after my head cleared.

"You have, and you're free to go *Spread Your Wings*," he spread his arms.

"So all of that talk about homosexuality being a sin is a lie?" I asked.

"Of course it's a lie," he replied, lowering one of his arms while pointing at the ceiling with his other hand. "God doesn't care who you love. The Almighty just wants you to find *Somebody to Love*. Gender is only important for procreation."

That made sense to me. Why would a celestial entity care so much about who we love?

"What happens now?" I asked. I felt awkward standing there, not knowing what to do with myself.

"You're going to have to figure that out on your own, but I feel it's only fair to warn you that once I'm done with your parents, the authorities will be looking for you." Freddie moved to stand next to my mother, placing his arm around her shoulders.

"Why would they be looking for me?"

"Who do you think they are going to blame when they find their bodies?" He ran the back of his hand down my mother's cheek. "You can stick around and watch if you want."

I wasn't sure that my parents needed to die, but I wasn't going to argue with Freddie. I was content to leave with my own life.

"No thanks. I think I'll leave," I said, walking out of the room.

"Hey, kid," Freddie called out as I stepped into the hallway.

I turned around.

"*Keep Yourself Alive*," he said, tossing me my father's wallet and car keys, "And thanks for this," he gestured at his body. "I haven't had this much fun in centuries."

I stared at him for what felt like an eternity. I had a million questions I wanted to ask him, but I wasn't sure I wanted to hear the answers to any of them.

"Better run along now," he said, breaking the silence and motioning for me to leave. "*The Show Must Go On.*"

TABLE FOR TWO

The doorman held the door open for Tom and Diane Donnelly as they left their high-rise apartment home for an evening out on the town.

"Have a good evening, Mr. and Mrs. Donnelly," the doorman smiled as they walked out onto the busy street.

The couple ignored his friendly remark, like they always did, and walked up to the waiting cab.

"Assholes," The doorman muttered under his breath.

"I'm sorry, did you say something?" Mr. Donnelly turned and snapped at the doorman.

You heard me, the doorman thought, but he couldn't say that. Instead, he lied and said, "Looks like snow." His smile never faltered.

He hated the Donnellys. Of all the residents in the building, they were the worst. They never tipped and rarely spoke to him. When they did find a reason to talk to him, it was usually to bark a command or to complain about something.

"Yes," Mr. Donnelly said, glancing at the dark clouds in the sky as he opened the back door of the cab, "It just might."

He held the door open for his wife then climbed in behind her.

"Where to?" The cab driver asked with a thick foreign accent.

"Uptown," Mr. Donnelly responded.

"Certainly," The driver smiled at them through the rearview mirror. "Would you like to hear some music?" He asked, trying to make his passengers feel comfortable.

"No, I wouldn't. I'm not interested in hearing your music," Mr. Donnelly barked at the driver.

"My apologies sir, I just thought you or the lovely lady would…"

Mr. Donnelly cut him off before he could finish, "What I would like is for you to stop talking and drive....and keep your eyes off my wife."

The cab driver drove the couple uptown and didn't say a word until they arrived at their stop.

"That will be $7.85," The driver said, stopping the meter.

Mr. Donnelly pulled out his wallet and counted out eight one-dollar bills and handed them to the driver who accepted them without saying a word and put them in his collection bag.

"Keep the change," Mr. Donnelly said as he got out of the cab. "I don't like having loose change in my pocket.

"Thank..." Mr. Donnelly slammed the door shut before the driver could finish.

The driver pulled away as Tom and Diane walked up the block to their destination, a four-star French restaurant named Dufour's.

"Was that not the ugliest man you've ever seen?" Diane asked her husband as they walked.

"Who? The cab driver?" Tom responded. "He certainly wasn't handsome, but I've seen uglier. Remember that homeless man in the park? That guy was ugly."

"Yeah, he was." She remembered the homeless man and the collection of warts that covered his face. "But he wasn't ugly in a creepy way like the cab driver. He was so pale and thin, and did you see his teeth when he smiled? They looked like horse teeth. They were so long and blocky." She shuddered at the thought of him. "He looked like he was ill. You don't think he was contagious, do you?"

"I doubt it," Tom answered, "He is probably just poor. Lots of poor people look malnourished like that."

Tom and Diane were greeted at the entrance of Dufour's by an usher that held the door open for them. They walked into the restaurant and up to the hostess.

"Reservation for Donnelly," Tom said before the hostess could greet them.

"Donnelly," The hostess repeated as she ran her finger down the list of names in her reservation book. "I'm sorry, but I don't see your name on the list."

"What do you mean you don't see my name on the list? I made the reservation two weeks ago." Tom's raised voice caused a few diners to look towards them.

"I've looked twice. There is no Donnelly listed here for this evening. You can see for yourself," she offered, turning the book around so Tom could see it.

"I don't care if I am on your list or not. I made a reservation for tonight, and you are going to seat me." Tom declared.

A tall man in a black tuxedo quickly walked up behind the hostess. He used his fingers to flatten out his mustache before speaking. "What seems to be the problem, sir?"

"The problem is I made a reservation for tonight, and this young lady tells me I'm not on the list." Tom pointed at the hostess.

"What name is the reservation under?"

"Donnelly,"

The man ran his finger down the page, "I'm sorry, sir, but your name is not on the list for tonight. Are you sure it was for this evening?"

"I'm positive," Tom said through gritted teeth.

The man flipped through the pages of the reservation book. "Aha," He declared. "It would appear that your reservation is for next Friday night."

"I didn't make it for next Friday. I specifically said this Friday when I called and made the reservation."

"I apologize for the mix-up, sir, but my hands are tied. I'm completely booked this evening. If you wouldn't mind coming back in an hour, I might be able to seat you then."

"Might!" Tom yelled, "You might be able to find me a table! This is bullshit!"

The clatter of utensils on plates and the murmur of conversations coming from the dining room came to an abrupt stop as people took notice of the confrontation at the hostess's podium.

"Tom, please?" Diane whispered in his ear, finally breaking her silence. "We'll find somewhere else to eat." She hated it when he let his temper slip in public, especially when he felt the need to resort to such colorful language. It was embarrassing.

"I thought you wanted to eat here," He turned towards his wife, an annoyed look on his face.

"I did, but not like this. Let's just go somewhere else." She tilted her head and gave Tom her best doe-eyed look to defuse his temper. A look Tom had not been able to resist in the twenty years they had been married.

Tom sighed, "Alright, let's go." He motioned for his wife to lead the way and followed behind her. As he walked out, he stopped in the doorway and turned back to address the hostess, and the man he assumed was the manager, "My reservation better still be there when I return next Friday."

"I will see to it personally, sir," The manager smiled, thankful that the ordeal was over.

Tom and Diane walked up the street, neither one sure of where they should go.

"This is your night, where would you like to eat?" Tom asked Diane.

"I'm not sure. We've eaten at every restaurant in town. I want something new, something different."

"There's a McDonald's around the block," Tom joked.

"Haha. Very funny. You can eat there if you like. I know how much you love to mingle with the commoners." She joked back.

"I bet we'd get better service than the place we just left."

Diane didn't respond. Something had caught her attention. Tom had to stop and double back once he realized his wife had stopped walking.

"What do you suppose is down there?" She nodded towards the narrow, dimly lit cobblestone street wedged between two buildings. She could see the signs of several shops, but couldn't make out the names.

"I have no idea. I've never seen this place before. Of all the times we've walked this street, this is the first time I've seen of it, and I would've missed it if you hadn't pointed it out."

"It looks rather quaint, doesn't it? Like something out of the early 1900s." She reached out and grabbed Tom's hand and started to lead him down the street. "Let's go have a look."

They walked down the empty street, looking into the windows of the shops they passed. The first one they came to was a book store with a window display filled with books. *How to Get Away with Murder, The Art of Death, A Clean Kill,* Tom read the titles to himself as they passed by.

The next shop was a tailor and a launderer. The one after that was a combination of a sporting goods shop and hardware store. At least that's what Tom assumed as he viewed the collection of tools and weapons displayed in the window.

What an odd assortment of shops, Tom thought.

"Look! A restaurant," Diane pointed as she pulled Tom towards the open door. "Do you smell that?" She took a deep breath, inhaling the aroma, "It smells so good."

"I thought you wanted to look inside one of the shops."

"I did until I got a whiff of whatever they are cooking in there. I didn't realize how hungry I was. We can look after we eat."

"You're the boss," Tom said, following her into the restaurant.

He had to admit the smell permeating the place was mouth-watering. The image of a large steak, cooked over an open flame while the fat dripped off of it and sizzled in the heat, filled his mind. His stomach grumbled in anticipation of the meal to come.

"Welcome to Pickman's." A tall, thin, man with pale skin greeted them near the door. He was wearing a large white apron over a white button-up shirt with a black bow tie fastened around his neck.

"Table for two?" He inquired of the couple.

"Yes," Diane answered.

"Right this way." He led Tom and Diane across the hardwood floor to a candlelit table in the back corner. He placed two menus on the table and waited for his guests to sit down.

Tom pulled out a chair for Diane then sat down himself. He glanced around the small dining area. There was only one other person in the restaurant, a man sitting alone across the room from them. The man seemed familiar, but Tom couldn't make out his features very well in the dim light.

"Can I get you something to drink?" The host was also their waiter.

"Bring us a bottle of your finest," Tom said.

"Certainly, sir," The waiter said with an amused look on his face as he turned and walked off.

"What's up with him?" Diane asked as she watched the waiter walk into the kitchen.

"Who?" Tom was distracted, "The waiter?"

"Yes, the waiter," Diane's voice was tinged with annoyance. "Didn't you see the way he smiled when he took our drink order? It was like he was laughing at us."

"Sorry, I guess I missed that."

"Obviously," Diane sighed.

Tom looked at Diane and decided to try and change the subject. She was visibly annoyed, and he didn't want to make the situation worse. "Does he look familiar to you?" He nodded towards the man across the room.

She rolled her eyes then turned to look at the man, "I don't know, maybe. Why does it matter?"

"I know I've seen him before, and it bugs me that I can't remember where." Tom suddenly stood up.

"Where are you going?" Diane asked.

"To the restroom."

Tom walked across the dining room towards a narrow hallway in the corner where he assumed the men's room was. His path brought him past the lone diner's table where he paused for a moment, trying to get a look at the man's face.

Sensing he was not alone, the man looked up to find Tom staring at him. As their eyes met, the two men recognized each other. "Can I help you?" The cab driver asked. "If you are looking for a ride home, I regret to inform you that I am off duty for the night."

"No," Tom said, "I was just going to the restroom and didn't expect to see you sitting here." Tom continued to linger at the man's table, staring at him. He was trying to make sense of what he was seeing. The man no longer looked sickly and pale. He looked healthy.

Must be the light, Tom mused.

"I must confess to being surprised myself. I certainly did not expect to see you here. " The cab driver speared a piece of meat with his fork and held it up, "Pickman's is nothing like Dufour's." The comment sounded more like a warning than an endorsement.

"If it tastes as good as it smells, I expect it will be better," Tom said.

"Oh, I can guarantee that once you've had Pickman's, you won't want anything else."

Tom stood there for a moment, watching as the man returned to his meal. When the silence between them started to become awkward, he backed away from the table and returned to his.

"I thought you were going to the restroom," Diane said as Tom sat down. She had watched him walk over and talk to the man then return.

"That was just an excuse so I could get a better look at him." Tom nodded towards the cab driver.

"And?" Diane asked. When Tom didn't immediately respond, she clarified her question, "Do you know him?"

"It's the cab driver," He replied, "The one that dropped us off in front of Dufour's."

Diane turned and stared across the room at him, "That's the cab driver? He looks so different." Her voice was loud enough to carry across the room.

Before Tom could reply, the waiter returned and set two wine glasses on the table, one in front of each of them. Then he pulled the cork out of the bottle he was holding and poured a dark burgundy liquid into the glasses.

Tom picked up his glass and sipped the thick liquid. He puckered his lips at the unexpected saltiness of his drink.

"Oh, that's awful," Diane said with a grimace.

"What kind of wine is this?" Tom held his glass out to the waiter.

"It's a hybrid red wine," The waiter said, emphasizing the word red.

Tom had heard of hybrid wines, but the idea of wine mixed with other types of alcohol disgusted him. Now that he had gotten his first taste of the salty and metallic mixture, it had confirmed his suspicions. It was disgusting, and he would never order a hybrid wine again.

"I can't believe people drink that." Tom's severe dislike for the drink was evident on his face.

The waiter smiled, showing his teeth. They looked unnaturally long, yet they were familiar. Tom had seen teeth like that before. He glanced across the room as he recalled the conversation he had with his wife when they got out of the cab earlier, the one where they discussed the cab driver's large horse-like teeth.

"Do you have anything else to drink?" Tom asked.

"Yes, but I am afraid you will find it equally displeasing," The waiter continued to smile as he spoke, "At least until you've eaten something."

"Can we just get two glasses of water instead?"

"Of course, sir," The waiter removed the wine glasses and returned to the kitchen.

"That was the worst wine I have ever tasted," Diane remarked once the waiter had walked away. "It was so salty and metallic. Why would someone mix perfectly good wine with something else?" She rested her forearms on the table and leaned forward as she whispered, "Honestly, I thought I might have cut my lip on the glass because it tasted a little like blood."

Now that he thought about it, he agreed, "Yeah, it really did."

The waiter returned and place two glasses of ice water on the table. Tom and Diane both picked up their glasses and took a sip, trying to wash the aftertaste of the wine out of their mouths.

"Are you ready to order?" The waiter asked.

"Not quite," Tom replied, "I haven't had a chance to look at the menu yet."

"Do you have anything besides entrees?" Diane asked, not bothering to look up as she looked over her menu. "I don't see any soups or salads…and is long pork the only protein you have.?"

"All that is listed is all that we serve."

"Why is that?" Tom looked up at the waiter, puzzled. "I would think more options would bring in more diners." He looked around the empty dining room.

"We are a small establishment that caters to a select clientele."

Tom picked up his menu and quickly scanned the list of entrees. "I'm not that fond of pork, but if that is what I smell coming from your kitchen, I'm willing to give it another try."

The waiter smirked at Tom's comment, "I'll give you a few moments to make your selection." He then walked across the room to the cab driver's table.

"He gives me the creeps," Diane whispered, "The way he smiles…and those teeth? What is up with those teeth? I bet he and the cab driver have the same dentist."

"We can leave if you want to," Tom offered.

"No, it's okay." She waved the idea off. "I'm starving and don't feel like trying to find another restaurant. Plus, whatever they are cooking back there smells so good."

"I agree."

"You need to hurry up and pick something so we can order."

Tom scanned the menu, trying to decide what to order. Everything listed sounded appetizing to his hungry stomach, and the aroma of the place wasn't making it easy to think. He read the menu a dozen times before he was able to make up his mind.

Tom looked up and waved the waiter back to the table. The waiter raised his finger to indicate he would be over in a minute.

The gesture annoyed Tom, as did the way the two men smiled at each other while looking over at him. He couldn't help but feel like they were sharing a private joke, one where he and Diane were the punch line.

"What can I get you, folks?" The waiter asked once he finally returned.

"You go first," Tom nodded at Diane.

"I'll have the fillet," Diane told the waiter while handing him her menu.

"And for you, sir?"

"I'll have the ribs."

"Excellent choices," The waiter proclaimed as he took Tom's menu. "Is there anything else I can get you while you wait?"

Tom looked over at Diane, who was shaking her head. "I think we're good," he replied.

"Very well," The waiter said, "Your food will be out shortly." Then he turned and walked off towards the kitchen.

Ten minutes later, the waiter returned, carrying two large plates, one in each hand. He placed the first plate in front of Diane and the other one in front of Tom. He then reached into his apron and pulled out two rolled sets of silverware and set them next to the plates.

"Enjoy," He said with a smile and then walked away.

Tom leaned over his plate and took a deep breath inhaling the aroma of the ribs. He looked over at Diane, who had begun to cut her fillet into little pieces. She liked to cut her meat before she ate it, whereas Tom preferred to cut off pieces as he ate.

He grabbed one of the ribs and pulled it away from the rest of the rack, biting off a chunk. The meat was so tender and juicy and seasoned perfectly. He took another bite, then another. In a matter of seconds, he had picked the bone clean and was sucking the greasy residue off of it.

"Tom!" Diane chided. He didn't normally eat so noisily. The slurping sound was irritating her, more so than it usually would.

Tom looked down at the cleaned bone and slowly set it down on his plate. "Sorry," He apologized. "I didn't realize I was making so much noise." He pulled another rib off the rack and took a bite out of it. "These are the best ribs I have ever eaten," He said around a mouthful of meat.

"I can tell, but that doesn't mean you have to eat them like a caveman."

Diane was also enjoying her dinner, more than she ever thought possible. That is why she was cutting her fillet into small pieces and savoring every bite like it was a sip of fine wine. She didn't see how Tom could be enjoying his meal the way he was inhaling it.

Tom continued to devour his ribs, trying to be quiet about it. As he ate, he watched Diane daintily cut a small slice off her fillet and put it in her mouth. Watching her was annoying. It was like watching a bird eat a bowl of seeds, one seed at a time. He could have devoured her entire steak in no time. The way she was eating, it would take her all night.

"Something wrong?" Diane asked, wondering why her husband was glaring at her.

"No, just wondering if you liked your dinner."

"Yes, it's delicious. I dare say it might be the finest cut of meat I have ever had, but I don't think it is as good as your ribs," she said, pointing at his plate with the fork she was holding.

"Why do you say that?" he asked, pulling a chunk of meat off the rib he was holding and popping it into his mouth. He smacked his lips as he chewed.

Diane glared back at Tom. The answer to his question would be apparent to him if he could watch himself eat.

"Why are you looking at me like that?" He narrowed his eyes at Diane.

"If you could see yourself, you wouldn't have to ask." She cut a small piece of meat from her steak and speared it with her fork.

Tom looked down at his plate of half-eaten ribs and then at his grease-covered palms before returning his disdainful gaze to Diane. "Are you calling me a pig?"

"I'm not calling you anything, but it wouldn't hurt to chew with your mouth closed and use your napkin every once in a while," She pointed at the folded up piece of cloth sitting on the table in front of him.

"Excuse me for actually enjoying my food."

Tom's raised voice got the attention of the waiter who was sitting in the corner rolling silverware. He looked over at the couple, a smile slowly creasing his cheeks. *It won't be long now*, he thought to himself.

"At least it doesn't take me an hour to eat," Tom continued, his voice drowning out all other sounds. "Daintily cutting your steak into teeny tiny pieces." He made a cutting motion with the rib he was holding. "Your food will be cold before you've eaten half of it."

Diane clenched the knife and fork she held in her hands, her knuckles white from the intensity of her grip, "What the hell is your problem?" She hissed as she rested her arms on the table and leaned towards Tom.

"My problem?" He scoffed, "You're the one who started this." He jabbed the rib at her.

"I was just trying to get you to show some manners. In the twenty years that we've been together, I have never seen you act like this. It is embarrassing."

"Well, you better get used to it, because this is the new me." He picked up a fresh rib, bit off a large chunk of meat, and started to chew with his mouth open.

"Knock it off, Tom. It's not funny," She warned him.

"I wasn't trying to be funny," He said before starting to suck the grease from his fingers.

"You better stop," Diane turned her hands so that the knife and fork she was holding pointed at the ceiling.

"Or what?" Tom asked as he reached out for his knife and fork.

Diane lashed out and speared Tom's hand to the table with her fork before he could grab his knife.

"What the fuck did you do that fo…." Tom was unable to finish the thought as Diane's knife plunged through the top of his head, freezing his mouth in the shape of an O.

Diane slowly withdrew her hand from the knife and watched as Tom's lifeless body slumped face-first onto the table.

I had to do it, she thought, *It was him or me. I was just defending myself.*

The moment Tom started to reach for his knife, she knew she had to stop him. She saw the look in his eye and what he intended to do. If she hadn't acted, it would have been her lying face down on the table.

Diane sat for a moment, trying to make sense of what had just happened. She should be horrified, but she wasn't. She was relieved. All she wanted was to enjoy her meal, to be able to eat it in peace, and savor each delicious bite. Now that Tom was dead, she could.

Diane couldn't believe that she still had an appetite after killing Tom, but she did. She felt ravenous. In addition to being hungry, she also felt a little aroused. There was something about the way the knife slid into Tom's skull that made her feel alive. It had awakened something within her.

I wonder how he would taste pan-fried with butter. The unexpected thought made Diane smile.

She dipped her index finger in the pool of blood that was collecting on the table and put it in her mouth.

"Mmm," she said, closing her eyes and savoring the taste.

"Shall I take this away for you?"

The sudden voice snapped Diane back to reality. She opened her eyes and looked across the table to where the waiter was standing behind Tom. It took her a moment to realize what he was asking before she nodded her head, "Yes, please."

The waiter removed the fork from Tom's hand then grabbed him by the shoulders. As he was about to pull Tom's body away from the table, Diane stopped him with an outstretched palm.

"Just a moment," she called out and leaned across the table to retrieve her knife from Tom's head. "Okay, you can take him now." She flicked her hand at the body.

As the waiter dragged Tom into the kitchen, Diane picked up her fork and resumed eating her meal. Now that she had eaten long pork, she was never going to eat anything else. She didn't think she had a choice.

When she finished eating, she set her utensils down on the plate. Noticing her plate was empty, the waiter came over and started to clear the table.

"I take it everything was to your satisfaction?" The waiter eyed the empty place at the table that was once occupied by Tom as he asked.

"It was. Thank you for asking."

"Can I get you anything else?"

Diane shook her head, "I'm fine. Better than I've ever been," She smiled and exchanged a knowing look with the waiter. "How much do I owe you?" She asked, reaching for her purse.

The waiter returned her smiled, "The first one is always free."

Diane reached into her purse, intending to tip the waiter for his exceptional service, but he shook his head.

"Tipping is not permitted," He said, "Besides, you gave us plenty." He nodded towards the kitchen.

"It has been a pleasure," Diane said as she got up. The waiter bowed at the compliment.

As Diane walked towards the exit, the cab driver stopped her. In all of the excitement, she had forgotten he was there.

"One moment, ma'am," The cab driver said as she walked by his table. "Let me give you a ride home." He stood up, "There is much to discuss if you are going to be joining us."

"That would be wonderful," she said, heading for the door. The cab driver was a couple of steps behind her.

Before she opened the door, she turned and called out to the waiter, "How long until you've updated the menu?"

The waiter smiled. He knew she was asking when her husband's body would be prepped and ready to eat.

"Our menu is updated daily," he replied.

"Care to join me for dinner tomorrow night?" she turned and asked the cab driver, "I don't like dining alone."

"It would be my pleasure," he said.

"I'd like to make a reservation." She looked over at the waiter then back to the cab driver, "A table for two."

THE BATTLE FOR BAGWELL PARK

The playground at Bagwell Park was the local hangout for my friends and me after school. It was located at the back of the park, behind the baseball diamonds and tennis courts.

We would spend hours on the large wooden structure making believe it was a castle, or a spaceship, or whatever our imaginations required it to be. The swings were our escape crafts and the sand they were built upon the uncharted ground of faraway places.

The park no longer exists. It was demolished a couple of decades ago to make way for a new subdivision. My friends and I were sad to see it go, but we all agreed it needed to be put to rest. We had a lot of great memories from our time in that park, but it was also where we experienced the worst afternoon of our lives.

I remember it like it was yesterday.

"Antonio needs to stop showing off and hurry up," Jeff complained when he saw our friend walking across the grass on his way to meet us.

Antonio had his butterfly knife in his hand, flipping it open and closed like he was Two-Bit Matthews from *The Outsiders*, a favorite movie of ours.

My friends and I had gathered at the playground like we always did after school that day. Antonio was usually the last one to show up because he didn't have a bike and had to walk to the park from his house.

"I see Mr. Magoo is still here," Antonio said, shoving the knife in his back pocket as he walked over to the swings where Callie, Jeff, and I were sitting. He glanced back over his shoulder at the old man sitting on the park bench.

We had dubbed the stranger Mr. Magoo because he was short, bald, and had squinty eyes, just like the cartoon character whose show sometimes played on Saturday mornings.

The old man had been there every day that week when we got to the park. He was always sitting in the same spot, wearing the same out of date tweed jacket and black fedora. He would be there when we arrived and would still be there when we got on our bikes and rode off. He never got up. He would just sit on the bench, writing in his book, and glancing over at us every once in a while.

"What do you think he wants?" I asked.

"He's probably trying to decide which one of us he wants to kidnap," Callie answered.

"Well, I'm tired of him staring at us," Jeff got up off his swing and walked towards the man on the bench. "Hey!" He yelled while waving his hand in the air to get the man's attention, "Hey, mister."

The man put down his pen, looked up at Jeff, and smiled.

"What's your deal?" He asked, putting his hand on his hips. "Why do you keep staring at us?"

The man stood up, put his pen and book into his pocket, picked his hat up off the bench, and walked to the large wooden beams that marked the border of the playground, "I was just wondering which one of you was going to die first." He placed his hat on his head and thumped it down into place.

Jeff didn't know how to respond to the odd comment and just stood there and stared.

"You might want to get back onto your...what are you calling the playground today?" He held his chin in his hand as he tried to recall the answer to his question, "Now I remember," He pointed to the large wooden structure behind us, "It's a submarine this week, isn't it? The Nautilus, right?"

The rest of us walked up and stood behind Jeff so we could hear what the old man had to say. He was right. We had been pretending the park was Captain Nemo's Nautilus from the movie *20,000 Leagues Under the Sea*. It was the Sunday night Disney movie and was all we talked about at school Monday morning. Naturally, it became the focus of our playground adventures that week.

"Better run along," He said, shooing us towards the playground equipment behind us, "Things are about to get very interesting."

None of us moved. Why would we? He sounded crazy. I'm sure I wasn't the only one who considered running over to the payphone and calling the police.

The old man just stood there smiling at us while he removed a pocket watch from his jacket. "Suit yourselves," He said and pressed a button on the top of the old device before returning it to his pocket. "Good luck," That was the last thing he said before he tipped his hat at us, winked, and then vanished.

"Holy Shit! Did you see that?!" Antonio pointed to the spot where the old man had disappeared.

"Yeah, captain obvious, we saw it," Jeff turned to look at Antonio.

"What just happened?" Callie asked.

I glanced around, looking for where the old man was hiding. It had to be a trick of some kind. I was sure of it. It felt like we were the victims of some sort of hidden camera show like *Candid Camera*. The only problem with that idea was that nobody had appeared to let us in on the joke.

I started to take a step back towards the others, but I couldn't lift my leg. When I looked down, I noticed that my feet had sunk into the sand.

"What the hell?" Jeff cried out, noticing the same thing happening to him.

"We're sinking!" I heard the panic in Callie's voice.

"Get off the sand!" I yelled as I frantically tugged my feet free and tried to run to the nearest piece of playground equipment.

Every step I took caused my feet to sink back into the ground as if I were trying to run through quicksand. I was exhausted by the time I grabbed hold of the metal bars on the edge of the merry-go-round and pulled myself up.

Callie and Antonio were able to help each other make it to the large wooden structure in the center of the playground, while Jeff slogged his way over to the tire swing. Once we were all safely on solid ground, the four of us looked at each other, hoping one of us could make sense of what was happening.

"That was uncool," Antonio finally broke the silence, "That old fucker did something to the playground. You heard what he said, 'things are about to get interesting' he knew we were going to start sinking. That's why he tried to get us to go back to the fort." The fort was our generic name for the large wooden playground structure.

"Thanks for pointing out the obvious again," Jeff rolled his eyes.

Antonio saluted him with his middle finger.

"Is that your IQ or your age?" That was Jeff's standard reply when one of us flipped him off.

"It's the size of your dick," Was Antonio's retort.

Before the war of words could escalate from there, Callie stepped in front of Antonio, "Knock it off," she said. "Arguing with each other isn't going to help us get out of here."

"We might be able to make it to the edge if we ran fast enough," Antonio suggested.

"That won't work," I said.

"Why not?" Jeff challenged my claim.

While Jeff and Antonio were trading insults, I had rolled over onto my stomach and leaned my arms over the side of the merry-go-round so I could reach out and touch the sand. My hand passed through it with little resistance. It was a weird sensation. It still felt like sand to me, but it had the consistency of water. Instead of answering his question, I showed him what I had discovered.

"Maybe we can swim to the edge," Another suggestion from Antonio.

"Sure, if you think you can swim through quicksand," I replied.

"Then how do we get out of here?" Jeff asked.

"I don't think we are supposed to. Not that way, at least."

"What is that supposed to mean?" Jeff stood on the edge of the tire swing, using the chains to keep himself balanced.

"I think the old man trapped us here for some reason."

"Why?" Jeff wanted answers I didn't have.

"I don't know," I snapped at him. "You know as much as I do."

"Maybe we should yell for help," Callie spoke up.

"Good idea," Antonio said as he climbed to the highest point of the fort. "HELP!" He yelled and waved his arms towards the parking lot, hoping someone would notice him.

Callie and Jeff added their voices to his.

I didn't join them. Instead, I plunged my hand into the sand and pushed the merry-go-round in a circle.

"Why aren't you helping?" Callie asked once she noticed I wasn't calling out with them. "Don't you want to get out of here?"

"I do," I sat up and dangled my legs over the side of the merry-go-round to stop it from turning, "I just don't think anyone can hear us."

"Why not?" She asked.

"Listen for a second," I tilted my head. "What do you hear?"

"Nothing," She responded after a few moments.

"Why can't we hear any birds, or the cars out on the street?" I pointed to the road where several cars were driving by. "Why can't we hear the people playing baseball or tennis?" I pointed over to the baseball diamonds and the tennis courts, half of which were in use.

The park was always filled with a cacophony of sounds. We were generally too busy playing and making a lot of noise ourselves to care about anything else that went on around us. Now that it was gone, it was hard not to notice that it was missing.

"They might not be able to hear us, but maybe they can see us," Antonio continued to wave his arms in the air from his perch atop the fort.

"Maybe," It was possible, but I doubted it. Given everything else that was happening, I assumed we were on our own.

While the three of us discussed the lack of sound, Jeff was oddly quiet. When I noticed he wasn't joining in the conversation, I kicked at the sand with my foot, causing the merry-go-round to turn until I was facing him.

"Did you see that?" He asked when he noticed me watching him. He was pointing to the far end of the playground.

I turned around and scanned the area, but couldn't see anything. I was about to turn around and ask Jeff what he saw when I noticed the area beneath the teeter-totter swell up like a wave. The sand rose, pushing the end of the teeter-totter into the air, which in turn caused the opposite end to drop into the sand.

It was weird how the sand was like water when we touched it, and would swallow us up like quicksand if we tried to escape, but the playground equipment stayed cemented in place.

"There!" Jeff yelled, noticing the rising sand at the same time I did.

"What was that?" Callie called out. She had joined Antonio at the top of the fort, trying to get a better look at what we were seeing. She didn't notice the sand rise and fall, but she did see the teeter-totter move.

"We need to get away from the sand," I said.

I backed away from the edge of the merry-go-round until I was sitting in the middle of it with my legs tucked against my chest.

"Why? What is it?" I could hear the growing concern in Jeff's voice.

"Don't you remember what the old man called the fort?" I responded with a question of my own.

"He called it the Nautilus," Antonio answered before Jeff had a chance to.

I turned and looked at Antonio and Callie then back to Jeff. "Remember what happened to the Nautilus in the movie?"

"Oh shit," Jeff looked down at the ground and realized how vulnerable he was, standing there hanging onto the tire swing. "What do we do?"

As Jeff spoke, the sand next to the merry-go-round began to rise. I held my finger to my lips to quiet everyone. Then, after making sure I had Jeff's attention, I jabbed the same finger into the air several times, hoping he understood what I was trying to tell him.

He nodded his head and began to climb up the chains that held the tire swing in place. It was something he had done many times before. We'd all done it, even Callie. Climbing up and sitting on the crossbeam started as a rite of passage for our little group, but later became a way for us to show off to anyone else that happened to be in the park.

The chains rattled as he pulled himself up and grabbed onto the beam, wrapping his arms and legs around it, dangling like a sloth on a tree branch. The noise he was making didn't go unnoticed. The swell of sand surged forward then dropped quickly as the thing beneath the playground made its way towards him.

Hurry, I silently urged Jeff to move quickly. All he had to do was pull his body upright, but for some reason, he stopped and sat there, clinging to the underside of the beam while staring at the ground. I followed his gaze, wondering what was keeping him from moving.

I gasped when I saw the enormous lidless eye protruding out of the sand beneath him. It was colorless except for the dark pit of its pupil, which was a solid black void.

None of us moved or made a sound as we waited to see what would happen next. The seconds stretched into minutes, but the eye never moved. It stayed where it was, fixated on Jeff.

I didn't know how long he could maintain his position, clinging to the underside of the beam like that. Jeff was the most athletic out of all of us, but I could tell he was starting to reach his limit. I could see his arms begin to tremble from the strain of holding on. If we didn't do something soon, he was going to fall.

I glanced over at the fort as an idea began to take shape in my mind. It was tricky, but if anyone could do it, it would be Jeff.

I waved my arms in the air until I got Antonio and Callie's attention. Once their eyes were on me, I proceeded to pantomime my idea to them. It took me several attempts to get the basic idea across, but once they were able to decipher what I was planning, they nodded their heads in understanding.

If my plan didn't work, Jeff would fall into the sand where he would drown or be dragged away by the giant squid. The same thing would happen if we did nothing, so we at least needed to try.

I waited until Antonio and Callie made their way down to the platform closest to the tire swing. They were careful not to make any noise. For this to work, the squid needed to stay focused on Jeff, at least until they were in position.

Once they were ready, I slipped my sneakers off and quietly made my way to the edge of the merry-go-round. As I aimed my shoe at the eye, two tentacles snaked their way out of the sand, climbing up the side of the beams that anchored the tire swing to the ground.

I could see Callie and Antonio silently motioning for me to hurry up as the tentacles closed in on Jeff. If the squid got hold of him, there was nothing we could do to stop it from pulling him down.

I took a deep breath, pulled my arm back, and threw the shoe as hard as I could. It seemed to move in slow motion as it sailed through the air. *Come on, come on.*

My aim was perfect. The shoe hit the squid right in the center of its eye, forcing it to withdraw its tentacles and submerge.

My mom is going to kill me, I thought, watching my shoe get dragged into the sand with the squid. But I didn't have time to worry about that now. We still needed to save Jeff.

"Move!" I yelled at him.

Jeff didn't need to be told twice. He pulled himself up and into a sitting position so that he was straddling the beam.

"Run!" I yelled and pointed to where Callie and Antonio were motioning him forward. He needed to get moving before the squid returned.

At first, Jeff was confused. He didn't understand what we were urging him to do. As he looked across the open stretch of sand between the structure that held the tire swing and the platform where Callie and Antonio stood on the fort, it started to dawn on him.

He turned and gave me a look that said, *"You can't be serious."*

I nodded my head emphatically to let him know how serious I was.

He looked back at the wide-open space between him and the fort. Even though he was shaking his head, he stood up. With his arms held out for balance, he bent his legs and prepared to run.

I turned when I heard Callie gasp. She was pointing at the under the tire swing. It was swelling up.

"GO! GO! GO!" I waved my arms in the direction of the fort.

Jeff looked down at the rising sand in wide-eyed alarm. He knew if he didn't move, the squid would surely get him this time. Without hesitation, he started running along the top of the beam. Beneath him, the sand continued to rise. I held my breath when he ran out of room to run and jumped.

As Jeff sailed through the air, several tentacles burst out of the sand and began flailing around him. The squid couldn't see its target and seemed to be hoping for a lucky strike that would knock him to the ground. But Jeff was the lucky one.

Along the side of the fort was a series of metal bars that acted as a ladder, allowing kids to climb to the higher levels of the fort a lot faster than using the winding walking ways. That is what Jeff was aiming for when he leaped off the beam. It was also where Callie and Antonio waited to assist him.

He hit the side of the fort with enough force to knock the wind out of his lungs. I heard him grunt then watched as he clawed at the rungs of metal, trying not to fall back into the sand. I felt helpless at that moment. If he fell into the sand, it would be my fault since I'm the one that encouraged him to jump.

If it weren't for Callie and Antonio's quick reflexes, Jeff would have fallen. When he landed against the fort, the two of them quickly reached through the bars and grabbed hold of him until he was able to pull himself up and over the wall that separated them. Once he was on the platform, he dropped to the floor, panting in fear and exhaustion.

But he wasn't out of danger yet. None of them were. The squid's tentacles were sliding up the sides of the fort, reaching through the bars of the ladder, searching for them.

"Get to the lookout!" I pointed to the highest platform in the fort. The squid's tentacles weren't long enough to reach them there.

Antonio leaned down and helped Jeff get to his feet, and then the three of them ran up the winding walkway of the fort until they reached the lookout. As they ran, the squid gave up and submerged beneath the sand.

Now that Jeff was safe, I laid back on the merry-go-round, looking at the clouds, and wondering how we were going to get home.

I didn't stay like that for very long. Antonio, Callie, and Jeff were excited about something. I could hear them calling out my name.

When I sat up and looked over at them, they were waving their arms and jabbing their fingers in the direction behind me. I whipped my head around, looking for the source of their excitement.

Oh shit!

I watched the mass of tentacles rise over the edge of the merry-go-round and make their way towards me. My pulse started to race as my body reacted to the overwhelming fear that had taken hold of me.

Move, move, move, I pleaded with my body. I wanted to run, but my arms and legs wouldn't respond. I was frozen in place, too scared to flee. I started to tremble as the tentacles closed in on me.

"Don't die, don't die, don't die…" Callie's pleas were the one thing I seized upon as Antonio and Jeff tried calling me every insulting word they could come up with to get me to move. In any other situation, their lame attempts would have been funny.

I don't want to die. The tentacles were inches away from my feet. All of the things I had planned to do that summer suddenly flashed through my mind. *I don't want to die.* The first tentacle to reach me brushed against my shoe. I instinctively pulled my foot back and out of reach. That one small movement freed the rest of my body from its paralysis. "I am not going to die!" I yelled at the tentacles, scooting back towards the opposite side of the merry-go-round.

My victory was short-lived when my back collided with something large and rubbery. I didn't want to turn around, knowing that the squid had risen from the sand behind me while I was distracted by its tentacles, but I didn't have a choice. Not if I wanted to survive

I turned my head first and found myself looking right into the eye of the squid. It was as big as my head. I took a couple of steps away from it as I turned the rest of my body around.

It knew I was trapped and was toying with me. Every direction I looked, there was a tentacle hovering just over the edge of the merry-go-round, waiting to snatch me up if I tried to escape.

I stood in the middle, trying to keep my balance as the movements of the squid jostled the large metal disc back and forth like a turntable. With no other option available to me, I waited for the sea creature to make its move. I didn't have to wait long.

It wrapped two of its tentacles around the handles of the merry-go-round, bracing itself while it titled its massive head back. The sound of its beak clacking open and closed could be heard long before it came into view. As it lowered its head, bringing its mouth level with the merry-go-round, I was able to catch a glimpse of Antonio, Callie, and Jeff, where they stood on the fort.

The three of them were waving their arms at me, yelling at me to run.

Run where?

I was trapped on a spinning disk in the middle of the playground, surrounded by tentacles.

Then I saw it, a possible way out. My friends had seen it too and were motioning for me to take the opportunity before it was too late.

You can do this! I tried to psyche myself up. *Just pretend it's a ramp and not the head of a giant squid.*

If Jeff could run along the beam of the tire swing, I could do this.

I bent my legs, leaned forward, and took off running. The squid reacted by swinging several of its tentacles in my direction, trying to stop me. I had to jump over the first one that blocked my path and duck beneath the second. The third one came down behind me and would have landed on top of me if I hadn't kept moving. Once I made it through the obstacle course of tentacles and to the edge of the merry-go-round, I leaped into the air.

When I landed on the squid's head, I fell to my knees. I wasn't expecting its body to be as soft and spongy as it was, which caused me to lose my balance. That was when I realized the squid wasn't even real. It was a giant prop made out of foam and rubber, like the one in the movie. The only difference between the two was that this one wasn't a puppet, it was moving by itself, and it was trying to kill me.

"Get Up!" I heard Callie yell.

"Run!" Antonio cried out.

"Look out!" Jeff warned while pointing behind me

I turned just in time to see one of the tentacles reaching out, inches away from wrapping itself around my ankle. Tucking my legs underneath me, I tried to stand up but couldn't. The movement of the squid and the composition of its body made it impossible to keep my balance. I was forced to crawl.

As I got closer to the fort, Jeff and Antonio leaned over the railing, reaching their arms out towards me. I kept crawling as fast as I could, reaching out to Jeff once I was within reach of his outstretched hand. I felt my fingers brush against his.

I made it! I celebrated, feeling Jeff's hand close around mine.

"NO!" Callie cried out.

I thought the weightlessness I was feeling was Jeff pulling me to safety, but it wasn't. Instead of being pulled closer to the fort, I was being lifted into the air and away from it.

The squid had managed to wrap one of its tentacles around my leg. I kicked at it with my free leg, trying to pull myself free, but its grip was too tight.

"JEFF!" Antonio yelled.

I whipped my head around when I heard Antonio. I was horrified to see Jeff being lifted into the air, suspended by a tentacle around his waist. The tables had turned against us.

The two of us were caught, and there was nothing we could do. If we managed to get free, we would fall into the sand and drown.

I stopped struggling after a few minutes. All it was doing was exhausting me. Jeff gave up shortly after I did. The same look of defeat plastered on both of our faces.

I could hear Callie crying and Antonio repeating the phrase, "What do we do?" over and over again.

What happened next was a bit of a blur because of how fast it happened. From where I was dangling, I was able to see Callie snatch something out of Antonio's back pocket and clutch it tightly to her chest. Then she did the craziest thing I had ever seen her do. She jumped over the railing of the fort and began to slide down the body of the squid.

When she got about midway down, she flipped her wrist, revealing the object she had taken from Antonio. It was his butterfly knife. I had forgotten about it until I saw the blade flick open in Callie's hand.

She kept sliding until she was between the squid's eyes and then used her sneakers to bring herself to an abrupt stop. The look on her face, as she repositioned the knife, was one of determination and rage. Callie was ready to put an end to this shit.

With a yell, she raised the knife and brought it down upon the squid's left eye. She continued to stab it again and again until all that remained was an empty socket of torn rubber and foam. Then she did the same thing to the other side. Callie's attack happened so fast that the squid didn't have time to react. By the time it came to its senses and started reaching out to grab her, the attack was over. Once she destroyed the right eye, the squid disappeared, leaving Callie, Jeff, and I suspended in midair when it happened.

I fell the furthest and hit the sand like a brick, which forced the air out of my lungs. That left me dazed for a few minutes. When I came to my senses, I saw Antonio help Jeff get to his, then make their way over to where Callie was sitting on the ground, staring at the knife where it lay in the sand.

"Bravo," A voice called out from the edge of the playground, accompanied by the sound of clapping.

The four of us turned to find the old man standing near the bench he was sitting on when we first arrived at the park.

"I didn't expect all four of you to survive. That is quite the accomplishment. You should be proud of yourself. You've passed the first test."

"What test?" Jeff asked

"I'm sorry, but you will have to save your questions until after the exam is completed."

"What the fuck is that supposed to mean?" Jeff took a step towards the man.

The old man didn't answer. He just tipped his hat to us and said, "I'll be in touch." Then he disappeared.

Our childhood was never the same after that. That afternoon took its toll on us and forced us to face our mortality much sooner than we ever should have had to. That drove a wedge between our friendship, which divided us and caused us to drift apart. We never went back to the park after that, fearing the man would trap us again. That was also why we stopped hanging out with each other. If we weren't all together in one place, he couldn't catch us.

That was thirty-odd years ago. I had hoped I would never have to relive that nightmare, but it seems it has found me again. Yesterday, I received a postcard in the mail. Written on the back of it was a simple message: *See you soon*, it said. It wasn't signed, and there was no return address. Those things weren't needed. The person who sent it knew I'd understand where it came from the moment I turned it over and saw the faded picture of the playground and the old man waving at the camera from where he sat on the bench.

A HOLLY JOLLY CHRISTMAS

"If you are going to keep me tied to this chair, at least give me the dignity of letting me wear my hat," my wife hissed at me while she nodded to the green stocking cap at her feet—the one shaped like a Christmas tree.

I picked up the hat and placed it gently on her head. Then I positioned it just how she liked it, slightly to the left side with the top folded neatly, so the giant golden bell rested against her shoulder.

"Thank you," she said as I adjusted the strings of light that bound her to the dining room chair.

"Are they too tight?" I asked. I felt terrible that I had to tie her up. "I can go out to the garage and get that nylon cord we use to tie the tarps down."

"I'm fine, but I'd feel much better if you'd just untie me. I'm not going to hurt anyone. I just want to spread a little Yuletide cheer."

"I love you, but you know I can't do that. You can't leave the house since you decided to sneak into the Johnson's home and redecorate their tree."

"Have you seen their tree? It was hideous!"

"What about the Greenberg's house?"

"They didn't have a tree at all, so I gave them one."

"They are Jewish."

"Jewish people don't like trees?"

I couldn't tell if that was supposed to be a joke or not. I could have continued to list the neighbors she had scared or annoyed, but there wasn't any point. She felt justified in everything she had done.

"We are lucky everyone declined to press charges as long as you agreed to stay under voluntary house arrest until Christmas was over," I reminded her.

"I didn't agree to that, you did," she spat the words at me. "I would never agree to something that would prevent me from enjoying the holidays."

"I didn't have a choice. Your version of enjoying the holidays involved breaking into our neighbors' homes."

She turned her head away from me, clearly annoyed that I had sided against her.

"If you won't untie me, could you at least plug these in?" she asked and indicated the strings of lights I used to tie her up. Several seconds later, she added, "...please."

"If it will make you happy, then I will gladly plug them in for you," I said as I grabbed an extension cord from the closest.

"Let me know if they get too hot," I said after plugging the lights into the outlet. I waited a few minutes to make sure she was ok before going into the kitchen to pour myself a drink. As I walked away, I could hear her start to hum the tune of *O Christmas Tree*.

I poured a shot of whiskey and downed it in one gulp. I was about to pour another when I heard the doorbell ring out the tune *Carol of the Bells*. My wife replaced the old bell shortly after she became obsessed with decorating for the holidays.

I opened the door to find two gentlemen standing on my porch, both dusted with a fine layer of snow. I was only expecting the Magister and was surprised to see the priest standing next to him. I didn't know the two churches worked so closely together. I figured their work would put them at odds with each other, but I wasn't going to question it. I was willing to accept any help I could get.

The Magister's number was given to me by an anonymous member of an online forum where I had gone to ask for help as I tried to figure out what was wrong with my wife. I had already taken her to several specialists. They all said there was nothing wrong with her. She was just getting into the spirit of the holidays.

I couldn't convince any of the doctors that the person they were talking to was not my wife. One of them even suggested that maybe I was the one that needed help. Perhaps I was under too much stress and seeing things that weren't there. That was when I gave up and turned to the internet for help.

It took a lot of courage, of the liquid variety, to make the phone call that brought the Magister and the priest to my doorstep. I laughed when I initially received the message that prompted me to call. *Your wife might be possessed. If you genuinely want to help her, call (555) 555-XXXX and ask for Magister Alexander.*

My wife had been tested for everything else, so I might as well make it official and have her checked for possession as well. At least, that is how my liquor addled mind justified making the call.

"Mr. Hudson?" The man I assumed was the Magister reached out with his left hand, "I'm Theodore Alexander, and this is Father Cooke," he said and nodded towards the priest beside him.

"Please call me Ben," I said and shook the Magister's hand then offered my hand to Father Cooke. "Come on in."

"Should I call you Magister?" I asked after shutting the door, "I'm a little confused on the protocol here. I didn't know Satanic priests like you existed until someone gave me your phone number."

He laughed, "Mr. Alexander is fine if that makes you more comfortable."

"I'll call you whatever you want if you can help my wife," I said, leading the men further into the house.

"Wow, you weren't kidding," Mr. Alexander exclaimed as he took in all of the Christmas decorations.

Every available space was filled with a variety of holiday ornaments.

"Is every room decorated like this?" he asked.

"Yep, she even replaced the shower curtains with holiday ones. I can't even take a shower without being reminded of the holidays." I didn't intend for the answer to come out as snarky as it did.

"I see that most of the decorations are of commercial characters. There are different versions of Santa, Frosty, the reindeer, and elves, but I don't see any of the usual religious decorations. No manger, no crosses, not even any angels," Father Cooke noted while he surveyed the room.

"…And trees," Mr. Alexander added, "There are a lot of Christmas trees."

"Is that significant?" I asked

"Potentially," Mr. Alexander replied, "The entities we deal with tend to surround themselves with religious symbols that can often be used to identify where they came from."

I hung their coats on the rack and led them into the living room where my wife was tied up. When they saw her bound to the chair, Christmas lights blinking all around her, they looked at each other than over at me.

"She asked me to turn the lights on," I said while I took a detour to the kitchen to grab the whiskey and some glasses. "When I got your message, I didn't have much time to prepare, and I couldn't find any rope. But there were plenty of lights lying around, so...," I shrugged. The rest they could figure out for themselves.

I returned to the living room and set the whiskey and glasses down on the coffee table. I sat in the recliner next to the couch and poured myself another drink. Mr. Alexander and Father Cooke waved off my offer to pour one for them.

"I like the lights," she said to the men as they sat on the couch facing her. "They help illuminate all of the beautiful decorations, and they make me feel festive."

"They are quite lovely, Mrs. Hudson," Mr. Alexander said, "I have to ask why all of the trees?"

"Thank you," She responded politely before answering his question. "I figured two religious boys like you would already know the answer to that. It was after all your religion that appropriated the tree for yourselves."

"Our religion?" Father Cooke asked before glancing over at Mr. Alexander. The look they exchanged signified that they had just learned something important.

"Don't be coy Father, you know I am talking about Christianity," She sounded a little annoyed. "You boys are different sides of the same coin as far as I'm concerned. Your patchwork religion was built out of the pieces of the ones you destroyed. That tree and its place in the home was a tradition long before your God showed up."

I sat quietly in my chair and sipped my whiskey while I listened and wondered where the conversation was headed. It was clear to me that the person sitting in that chair was no longer my wife, and it frightened me. I had shared my bed with whatever she had become. That gave me chills.

"Ben?" Mr. Alexander raised his voice to get my attention when I had failed to answer the question he'd just asked me.

"What?" I asked as I returned from my muddled thoughts. The alcohol had started to take effect.

"Is there someplace we can talk in private?" he repeated.

"Uh...yeah," I thought for a moment, "How about the garage?" I suggested. Our house was small, and the interior walls didn't block sound very well.

"Bring the icicles when you come back inside," my wife said as we filed past her on our way to the garage. "There should be a box of them in the trunk."

Once we were all in the garage, I leaned against the hood of the car, arms crossed, and waited for one of them to speak.

"This is much easier on the eyes," Father Cooke remarked when he noticed the garage was free of Christmas decorations.

"I come out here sometimes to get away from all that," I nodded towards the house. "It's the only place I could keep her from decorating."

"I would spend a lot of time out here as well under the circumstances," Father Cooke smiled.

"I know Christmas decorations are the last thing you want to talk about, but I do have to ask about them, specifically the bells. It didn't occur to me until just now how many of your decorations have been enhanced with bells. Have bells always been a big part of her decorations?" Mr. Alexander asked.

"Not that I recall…I mean, we always had a few decorations with bells, but nothing like what you see in there now."

"The doorbell, I noticed it played the Carol of the Bells, how long have you had that?" Father Cooke asked.

"She bought that a couple of days ago?" I couldn't keep my curiosity contained. "What do the bells have to do with all of this?" I asked.

"Bells have been known to play a significant role in many ancient religions, and they may be the religious symbol we overlooked when we walked in," Mr. Alexander placed his hand on his chin as a thought occurred to him. "When you called, you mentioned that your wife was a music teacher, right?"

"Yes, well, she is currently on a leave of absence," I waved my hand in the air, "For obvious reasons."

"Has your wife come into contact with any strange instruments recently?"

"Strange? No, I don't think so."

"Strange might not be the right word, it could be something simple like an antique," Father Cooke elaborated. "A better question might be, 'has she brought home any new musical instruments'?"

"No…" I started to say, but all of the talk about bells triggered my memory. She did bring home some bells. I didn't really think of them as musical instruments, but technically they were.

"Now that I think about it, the day she started acting weird, she'd brought home this little wooden box with three bells in it. The kind with the handles on them." I tried to pantomime what they looked like, as I described them. "There was also a little piece of sheet music tucked to the side. I remember her showing it to me. She picked it up at the thrift store."

I rushed back into the house, which left the two men with puzzled expressions on their faces. I ran into the front room and grabbed the box where my wife left it sitting on the table in the foyer. When I returned, I held it out to Mr. Alexander with two hands. "This is it."

In my excitement to show them the box, I accidentally left the door open, which prompted my wife to yell out, "What about the icicles?"

I went and closed the door as Mr. Alexander inspected the outside of the box.

"It appears to be hand-carved, and these patterns along the outside appear to be Germanic or possibly Norse. If this is authentic, it is very old and very valuable. I'm surprised someone would donate this to a thrift store."

He carefully opened the lid to reveal the three ornate bronze bells nestled inside. Instead of removing a bell, he slid the piece of parchment out and handed the box to Father Cooke.

He started to smile as he looked over the single piece of sheet music. I could tell he found the answer he was hoping to find. When he finished with his examination, he retrieved the box from Father Cooke and handed him the piece of paper.

"These are summoning bells," Mr. Alexander indicated the box that held the instruments, "And that," he pointed at the sheet of music, "Works as the incantation. Your wife must have used the bells to play the song. That is what allowed the solstice spirit to possess her."

"The what?" I inquired.

"Old nature spirits," Father Cooke explained. "Thousands of years before God came to Earth, primitive humans worshipped various nature deities. Solstice spirits were the emissaries for many of those old gods."

"But our God is a jealous God," Mr. Alexander cut in. "When He arrived, He demanded loyalty from everyone, including those entities. Most of them were powerless to resist Him and were forced to join his cause. Today we call some of those spirits angels. Those that opposed him joined the ranks of The Serpent's demon horde or were driven into the deepest and darkest crevices between heaven and hell, rarely to be seen."

"OOOkkkaaayyy…" I said, drawing out the word. "But what does that have to do with Christmas and all of these damn decorations?"

"Solstice spirits are not normally malevolent. Many of them were summoned to help in times of need, or to give thanks, or to celebrate the changing of the seasons," Father Cooke explained.

"The problem with this spirit," Mr. Alexander continued where Father Cooke left off, "Is that it has probably been thousands of years since it has seen the world and now it is feeling like a kid in a candy store. It thinks it was summoned to celebrate the winter solstice. That is why it focuses on the non-religious symbols of Christmas. That is also why it has been trying to force those things on your neighbors."

"Let me stop you right there," I said before he could continue. "Assuming everything you just told me is true…can you save my wife?"

"I've never encountered a solstice spirit before, but I do believe we can save her," Mr. Alexander answered.

"So, if this isn't an angel or a demon, how do you go about exorcising it?" I asked.

"An exorcism won't work on your wife. Solstice spirits aren't bound by the same laws of order that govern angels and demons," Father Cooke answered.

"Then how are you going to save her?"

Mr. Alexander smiled.

"That smile tells me I am not going to like the answer to that question," Father Cooke said.

"If the lore is correct, solstice spirits are essentially bullies. They don't like to be told what to do. They want to be able to do what they want whenever they want, and they will do everything in their power to have things their way. So, if you are faced with a bully, what's the best way to make that bully stop?" Mr. Alexander's smile grew, "You get a bigger bully."

"What?" I ran my hand through my hair. "Maybe I've had too much to drink, but I'm not following you."

"What he is saying," Father Cooke said, "Is that he wants to scare the spirit out of your wife."

"How does that work?" I was extremely skeptical. "It's a spirit, what could possibly scare it off?"

"Christmas is all about celebrating, spreading joy to those around us, and forgiving the small trespasses of life. That is what the solstice spirit wants to embody in its twisted way. I plan to summon a spirit that is the opposite of that," Mr. Alexander explained.

"I figured that is why you were smiling," Father Cooke pointed his finger at Mr. Alexander. "If you are going to do what I think you are going to do, you need to warn him about the risks. This situation can quickly go from bad to worse if we make the slightest mistake."

"True. That is why we need to make sure Mrs. Hudson is an unsuitable host for the entity we plan on calling forth."

"What are you talking about?" I was getting tired. I didn't know how much more of this craziness I could take.

"There is only one spirit I know that is capable of sending the solstice spirit running back to whatever dark cave it crawled out of, a spirit that embodies fear, death, and isolation. A Samhain."

I just stared at Mr. Alexander until he explained.

"A Samhain is a type of harvest spirit. Like the solstice spirit, it is free from the rules of religion that govern us." He pointed to Father Cooke than back to himself as he said the last word.

"You would probably know it better as a Halloween spirit." He looked over at the priest when he spoke again. "Father Cooke is concerned that we won't be able to banish it before it tries to fill the vacancy left in your wife when the solstice spirit flees."

"That sounds insane. Can't we just bargain with it and get it to leave on its own? If it is a Christmas spirit, won't it just leave when Christmas is over?"

"It might. It might not. Think about it this way, if I gave you the keys to your favorite car and said 'bring it back whenever' how long would you drive it before giving it up?" Mr. Alexander had a point. Plus, I didn't think I could handle another day of her holiday cheer.

"There is no telling how long that thing plans on staying. We can try and wait it out, or we can force it out tonight."

I took a deep breath and exhaled. "Alright, let's do it," I said. "If I were in her place, I'd want you to get it out of me as quickly as possible." I couldn't believe this was happening.

"What next? Is there some sort of contract I have to sign?" I remembered reading that the woman who saved her son had to sign a contract.

"No contract required." The question seemed to amuse Mr. Alexander. "What we are about to do is not sanctioned by either of our churches, so no payment is required." He held up the box of bells, "but I will be taking these with me. You can think of that as payment if you like."

"That is fine with me," I said, "When do we get started?"

"First, we need to make sure the Samhain spirit feels welcome when it is summoned. That will help to ensure it remains tethered to the house long enough for it to become aware of the solstice spirit's presence."

"How do we do that?"

"We need to clear the house of all the Christmas decorations," Mr. Alexander explained. "Then we need to redecorate with those," he pointed to the large boxes labeled HALLOWEEN stacked in the corner of the garage.

"...and just in case," Mr. Alexander turned and looked at Father Cooke, indicating what he was about to say was for his benefit. "...we need to lock up all of the knives," he paused for a moment before adding "...and the forks."

"Aren't you forgetting something?" Father Cooke looked at him with raised eyebrows.

"I was going to get to that...I just wanted to wait until everything else was ready," Mr. Alexander seemed mildly annoyed.

"What is he talking about?" I asked

"Summoning a Samhain spirit requires a certain type of investment," Mr. Alexander explained, "It takes a little more incentive besides a few ancient phrases to get it to appear."

"What kind of investment?" I was afraid to ask.

"Was that cat food in the bowl I saw sitting on the kitchen floor?"

WEIRD WOLF

"No, no, no," I said, shaking the steering wheel, hoping that simple action would keep the old Honda from dying on me.

It didn't work. The engine sputtered a few more times before finally dying with a pathetic wheeze. As the car rolled forward, I pulled to the side of the road and coasted along the shoulder until it finally came to a stop.

"Well shit," I muttered, grabbing my phone from the cup holder and unlocking it with my thumb. My wife had a habit of waiting up for me when I was driving home late, so I wanted to let her know what had happened before I called our roadside assistance service.

"That figures," I said, staring at the *No Service* message displayed in the top right corner of the phone screen. I guess I wasn't going to be calling anyone.

The car door groaned as I swung it open and stepped out into the street. *Piece of shit*, I slammed the door shut, looking up and down the road, trying to see if I could see any lights in the distance. There was nothing but darkness in either direction. The only light was that of the full moon bathing everything in an eerie blue glow.

It was a little after midnight, and according to the map app, my last known position put me somewhere in the north Georgia mountains, about twenty to thirty miles from the nearest town in either direction. That meant it could be hours before I saw another driver if I saw one at all.

I walked up the road a bit, trying to see if I could get a signal for my phone, holding it up in the air as if that extra foot and a half would make a difference. On my way back to the car, I looked to the hills on either side of the road, wondering if climbing one of them might get me clear of whatever was blocking service to my phone.

The sound of a stick snapping in the woods behind me reminded me that I might not be alone out there in the middle of nowhere. *Probably just a deer*, I thought, trying to calm myself. *Or a bear*, my imagination whispered.

I quickly got back into the car and locked the doors. *I think I'll just wait a little bit.* I hadn't been there that long, and it was possible someone might drive by. There was no sense in running off into the woods if I didn't have to, right?

I sat in the car for almost an hour, jumping at every little sound I heard. I eventually got desperate enough to make a deal with whatever higher power might be listening. I promised everything I could think of if they'd just send someone to help me. It was pathetic, and I was starting to annoy myself.

"Screw this," I said, popping the trunk before getting out of the car. Sitting there doing nothing wasn't getting me any closer to home. If I wanted to get out of there, I was going to have to take a chance at climbing one of the hills. If I were lucky, I'd be able to make a call and be out of there within the hour.

I grabbed the tire iron from the trunk then went back to the front of the car. After opening the door, I leaned inside and pressed my hand on the horn for at least a minute. It was obnoxious, but that was the point. I was trying to scare off anything that might be lurking nearby among the trees.

"It's just a little walk up a hill and through some woods," I said, trying to convince myself I had nothing to worry about.

Here we go. With my phone in one hand and the tire iron in the other, I stepped off the road and started to climb the nearest hill. Thankfully, the full moon gave off enough light for me to weave my way around the rocks and through the trees without difficulty. I don't think I would have attempted the climb otherwise.

SNAP!

I was about halfway up the hill when I heard the sound of the twig snapping. I stopped and listened, raising the tire iron over my shoulder. The noise sounded like it came from the other side of a huge boulder sticking out of the ground like a broken tooth. *Probably just a raccoon or possum*, I silently hoped, but I didn't wait around to find out what it was. As quietly as I could, I started walking backward in the opposite direction.

Please let there be a signal, I prayed, hoping I would be able to make a call and get the hell out of there and back to civilization.

Yes!

The *no service* message was gone. In its place was a single signal bar. I rushed to unlock my phone, but the bar disappeared, replaced by the no service message, before my thumb touched the screen. *Dammit!* I was so close. I just needed to climb a little higher.

SNAP!

That time the noise came from directly behind me. I whirled around, holding the tire iron out in front of me, threatening to swing it. What I saw almost gave me a heart attack. Sitting on the ground, about ten feet away, was the biggest wolf I had ever seen. It must have run around the other side of the hill, coming up behind me while I was distracted by my phone.

"Easy now," I said, taking a step back.

The wolf cocked its head to the side and swiveled its ears forward to listen.

Wait, don't wolves run in packs? I quickly turned in a circle, scanning the hillside, expecting myself to be surrounded by a pack of hungry canines, but I didn't see any.

When I looked back at the wolf, it raised its eyebrows as if to say, *What the hell was that all about?*

"How about we both go on about our business?" I said, backing away from the wolf, moving further up the hill. "I'm just going to go up here and make a quick phone call," I held the phone out towards the wolf, "And then I'll leave."

The wolf remained sitting, following me with its eyes as I tried not to make any sudden movements while I walked up the hill.

The further away from the wolf I got, the more confident I became that it wasn't going to attack me. It seemed to be more curious than threatening. That didn't mean I was willing to turn my back on it. I kept the wolf in my line of sight the entire time I moved away from it.

Two bars, I stared at the screen of my phone, making sure they weren't going to disappear on me. They remained.

"Just a few more minutes, and you can have these woods all to yourself," I said to the wolf, unlocking the phone with my thumb.

I was initially going to call my wife but decided I should probably call 911 first. I was unfamiliar with the area, and I wasn't sure what was up with that wolf, better to be safe than sorry.

"911, what's your emergency?" the operator asked. Her voice sounded distant, probably from the weak signal my phone was receiving.

I explained my situation to the operator, leaving out the part about the wolf.

"I don't have any officers in the vicinity," she said. In the background, I could hear her furiously tapping away at her keyboard. "But," she paused for a moment while the tapping continued. "There should be a Ranger post not far from you. I am going to put you on a brief hold and see if I can get ahold of someone for you."

"Okay, thanks," I replied to the operator. To the wolf, who had decided to lie down on the ground, I said, "Not long now." He wasn't even paying attention to me. Instead, he was looking off into the night, his ears swiveling back and forth as he listened to sounds only he could hear.

"Did you say something?" the operator asked, coming back onto the line. I didn't know she could hear me while I was on hold.

"Uh…no, sorry, just talking to myself."

"Just give me a few more minutes," she said, placing me back on hold.

I paced back and forth, kicking the occasional stick or stone down the hill while I waited for the operator to return. The wolf didn't seem to like the noise I was making. He stood up and glared at me. I was sure he wanted me to stop.

"Sorry," I whispered, turning away from his judgmental stare.

You'd think the presence of a large wolf would have made me more nervous than I was, but I felt the opposite. He was behaving more like a dog than a wolf, and I didn't feel threatened by him at all. I kind of liked having him around. He made the hillside feel a little bit safer and a lot less lonely.

"Great news, Mr. Coletti," the operator said, coming back onto the line. "I was able to get in touch with the ranger station. They are sending someone out to help you."

"Thank you," I replied while giving the wolf a thumb's up.

"If you like, I can stay on the line until they arrive," the operator offered.

"I don't think that will be necessary." I still needed to call my wife, plus I was anxious to get out of the woods and back to my car.

"They said they'd be there in about thirty minutes. I would give them forty-five. If they don't show up by then, give us another call."

"Okay. I will."

"Is there anything else I can assist you with?" the operator asked.

"No, I think I'm good," I replied.

"Alright, you take care, Mr. Colletti."

"Will do," I said, tapping the red phone icon and ending the call.

"Mind if I sit?" I said to the wolf, pointing at a small cluster of boulders with the tire iron. The muscles in my legs were starting to ache from all of the limbing I had done. I needed to rest my feet for a moment before I hiked back to the car.

I didn't think I needed the tire iron for the time being, so I leaned it up against the rocks as I sat down and prepared to call my wife.

"One more call, and then I am out of here," I said to the wolf, scrolling down my list of contacts until I found my wife's number.

SNAP!

The wolf and I shared a look before turning our gazes to the dark woods, searching for the source of the sound.

SNAP! SNAP!

The wolf raised its hackles and began to growl, turning away from me to face the coming threat.

The snapping of branches and rustling of pine needles grew louder and louder as whatever was out there began to run towards us. It was big, whatever it was.

I wrapped my hand around the tire iron and jumped to my feet, pocketing the phone so that I could hold my weapon in a two-handed grip. I couldn't see what was coming, but I could hear its labored breathing. It was huffing and grunting its way up the hillside.

The wolf looked back at me for a moment before he bolted into the woods to confront whatever was coming.

"Wait," I tried to call out, but he was out of sight before I could speak.

Even though I couldn't see what happened when the wolf caught up to the thing out in the woods, I could hear it. The sound of their scuffle was a loud chorus of breaking branches, tumbling rocks, menacing growls, and guttural yells, yells that sounded almost human.

Run! Get out of here while you can! My mind screamed at me. *The wolf is buying you some time, don't waste it!*

I turned and hurried down the opposite side of the hill away from the conflict, but I didn't get very far. The slope on that side was too steep and rocky to make my way down in the moonlight. One wrong step and I could tumble to my death.

I circled back, trying to keep as much distance between me and the intense scuffle that was taking place a short distance away. Once again, I had to stop, but not because I couldn't get past them. It was a voice that stopped me.

"NOOOOO!!!"

That was not the sound of an animal. I stopped and turned towards the snarling and grunting. All I could see was the constant movement of a massive shadow, making it impossible for me to distinguish the wolf from whatever was grappling with him.

Ignoring my common sense, I moved closer to get a better look at them. What I saw confused me. The wolf, which I assumed was harmless, had its jaws clamped around the ankle of a man, trying to drag him off into the woods. The man was on his stomach, kicking at the wolf with his free leg, clawing at the ground as he tried to pull himself towards me.

"Get away from him," I yelled, running up and swinging the tire iron at the wolf.

The wolf released his hold on the man's leg, backing away from my wild swings while he barked and snarled his annoyance at me.

I expected the man to get up and thank me, but he didn't say a word. Once he got to his feet, he yelled something incoherent and came running at me, spittle flying from his lips. I didn't have time to react before he barreled into me, knocking us both to the ground.

The momentum of the collision sent the tire iron flying from my hand, and the two of us tumbling down the hill. When we finally came to a stop, I was pinned beneath the man who was at least fifty pounds heavier than me.

I braced my hands against the man's chest, trying to push him off. I only needed to lift him a few more inches before I'd have enough room to wiggle out from underneath him. That was when he turned his head and latched onto my forearm with his teeth.

"What the fuck is wrong with you!" I yelled at the man, frantically pounding my free hand against the side of his head, trying to make him let go.

He growled in response, biting down harder. Rivulets of blood began running down my arm as his teeth grated against the bone in my wrist. The pain was excruciating. No matter how hard I hit him, he wouldn't let go.

This isn't working.

I needed to try something else and fast. I couldn't pull my arm free, not without tearing off a chunk of flesh in the process.

Think!

I reached out, running my hand through the dirt and pine needles next to me, searching for a weapon.

My hand brushed against something. Desperate for anything I could use to defend myself, I wrapped my fingers around it, ignoring the barbs digging into my palm. I would have preferred a rock or a stick but was going to have to make do with the pinecone.

I rolled the pinecone in my hand until I had the pointy tip of it turned towards the stranger. *Please let this work.* Wielding the pinecone like a knife, I swung my arm towards the man's eye. He pulled his head back. The pinecone scraped across his cheek before being stopped by the bridge of his nose.

The man yelped in pain, releasing his hold on my arm, but I wasn't free yet. He still had me pinned beneath the bulk of his body.

Ignoring the stinging pain of the pinecone's barbs biting into my palm, I continued to drive it into the corner of his eye. I was hoping the attack would force him to roll off of me, but it didn't work that way. It only made him madder.

The stranger roared his frustration at me, spraying my face with spittle. Desperate to escape, I started to flail my arms against his chest and face. He was unfazed by the assault, waiting for me to exhaust myself before grabbing my arms and pinning them to the ground.

"What the fuck is wrong with you?" I yelled at him, renewing my struggle to get free.

He didn't answer. I didn't expect him to. The crazed look in his eyes told me he was beyond reasoning. When he leaned forward, bringing his face close to mine, I had a strange thought that he was going to try and kiss me. I turned my head to the side, hoping to avoid whatever he was planning on doing, but that was a mistake. He opened his mouth as wide as he could and lunged for my exposed neck.

I closed my eyes, bracing myself for the worst. The man's teeth were less than a second away from tearing into my throat, a bite that would mean certain death for me. Using what little strength I could muster, I tried one final time to buck him off of me.

It worked!

I was momentarily stunned as the weight of the man was suddenly lifted from my body.

I can't believe that actually worked!

But it hadn't worked. When I opened my eyes, I saw what had really happened. It wasn't me that had knocked the man off. It was the wolf. While the man kept his focus on me, the wolf had blindsided him, knocking him further down the hill.

The man bellowed his frustration at being thwarted, wasting no time getting back to his feet and running towards me.

The wolf, who had taken up a position between the psychopath and me, ran to meet him.

The man tried to dodge around the wolf, hell-bent on reaching me, but the animal was quicker. The large canine threw itself into the path of the man, causing both of them to stumble to the ground. The wolf regained its footing first, looking back at me over its shoulder. I knew what that look meant. He was telling me to get the fuck out of there

You don't have to tell me twice.

Hugging my injured arm against my chest, I got to my feet. *Thank you*, I gave the wolf one final look, but he had already turned back to face the man, teeth bared, ready to bite. I didn't stick around to see what happened next. The wolf could take care of itself, of that I was sure.

Moving as fast as I could, I ran, trying to put as much distance as possible between that crazy hillbilly and me. I slid and fell on more than one occasion, but I didn't let that slow me down. *I am never going back out into the woods again*, I promised myself. Somewhere behind me, I heard the wolf yelp. *Just give me a few more minutes, buddy.* I hoped he wasn't seriously injured.

When I made it to the bottom of the hill, I didn't stop running. I burst from the trees and right into the path of an oncoming truck. I was so intent on getting back to my car that I didn't think to look to see if there was anyone else on the road.

I froze, raising my arms in a feeble attempt to protect myself as the headlights closed in on me.

The driver of the truck slammed on the brakes and swerved to the side before screeching to a halt. The truck passed by so close that I could have reached out and touched the park ranger decal prominently displayed on the passenger door.

I dropped to my knees. The excitement of narrowly avoiding death for the second time that night had taken the strength out of my legs.

"What the hell are you doing in the middle of the road," the ranger said, slamming the door of his truck.

The look I gave him was enough to diffuse his anger.

"Are you ok, mister?" he asked, seeing my bloody hand curled against my chest.

I shook my head, trying to catch my breath and calm my beating heart, "No, I am most definitely not ok."

"Let's get you over to the truck so that I can take a look at that arm," the ranger said, helping me get to my feet.

He kept one hand on my back to keep me steady as we walked over to his vehicle. "Have a seat and tell me what happened," he said, opening the door.

While he pulled the first-aid kit from beneath the seat and tended to my injured wrist, I told him everything that had happened. The ranger didn't say a word as he cleaned the wound and bandaged it. His silence was a bit unnerving. I couldn't tell if he believed me or not.

"The man that attacked you," the ranger asked, finally breaking his silence. "Would you recognize him if you saw him again?"

"Yeah," I replied. "I don't think I could forget his face if I tried."

After the ranger put the first aid kit back under the seat, he reached up, popped open the glove compartment, and pulled out a piece of paper. "Is this him?" he asked, holding up the paper so I could see it.

"That's him," I said.

"Are you sure?"

I'm positive," I said, taking the sheet from him and examining it. "His hair is a bit longer now, and he has a bit of a beard, but that's him."

"I'm going to have to call this in," he said, reaching across me to grab his radio, which was sitting on the seat next to me.

"Who is he?" I asked, continuing to examine the picture, wondering how someone who looked so normal could act so crazy.

"That is Wayne Reynolds," he tapped the photo with his index finger. "He's wanted for the murder of his wife and kids."

After I heard the name, I realized I had heard it before. It was all over the news a couple of months ago. Wayne Reynolds woke up one night and brutally butchered his wife and daughters. "He dismembered them, right?"

"And ate them," the ranger replied. "At least that's what the medical examiner thinks. It seems they couldn't find all of the pieces."

I felt queasy as the image of Wayne Reynolds leaning in to bite my neck flashed before my eyes. *Was he planning on eating me too?*

"You alright?" the ranger asked.

"Yeah, I'm fine. Just a little light-headed."

"Once I call this in, we can get you set up in town. In the morning, you can see about getting your car towed."

"Alright," I said.

"Sit tight," he said, thumping the roof of the truck with his hand before shutting the door and calling the cavalry.

I watched the ranger through the windshield as he paced back forth in front of the truck, talking on his radio. Every once in awhile, he'd look back at me. That went on for about ten minutes until I saw him drop the radio to his side and stare off into the woods. I could tell the conversation was over, and the ranger wasn't happy about something.

"You ready to go?" he asked, climbing into the driver's seat and setting the radio on the dashboard.

"We're not staying?" I asked. I figured I'd have to hang around until the cops arrived so I could tell them what happened.

"Nope," his curt reply told me he wasn't happy about leaving.

"Why?"

"We're nonessential, that's the term the state police used. They told me to take you into town and let the doc look you over. Someone is supposed to meet us there to take your statement." He turned the key, starting the engine. "Is there anything you need to grab from your car before we head out?" He pointed at my Honda.

"No," I replied, and then suddenly remembered my phone. I reached behind me, intending to pull it out of my back pocket, but it wasn't there. "Shit! I lost my phone," I said. "It must have fallen out of my pocket when I was wrestling with that psychopath." I looked over at the hill.

"If you're thinking about going back out there to find it, forget it," the ranger said, putting the truck in gear and easing back onto the road.

"Don't worry," I gave a humorless laugh. "I have no intention of going back out there."

I kept my eyes on the hill as we drove off, wondering about my strange encounter with the wolf. If it weren't for him, I would have just been another victim of Wayne Reynolds.

"Can I ask you a question?" I asked, breaking the silence of the last few miles.

"What's on your mind?" He replied, turning to look at me.

"I'm assuming you're pretty familiar with this area."

"I've lived here my entire life. I know these woods like I know my own backyard." Without taking his hand off the steering wheel, he extended his index finger, indicating the dark shadows of the hills looming in the distance.

"How much do you know about wolves?" I asked.

"Is this about that wolf you saw, the one that helped you?"

"Yeah," I held his gaze for a moment. "Have you ever heard of anything like that happening before?"

"Never," he said, pausing to collect his thoughts. "If I'm being honest, I don't think what you saw was a wolf."

"Why do you think that?"

"There hasn't been a wolf sighting in this area in over forty years. Plus, the animal you described is much larger than any wolf that ever roamed these hills. Do you think it's possible that maybe what you saw was a dog? It's not uncommon for hunters and hikers to let their dogs roam free out here."

"I suppose it's possible," I said. "It did act more like a dog than a wolf, but it wasn't wearing a collar."

"Lots of owners around here don't have collars for their dogs," the ranger said.

I wasn't an expert on wolves or dogs, so I let the conversation drop, keeping my thoughts to myself. The ranger knew the area better than I did, and if he thought it was a dog, it probably was a dog. I was just trying to make sense of the weird encounter. It didn't matter what type of animal it was. I was grateful for its help.

"Here we are," the ranger said.

The trees that lined the road were suddenly replaced by houses and small businesses, many of which looked like they were built before I was born. Quite a few of them had their doors and windows boarded up or in disrepair. It was depressing.

"The town has seen better days," he said, sensing my mood. "The last thing it needs is any publicity from Wayne Reynolds."

The ranger pulled the truck up to the front of a small clinic. The design of it made me think that it may have once been a school at one time. Through the door I could see a bored-looking receptionist, staring at her phone.

"This is where we part ways," the ranger said, "At least for the time being."

"You're not staying?" I asked.

"I've got to get back to my post and finish my shift." He took one of his hands off of the steering wheel and reached into the breast pocket of his uniform and pulled out a business card. "I'll stop by and check on you in the morning. In the meantime, if you need anything, give me a call," he said, handing the card to me.

"Thanks, Boyd," I said, reading the ranger's name off of the card.

"Just doing my job," Boyd replied. "Now go get that arm looked at before the state police arrive and ruin the rest of your evening." He nodded towards the clinic.

"It can't possibly get worse than it already has," I said, opening the door of the truck and getting out.

"Knock on wood," Boyd said, wrapping his knuckle on the dashboard of the truck in an attempt to ward off any more misfortune for me.

I shut the truck door and raised my hand in a wave as Boyd drove off. Once he was back on the road, I pocketed the business card he gave me and walked through the automatic doors into the clinic.

"How can I help you, sir?" the lady behind the desk asked, putting down her phone. I could see she was wearing scrubs under her sweater. She looked like a nurse. The clinic must have had her pulling double duty as the receptionist as well.

"I've had a bit of an accident," I said, holding up my bandaged arm. Spots of blood had already started to seep through the gauze. "But first, I was wondering if I could use your phone to call my wife and let her know where I am?"

"Of course," the nurse said. "There's a phone right over there." She pointed to a table in the tiny waiting area.

I walked over to the phone, not bothering to sit down as I dialed my wife's number. Her phone rang four times before going to her voice mail. I didn't expect her to answer. She often set her phone to *Do Not Disturb* when she went to sleep.

I left her a message, telling her that I had car trouble and that I was going to be late getting home. I also told her that I had lost my phone, but I left out the part about the wolf and being attacked by Wayne Reynolds. I didn't want to worry her needlessly. There would be plenty of time to tell her all about it when I got home. I ended the call by telling her that I loved her and the kids and that I would call them in the morning.

When I turned back around, the nurse was standing there waiting for me, a clipboard in her hand.

"I just need you to fill out these forms," she held out the clipboard, "And I'm going to need to see your insurance cards."

I pulled my insurance card out of my wallet and traded it for the clipboard.

"Thank you, Mr. Coletti," she said, reading my name off of the insurance card. "I'll be right back."

While the nurse pulled up my insurance information on the computer, I sat down and filled out the paperwork.

"You all set?" the nurse asked ten minutes later, walking over to the waiting area to check on me.

"Yeah," I said, handing her the clipboard. She returned my insurance card.

She flipped through the paperwork, making sure I had filled everything out correctly and that I had signed and dated all of the appropriate forms.

"Alright, follow me," she said, leading the way through a set of double doors next to the reception desk. "My name is Amanda, I'm a nurse practitioner, and I'll be taking care of you."

She led me down the hallway and into a small examination room.

"Go ahead and hop up here," Amanda said, patting the table. I just need to check your vitals before we take a look at your arm."

She checked my temperature then put that little device on the tip of my finger to measure my pulse and oxygen. After that, she took my blood pressure. All of my results were normal. I was surprised when she told me what my blood pressure was. The last few times I've had it checked, it was elevated. My doctor had told me that I was likely going to have to take medication to manage it.

"Let's see what we've got here," Amanda said, slowly unrolling the bandage the ranger had wrapped around my hand.

"Are you the only one here?" I was just trying to make conversation.

"Edgar, the janitor, is around here somewhere," she replied, pulling the last of the bandage off my wrist. "Other than that, it's just me."

"Oh," was all I could think of to say.

"Most nights, I just sit at the desk reading or playing games on my phone. The weekend is when we tend to get most of our business, but that's just because the idiots that live here can't find anything else to do on a Saturday night besides getting drunk and picking fights."

"What happens if you have an emergency?"

"The serious cases get rerouted to the county hospital if it's something we can handle here, Doc Webber is the doctor on call. He lives just up the road."

While Amanda spoke, she examined the bite wound, gently turning my arm to get a better look at all of the teeth marks on my wrist.

"So, what happened here?" she gestured at my wrist with her gloved hand, "And don't try to tell me it was an accident like you said before. That's a pretty nasty looking bite mark, and judging from the pattern, I'd say the animal that bit you was a human."

"It wasn't an accident. I was attacked." There was no reason to keep the truth from her. I told her what happened, leaving out the part about the wolf. I don't know why I didn't mention it, I was about to but suddenly changed my mind.

"Wayne Reynolds? Holy shit! You're lucky that guy didn't kill you. I can't believe what that sick bastard did to his family. How did you get away?"

"I…Uh…I…" I searched my mind for a reasonable explanation, once again not wanting to mention to the wolf. "I had my tire iron with me." I pantomimed, swinging the tire iron. "When he let go, I pushed him off and ran."

"And that happened tonight?" She sounded skeptical.

"Yeah," I said, "About an hour ago. Why?"

"This wound doesn't look that fresh." She had a puzzled look on her face.

"What do you mean?" I said, looking at my arm, trying to make sense of what she was saying.

"These puncture wounds are already in the second stage of healing." Amanda pointed at a few of the bite marks. "See how they are enflamed and already starting to pucker around the edges?"

"Yeah," I said.

I could see what she was talking about, but I didn't understand why that was such a big deal.

"That usually doesn't happen for a few days, especially with wounds as deep as these," She nodded at my arm.

"That's a good thing, right?" I asked.

"It is a very good thing," she replied. "It means you won't need any stitches. But I'm afraid I'm still going to have to give you a couple of shots."

"A couple?" I raised my eyebrows. "As in more than one?" I didn't like needles.

"Afraid so," Amanda said. "The human mouth is a dirty place. Even though your wound is already healing, it can still get infected. To prevent that, I'm going to give you a tetanus shot and a shot of antibiotics. I'll also be sending you home with a prescription for some more antibiotics. But first, I'm going to clean and bandage your wrist."

"I won't be going home, not tonight." I still needed to call a tow truck and get my car fixed before I could go anywhere.

"If you need a place to stay," she said, wiping away the dried blood from my wrist with a damp cloth, "There's a motor lodge a short walk from here. I can give you directions before you leave."

"Thanks, I'd appreciate that."

After Amanda finished cleaning and bandaging my wrist, she gave me the two shots she promised, one in each butt cheek. I could still feel the sting from the shots as I followed her out of the exam room and back to the waiting room where a police officer was waiting by her desk.

"How can I help you, officer?" she asked.

"I think he's here to talk to me," I said.

"Mr. Coletti," the officer held his hand out to me. "I'm Deputy Landers. I'm with the state police."

I shook the offered hand. "Do you need me to go down to the station?"

"I don't think that will be necessary." He took off his hat and gestured towards the waiting room. "We can talk right here if it's okay with you, ma'am." He looked over at Amanda.

"I don't have a problem with that if he doesn't," she replied, looking over at me.

"It's fine with me," I said. "I'm ready to get this night over with."

Amanda gave me a sympathetic look, "I have to go tidy up," she said, pointing with one hand to the hallway we had just emerged from while handing me my antibiotic prescription with the other. "If you need anything, press the buzzer on the desk."

"Thanks," I said, watching her walk through the double doors and out of sight.

I followed deputy Landers over to the waiting room, taking the seat opposite from him so that we were facing each other. He pulled a pen and note pad from his shirt pocket. I waited while he flipped through the pages looking for a clean one to write one.

"Tell me what happened," he said.

"Where should I start?" I asked

He flipped, back a few pages, and read over some notes. "Start when your car died, and you had to pull over."

I assumed Boyd, the park ranger, had already given them a brief rundown of what I had told him when he radioed in calling for police assistance. With that in mind, I told Deputy Landers everything I had told Boyd.

When I got to the part about the wolf, I found that I had to force myself to talk about it. Something inside me wanted to keep my encounter with the animal a secret, which made me hold back on a few of the details. I didn't have the same issue when I was talking to Boyd. Thankfully, the deputy didn't question me on the wolf. He was more interested in who attacked me, asking me to describe the man as best as I could.

"You're sure this is the man that attacked you?" Deputy Landers held out his phone, showing me a picture of Wayne Reynolds.

"I'm positive," I replied. "Did you find him?"

"Not yet," he said. "But we will. He can't hide in those woods forever." Deputy Landers stood up, indicating the interview was coming to a close. "I just need to get some contact information from you, and then we're done here."

"I can give you my address and home phone number, but I lost my cellphone in the woods while I was running away from Wayne Reynolds. I don't suppose anyone found it?" I asked.

"Not that I know of," deputy Landers replied. "They did find a tire iron, which I'm assuming belongs to you. Which reminds me, we are going to have your car towed into town in the morning."

I was happy to hear that. That was one less thing I had to worry about.

"Go ahead and give me your address and telephone number." The deputy said. He had his pen and note pad ready

While I gave him my information, Amanda walked back into the waiting area and returned to her desk.

"I think I'm ready for those directions now," I said to Amanda, referring to the motor lodge she had mentioned earlier.

"It's called The Hunter's Hide if you walk out of here and…" She didn't get to finish what she was saying before deputy Landers interrupted her.

"I'm headed that way. I can drop you off if you like," he offered.

"Sure." I wasn't going to pass up a free ride. "That'd be great."

I followed Deputy Landers out to his car, where he opened the passenger door for me. Once he was inside the vehicle, he radioed his dispatcher to let them know he was leaving the clinic and heading back out to the scene.

He dropped me off in front of the office of the motel, handing me a card as I got out of the car. "Give me a call if you think of anything else that might help us."

"Will do," I said, pocketing the card. "And thanks for the ride."

The Hunter's Hide motel reminded me of the *Bate's Motel* from that old black and white movie *Psycho*. The only thing missing was a creepy old house looming in the distance.

I entered the office expecting to see a Norman Bates look like behind the counter, but was instead greeted by a bearded gentleman that looked like a member of *ZZ Top*. From the way he was rubbing his eyes and yawning, I must have woken him up.

He gave me the room at the far end of the motel, claiming it was the best of the bunch because it was the one closest to the vending machines. I took the key and thanked him, eager to get into the room so I could take a shower and try to get some sleep.

Taking a shower was a bit awkward. I had to wash with one hand while keeping the other one out of the stream of water. Once I was clean, I leaned my head against the wall and let the hot water run over my tired body. I stayed that way until I felt myself nodding off.

I climbed into the bed wearing nothing but my boxers, falling asleep the moment my head hit the pillow.

BAM! BAM! BAM!

I wiped the drool from my chin and opened my eyes, wondering where the banging was coming from. The sunlight streaming in through the crack in the curtains told me it was morning. I looked over at the clock. It was just after 8.

BAM! BAM! BAM!

Someone was banging on the door of my hotel room.

"Just a second," I croaked, trying to remember where I had tossed my clothes. I found them lying on the floor just outside the bathroom. I got dressed as fast as I could, tugging open the door. Whoever was knocking had better have a good reason for waking me up.

I had only gotten the door open a few inches before someone pushed their way into the room, knocking me into the wall. The intruder's face was instantly recognizable. It was Wayne Reynolds. His right eye was bruised and swollen from where I hit him with the pinecone.

Wayne placed his hands out in front of him, "I'm not here to hurt you," he said. "I just need to talk to you."

"We don't have anything to talk about," I said, casting a look over at the phone, wondering if I could get to it before he could stop me.

He knew what I was thinking and took a step to the side, blocking my path. He positioned himself in such a way that he could quickly stop me if I made a run for the phone or the door.

"I just want to talk. I swear." He kept his hands out in the open where I could see them. "Look, I'll prove it." He reached behind him and pulled my phone out of his back pocket. "I will give this back to you if you'll just hear me out."

There was something desperate about his demeanor. He had changed drastically since I last saw him. Gone was the crazy look from his eyes. In its place was the look of a tired and defeated man.

"Fine," I said, crossing my arms over my chest. "Make it quick."

Wayne put my phone back in his pocket. "You might want to sit down," he said, pointing at the chair in the corner of the room

"I'm fine where I am." Strangely I wasn't afraid of him any longer. There was something pitiable about the way he stood there with his shoulder sloped.

He took a deep breath and ran his hands through his hair. "This is going to sound crazy…"

"Crazy doesn't begin to describe what you did to me out in those woods," I snapped at him, holding up my bandaged wrist

"That wasn't me," he said.

"If it wasn't you, then who was it," I scoffed.

"It was the wolf," he replied, sitting down on the edge of the bed.

The wolf, hearing him speak about the wolf made me uneasy. He shouldn't be talking about it.

"I can tell it's already starting to affect you," he said, seeing the troubled look on my face. "The wolf doesn't like being the center of attention. It prefers to remain hidden."

"I don't know what are you talking about?"

"That's why I'm here. To help you understand." He paused, spending the next few moments staring at the floor. When his gaze returned to me, there were tears in his eyes. "I just hope you're a lot smarter than me and listen."

I didn't say anything. I just waited for him to get to the point.

"I didn't kill my family. I would never hurt them." He wiped his eyes with the back of his hand. "And I didn't do that." He pointed at my wrist.

I was about to refute his claim, but he held up his hand, quieting me.

"It was my body, but it wasn't me," Wayne said, fixing me with his good eye. "I was bitten two months ago. I was out late trying to finish some work on one of my construction sites when this crazy guy came out of nowhere and tackled me. When I held up my arm to defend myself, he sank his teeth into my forearm. If the wolf hadn't shown up and fought him off, he would have killed me."

The wolf again.

"I didn't tell anyone what happened. When my wife saw my bandaged arm, I just told her I cut myself at work. It happened often enough, so she didn't question it. A few days later, I was shocked when the man who had bitten me showed up at the construction site again. I threatened to call the cops on him if he didn't leave. Before I managed to chase him off, he threw a folded up piece of paper at me, begging me to read it. The last thing he said to me before he ran off was, 'If you love your family, you'll get as far away from them as possible.'

"This is what he threw at me," Wayne said, pulling a folded up piece of paper out of his pocket. It was yellowed with age, and the corners were flaking off. He held it out to me.

I took the paper and slowly unfolded it, doing my best to keep it intact. It was a handwritten note, and this is what it said:

The Weird Wolf has bitten you. When the full moon rises, your body belongs to the beast, and his body belongs to you. I could not stop his hunger. I pray you are more successful than me. Protect your loved ones. Get as far away from them as you can.

"The wolf," I forced the words out, "That was you trying to help me?"

Wayne nodded his head.

"This is...this is insane." I tried to hand the note back to him.

"That's yours now," he said, refusing to accept it. "This is also yours," he added, pulling my phone out of his pocket and holding it out to me. "I'm sorry this happened to you," he said. "I truly am. I did everything I could to stop him. I never thought we'd run into anyone out there."

I took the phone and stared at it, remembering when I attacked the wolf, thinking I was saving the man.

Had I sealed my own fate?

Wayne stood up and headed for the door.

"Where are you going?" I also stood up.

"I know you want answers, but I don't have them. All I can tell you is that note is real. If I had believed it, my family would still be alive." He opened the door.

"Where will you go?" I asked.

"I'm going to turn myself in," he sighed, turning back to face me from the doorway. "I'm tired of running, and it's time I take responsibility for the death of my family."

"But you didn't kill them."

"I might as well have. I might have been able to save them if I hadn't been home that night."

"Why didn't you turn yourself in earlier, once you found out what had happened?"

"I tried, but the wolf wouldn't let me. You'll learn soon enough that the wolf will do anything to survive and remain free. Plus, I'm not just turning myself in because I feel guilty. I'm turning myself in to protect myself from you."

"Me?"

"The wolf didn't just use my body to kill my family that night. It also killed the man who bit me. They just haven't found his body yet. The wolf will use you to track me down and kill me the first chance he gets."

"Why?"

"The fewer people that now about him, the greater his chances of survival are. If you love your family, you'll get as far away from them as possible. The ones closest to you are the biggest threat to its survival." That was the last thing Wayne Reynolds said to me before shutting the door and walking away.

BEST PATH FORWARD

"Right this way, Mr. Allen." Ted, the representative from Best Path Forward, held the door open and gestured for me to enter the small waiting area.

I stepped into the middle of the room and turned to face the three unmarked doors before me. Ted followed closely behind me with a thick manila folder clutched under his arm.

"Can I get you anything before we begin," Ted asked. "Coffee? Tea?"

"I'm good," I replied, keeping my eyes on the three doors before me, wondering which one I would choose.

"Okay then, let's begin," Ted wiped the sweat from his brow and smiled nervously.

I didn't know why he seemed so tense. I was the one about to make the most significant decision of my life.

"As you requested, we have screened all possible candidates and chosen the top three for you to interview. In each room, you will find a folder like this," Ted gestured to the folder he was holding, "Filled with all of the information you need to make your decision. Once you have read through the folder, you are allowed to ask each candidate three yes or no questions, but under no circumstance are you allowed to answer any questions they might ask you."

"Let's do this," I said, straightening my tie and adjusting my suit as I approached the first door.

"You have thirty minutes to complete your assessment. You can spend as much time as you like with each candidate. It doesn't matter as long as you finish within the thirty-minute timeframe. It is your time, spend it wisely," Ted said as I reached out and grasped the handle of the door. "Your time starts the moment you open the first door and walk inside."

"I know," I cast an annoyed glance back at Ted as I spoke. "I read the rules and regulations packet you gave me when I hired you."

"Sorry," Ted apologized. "It's company policy to go back over the rules before we begin."

I raised my eyebrows and gestured impatiently with my hand for him to get on with it.

"There's one last thing." Ted held up his index finger. "Once you leave a room, you cannot return to it."

"Understood," I said. "Can I open the door now?"

"If you don't have any questions for me, you can start whenever you are ready." The nervous smile returned to Ted's face.

I took a deep breath, opened the door, and walked inside.

Before me was a desk with a manila folder sitting upon it, above the desk was a blacked-out window designed to keep me from seeing the candidate. They didn't want any kind of physical deformity I might see to sway my decision.

Hanging on the wall to my left was an old fashioned telephone handset.

I sat down at the desk and opened the folder. As I began to read through the resume before me, I thought there must be some mistake. I couldn't understand how the man in this room could be one of my top three candidates.

I was about to get up and leave, having already decided there was no way I was going to choose this person when I decided to ask one of my three questions.

I picked up the handset from the wall and held it to my ear. While I waited for the man on the other side of the window to do the same, I flipped through the folder. I wanted to make sure I was reading it correctly, looking for something I missed that would make me understand why they had chosen him to be here. When I heard the phone click, indicting a connection had been established, I asked my question.

"Are you insane?"

There was a brief pause followed by a scoffing sound, "No," the person on the other end of the line responded. "Are you?" he asked. The phone distorted his voice, making him sound like a robot. That was another security measure to prevent bias when choosing a candidate.

I was about to ask him another question, hoping to get an explanation for the things I was reading in his file. But I knew they were monitoring the call, and I would be disconnected if I asked anything other than a yes or no question. Instead, I hung up the phone, closed the file, and left the room.

"Everything okay?" Ted's voice was shaky.

I ignored him and approached the door to the second room. Everything was not okay, and Ted already knew that. He was the one who had prepared the files in each room and already knew what was in them. That must be why he was so nervous. He knew I wouldn't be happy now that I only had two candidates left.

I threw the door to the second room open and then slammed it shut after I entered, making sure Ted knew just how upset I was.

Once inside, I adjusted my suit and then sat down at the desk and began to read the next candidate's file.

This has got to be some sort of sick joke!

I slammed the folder shut, knocking the chair over as I got up to leave the room. This candidate's resume was almost the same as the one in the first room.

I walked out and glared at Ted as I approached the third door. He gave a weak smile in return.

The third one better be the fucking charm, I thought sarcastically, yanking the door to the third room open.

After I walked into the room, I took a moment to compose myself before sitting down. Once seated, I took a deep breath and slowly opened the folder on the desk and began to read through the file.

"GOD DAMMNIT!" I yelled, grabbing the folder and storming out of the room.

"Is this your idea of a sick joke?" I yelled at Ted, slapping the folder against his chest. "I paid you a lot of money to find my top three candidates, and all you can find are three murderers."

"I'm sorry you are not happy with our service Mr. Allen, but I assure you, those are your top three candidates. Our technology is infallible."

"You expect me to believe that the three best men I can become all involve me killing my family?" I threw the file into the air, letting the pages within flutter to the ground.

"I know it is hard to accept, but that is what we found. We couldn't find any future in which you did not kill your family at some point during your life. The only futures where your family survived were the ones where your wife was able to kill you first."

I stepped closer to Ted, bumping into him with my chest. "I choose…" I paused, seeing the fear in his eyes. Now that I had read all three files, I knew why Ted was feeling so antsy.

"I choose candidate number one," I finally said.

Ted released the breath he was holding, relieved to hear my choice. "Yes, Mr. Allen. I will have the necessary paperwork ready for you before you leave."

"You better, Ted, or else I might change my mind and choose candidate number three."

"Of course, Mr. Allen," Ted said, practically tripping over himself to leave.

He knew that if I had chosen the third candidate, he would have been my first victim.

RETURN CARTS HERE

A few weeks ago, I got word that my store was going to be the field testing site for a new type of shopping cart. One that was supposed to make walking through the aisles feel like gliding through the air or skating on ice. Those aren't my words. That is what the email I received from corporate said.

In the twenty years I have been with the company, we have gone through three different sets of shopping carts, from metal to plastic, and they were all alike. They were the same basic shape, the same basic size, and they always developed the same basic problems.

I didn't think the store needed to waste money on a new set of carts. The carts weren't the problem. It was the inconsiderate shoppers who abused the carts that were the problem. But I was just a manager. My opinion didn't matter to the corporate decision-makers.

A few days after being notified about the new shopping carts, I received a large envelope in the mail packed with colorful, yet pointless, propaganda on the cart's design along with the manufacturing process. I also received a thick stack of survey cards to hand out to the customers once they had a chance to try the new buggies out.

I read through the material that night and was sort of blah about everything. They were just shopping carts, after all. I didn't care that they were made of some new eco-friendly polymer or that they could hold twice the weight of a traditional cart. I was pretty sure the customers weren't going to care much either.

When the carts arrived, I had to admit they had a visually pleasing aesthetic. At least as pleasing as a shopping cart could be. The baskets were made entirely out of black plastic, while the underlying frame was metal. The thing I liked most was that they weren't rectangular like most carts. All of the edges were rounded off, which made them look like an escape pod from a spacecraft.

The carts also had excellent maneuverability. I took one through the store for a test drive and was surprised at how well it handled. I was able to make tight turns into the aisles with no problem. When I took the corners fast, the cart didn't threaten to tip over as the old ones would. The wheels never lost traction, nor did they wobble or squeak. Now I know why corporate had used the words gliding and skating to describe them.

The customers seemed to like the carts. Every survey card I read gave them high marks with more than one shopper saying it was the best cart they've ever used. I was starting to develop a sense of pride in them and was happy that my store was picked to be the test site. But like all good things, the feeling didn't last very long.

The day everything went to shit, I had to park next to one of our cart corrals. I don't like parking next to them if I can help it, but I didn't have much choice. It was either that or parking near the street, which is a bit of a hike, and I don't like walking that far if I can help it.

After work, when I returned to my car, I found one of the new shopping carts pressed up against the driver's side door.

"Stupid, fucking, lazy people," I cursed the person who couldn't be bothered to place the cart in the corral.

I grabbed the handle of the cart, intending to put it in the corral where it belonged, but I stopped when I saw the sizable dent in my door.

"You have got to be fucking kidding me," I fumed.

I admit I have a temper, and I probably should have taken a moment to calm down and just push the cart into the corral like I was going to, but I let my anger get the better of me.

I'd be lying if I said it didn't feel good to kick the cart over onto its side. I felt even better when I noticed the kick had caused a significant crack along the side of the cart's basket. I smiled. That seemed like a fair trade-off to me, a crack for a dent.

I left the busted cart on its side, got in my car, and went home. I decided to let the opening manager deal with it since I had the next day off.

The next morning I contacted my insurance company to see about getting the dent fixed. After spending an hour on the phone arguing about whether or not my policy covered the damage, I decided it would be quicker and less of a headache just to pay to have it fixed myself, so that is what I did.

When I returned to work, I wasn't in the best of moods. Seeing all of the new shopping carts strewn about the parking lot just made it worse.

"Lazy ass people," I said, gathering up a few of the stray carts and slamming them into the nearest cart corral.

I told corporate we needed more hours for cart attendants, but they didn't think so.

On my way to the front office, I was stopped by Rodney, the stock manager, who informed me that we had a return truck the next day, and I needed to get my stuff processed. One of my duties is to sign off on all of the defective merchandise we have and get it boxed up so that it could be shipped back to the warehouse.

Once I dropped my stuff off in the office, I walked to the receiving bay at the back of the store. That is where we keep all of the unprocessed returns we've collected over the past week.

As I surveyed the pile of merchandise, deciding where to begin, I noticed a single cart parked in the corner of the truck bay with a handwritten note on it that said DAMAGED.

It looked like I was going to have to deal with the cart I had busted after all. I didn't mind, though. Nothing would have made me happier at that moment than to send that cart back to the warehouse, knowing it was going to get destroyed. I decided to process it last and savor my victory over it.

As I was filling out the forms to transfer the damaged merchandise back to the warehouse, I was interrupted by a short but loud squeak. It sounded like a rusty hinge being forced open too quickly.

I looked up and scanned the area but couldn't tell what had made the sound. I was in a large receiving bay with metal doors, metal racking, and various other metal objects. The squeaking could have come from any one of those things.

I returned to my paperwork. The moment my pen touched the form I was filling out, the squeak returned. I continued writing, trying to ignore the intermittent noise, but I couldn't. It was too annoying.

I waited until it started again and then whirled around, trying to pinpoint where the sound was coming from. When I turned, my elbow caught the edge of a box, sending merchandise falling to the floor, the sound of which made it impossible to tell where the squeaking was coming from before it stopped.

I bent over to pick up the contents of the box.

"Can this day get any worse?" I asked the empty room.

It could. While I was shoving things back into the box, the squeaking returned. This time it was louder and more insistent than before, and I was getting royally pissed off.

I looked up, a yell of frustration forming in the back of my throat, but it got cut short when the shopping cart slammed into my forehead knocking me back and onto my ass.

I was stunned for a moment and confused about what had just happened. Somehow, the shopping cart in the corner squeaked its way across the receiving bay until it rolled into me. It wasn't a casual roll either; there was some force behind it. If I didn't know any better, I'd say someone had pushed the cart, but there was no way someone could have entered the loading area without me noticing them.

I got to my feet, fingering the tender spot on my forehead, feeling the tight knot of a bump already forming.

That cart is going to pay. There was no way I was ever going to let it roll again.

Underneath the racking in the receiving bay behind the toolbox is a giant sledgehammer. For the longest time, I wondered why it was there. We've never had cause to use it, yet there it has sat for years. At that moment, I knew exactly what it was for and intended to make use of it.

I grabbed the hammer and walked over to the cart. I had the silly notion that it might try to flee, so I kicked it onto its side. Once I was sure it wasn't going to roll away, I raised the hammer over my head and brought it down on the cart's basket. I kept hammering it until it was a mess of broken plastic and bent metal. Then I picked up the pieces and threw them in the trash compacter.

Satisfied that the cart would never bother me again, I finished processing the damaged products and left the receiving bay, heading to the front office with a smile on my face.

As I turned down the toilet paper aisle, I had to move to the side to let a young woman wheel her cart by me. When she was about to pass me, the cart she was pushing unexpectedly turned to the side, causing the bottom bar of the frame to ram into the bony part of my shin.

I hissed in pain and lifted my injured leg.

"I'm so sorry," she apologized. "I don't know what happened. I was pushing it straight ahead, and it just suddenly veered towards you. I really am so sorry."

"It's okay," I managed to say through clenched teeth.

I continued walking, with a slight limp, until I made it to the central aisle and turned towards the front of the store. I made it past three more aisles before I was blindsided and knocked sprawling onto the floor. As I started to get up, ready to give someone a piece of my mind, a shopping cart rolled past me with an older gentleman hobbling after it as fast as he could.

"Sorry," the elderly man said once he had regained control of his cart, "These new carts move so fast. I guess it got away from me."

"Don't worry about it," I growled, getting to my feet and brushing my pants off before walking off.

For the rest of my walk to the front of the store, I stopped at each aisle to make sure no one else was going to try and run me over with a shopping cart. My actions got me several peculiar looks from the people I passed, but I didn't give a shit. I was in pain and had a growing suspicion the carts were out to get me.

When I made it to the front of the store, I had a clear view of the register lanes. The coast was clear, so I picked up my pace until I was practically running. I thought I was home free but suddenly found myself falling flat on my face as one of the kid-sized shopping carts, the ones designed to look like miniature versions of our standard shopping carts, managed to catch me in mid-stride.

"Why did you do that?" the mother of the girl who was pushing the cart yelled at her daughter.

"I'm sorry," the girl's mother said to me. "I don't know what she was thinking."

"I didn't do it," the girl started to cry.

The cashier came over and tried to help me to my feet, but I shrugged her off and limped to the office, holding my arms against my sore body. Once I was safely inside, I slammed the door and locked it.

I knew one of the other managers kept a small pharmacy in the desk, so I searched the drawers until I found a bottle of aspirin. I dropped two pills into my hand, then decided to add two more before popping them into my mouth.

What the hell is going on? Are the carts out to get me now?

That couldn't be true. Carts were inanimate constructs of metal and plastic. They don't think, and they can't feel pain. There was no sane reason they would be out to get me.

After I had calmed down and was able to think rationally, I was able to convince myself that I was just the victim of a series of bizarre events involving shopping carts. To be on the safe side of fate and circumstance, I avoided getting close to any shopping carts for the rest of the evening.

Once I got all of the registers closed and let all of the employees go home for the night, I let out a big sigh of relief. I couldn't wait to get home and put this day behind me. I was sore in so many places and just wanted to take a hot shower and go to bed.

When I walked outside, I was irritated to see that no one had bothered to bring in the carts. That was supposed to be done by the stock crew before they left, but they had a convenient habit of forgetting some nights. At least they were all corralled, and I wasn't parked anywhere near them.

Even though I knew I would get shit for it the next day, I was going to leave them where they were and let the morning crew bring them inside.

I approached my car feeling more and more relieved with each step I took, thinking the worst was behind me, but I was wrong.

I could hear a faint squeaking sound coming from behind me, which caused my heart to skip a beat. I turned around in a complete circle, scanning the parking lot, looking for any shopping carts nearby, but they were all still in the corrals.

I hurried to my car, dropping my keys as I tried to pull them out of my pocket. That damn squeaking had made me so jumpy my hands were shaking.

I knelt to pick up the keys, the squeaking starting the moment my fingers closed around them. It was loud, which meant it was very close. I began to rise, but my hands were shaking so much that I couldn't hold onto the keys. They fell back to the pavement. I tried to catch the keys as they fell, but I missed and ended up kicking them under the car.

I got down on my hands and knees, trying to see where the keys fell. What I saw on the opposite side of the car made me almost piss my pants. Several black rubber wheels quickly squeaked by, taunting me. They had done their job of distracting me long enough for the other carts to get into position.

The first cart hit me from behind and sent me sprawling onto my stomach. That caused me to scrape my hands on the asphalt as I tried to catch myself.

The second cart hit me on my side, right in the middle of my ribcage. There was a loud popping sound like someone was cracking their knuckle, then searing pain. I tried to roll over, but the pain was unbearable. That was when the bottom of the third cart hit me on the side of the head. The cart had hit me so hard that it flipped over and landed on top of me.

I could no longer hear the squeaking coming from the carts. It had been replaced by a loud, ringing sound coming from my ear. There was also a warm liquid running down my cheek, and I was starting to feel nauseous and dizzy. I was in so much pain that my vision began to blur and dim.

I tried to get up, but the muscles in my arms refused to cooperate. As I felt the darkness of oblivion closing in, I turned to the side and was able to focus my eyes long enough to see the line of carts waiting to take their shot at me. *They are out to get me.* That was my last thought before the darkness claimed me.

I awoke in the hospital three days later with a concussion, a ruptured eardrum, and several broken ribs, and an assortment of colorful cuts and bruises. I also had some form of amnesia and couldn't remember why I was in the hospital, but I was in a hell of a lot of pain and knew it must be for a very good reason.

Once the doctor found out I was awake, he came by and gave me a rundown of my injuries and his prognosis of my recovery after first assessing the extent of my amnesia. I was hoping he would tell me what happened to me, but before I could ask him, my memory was rudely returned to me by a familiar sound.

The squeaking started somewhere out in the hall then stopped. After a brief pause, it started again, then as quickly as it had begun, it stopped again.

"Is something wrong?" The doctor asked, noticing the large drops of sweat that began to snake down my forehead.

"Did you hear that?" I whispered. "...that squeaking." Right after I said that the squeaking began again, but now it was much louder.

I was terrified. Before the doctor could answer me, I jumped out of bed and ran to the door, tipping over my IV stand in the process. Just as I was about to slam the door shut, I was hit in the stomach by something rolling into my room.

"Oh my God, I'm so sorry; I didn't expect you to be out of bed." The nurse gasped as she ran over to help me.

Once she and the doctor helped me back into bed and made sure I hadn't added to my list of injuries, I was able to see the thing that punched me in the gut. It was nothing more than a little rolling cart used by the nurse to deliver medicine. I felt silly, but then I thought to myself, *maybe it knows.* That was when I started screaming for them to get it out of the room. It took two orderlies and the doctor to subdue me long enough to inject me with a sedative.

The next couple of days, they kept me sedated and did a few tests to make sure there wasn't anything wrong with my head that would make me lash out the way I had. During that time, I was able to keep myself under control, thanks mostly to the drugs.

By the end of the week, I convinced the doctor that my outburst was a momentary lapse of judgment, and it wouldn't happen again. He believed me and cleared me to go home, but first, I had to speak with a police officer about what happened the night of my accident.

"I don't know that I can help you," I said to the officer after he asked me to walk him through the events of that night. "I was walking to my car when I was jumped from behind. The next thing I remember is waking up in this hospital bed."

That was technically the truth, I was jumped, but I wasn't going to tell him it was the shopping carts that did it. He'd put me in the looney bin if I said that.

"But they didn't steal anything, right?" the officer asked.

"Not that I know of," I replied.

"Do you know of anyone that would want to hurt you? Maybe an angry customer or employee?"

"No," I said, shaking my head while in my mind I said, *Yeah, the shopping carts want to hurt me.*

"Well, you're lucky that street sweeper came by when he did," he stood up and pulled a card out of his pocket. "Give me a call if you remember anything."

I took the card and nodded.

On the day I was to be released from the hospital, the nurse came to tell me my ride was waiting for me in the lobby. I had called Rodney and asked if he could give me a lift back to the store so I could pick up my car.

"Would you like me to get you a wheelchair?" she asked.

"NO!" I said a little too quickly and a little too loudly. I didn't want to be near anything that remotely resembled a shopping cart. "No," I repeated in a calmer voice. "I'd prefer to walk."

I walked down to the lobby, trying to hide how much pain I was still in, and waved to Rodney when he caught sight of me coming off the elevator. As he helped me into his car and drove me to the store, we talked about nonsense and avoided the topic of what happened to me. It wasn't until we had reached the parking lot that I got up the courage to ask him about the carts and if the store was going to keep them. The trial period was supposed to be ending this week.

"Oh, don't worry about the carts," Rodney said. "The company has decided to add them to all the stores. They'll still be here when you get back."

That's what I was afraid of.

SAY IT SALLY

10:00 AM

I went into the kitchen, made myself a bowl of cereal, and carried it into the dining room to eat. If I had my way, I would have taken it back to my room, but my mother would have had a fit if she caught me doing that. The last time I tried, she disconnected my Xbox from the router for an entire weekend.

When I entered the room, my little sister Constance was already at the table playing with her crayons while she ate her toast. I pulled out my chair and started to sit down. I should have known something was up when Constance stopped what she was doing and started watching me with a sly smile on her face.

"What the fuck, Constance?" I yelled after I had I sat on her doll, sending one of its hard plastic limbs into the crack of my ass with enough force to bruise my tailbone.

Both Constance and the doll started laughing. I hated that doll. It was hideous and had one of the most annoying voices. If you squeezed different parts of its body, it would say different things. The laugh happened whenever you squeezed its stomach.

I stood up and grabbed the doll off the seat by its leg.

"Give it back!" Constance ran over and tried to snatch the doll out of my hand, but I held it over her head just out of arm's reach.

"You want it?" I said, holding the doll before me like a football. "Go get it." I dropped it then kicked it into the living room.

As the doll flew over the sofa, it giggled then said, "uh-oh, better get a diaper."

"Mom! Adam kicked Sally." Say it Sally was the name of her doll.

"Mom, Mom, Mom!" I mocked her.

"What have I told you about taking her doll away?" Our mother stormed into the dining room.

"I didn't take it," I said. "Constance left it in my chair, so I moved it."

"Don't push me, Adam. Go and get her doll." She pointed towards the living room.

"But."

"Do it," she said, turning and walking back to the kitchen. That was how she let you know the conversation was over. She would just walk away.

Constance stuck her tongue out as I walked by on my way to the living room. I pretended to pick my nose then reached out to wipe my finger on her tongue. She screamed and ran into the kitchen.

"Stupid doll," I said, reaching down to pick it up, but before I did, it said the strangest thing.

"No more days…will follow…for you…there's no tomorrow," It came out of Say it Sally's mouth like a poem, but the words seemed like they were cobbled together from different phrases the doll typically says.

I grabbed the doll by its hair and carried it into the kitchen, where I dropped it on the floor in front of Constance, who was telling my mother that I tried to make her eat a booger.

"Keep your creepy doll away from me," I said, leaving the room to go eat my cereal.

12:00 PM

"I need you to keep an eye on Constance while I run to the store," my mother called out as she walked down the hall.

I was sitting at my desk playing on my laptop.

"Did you hear me?" She stopped in my doorway.

"I heard you," I snapped back.

She glared at me for a moment and then stormed into my room and pulled something out from underneath my bed.

"I thought I told you to leave her doll alone," she said, holding up Sally for me to see.

"I didn't put it there," I protested. "Constance probably put it there to get me in trouble."

"I don't have time for this," she said, walking out of the room with the doll. "Just leave it alone."

1:00 PM

"Mommy said you have to play with me while she is gone," Constance walked into my room, hugging her ugly doll.

"No, she didn't. Now get out," I pointed towards the door.

"If you don't play with me, I'll tell mommy about the nudie magazines under your bed."

"What," I said, momentarily confused by how she knew about the magazines. A friend of mine stole them from his older brother and gave them to me. I kept them with my comic books in a box under my bed. "Have you been going through my things?" I stood up and approached her.

"No," she said, holding her doll out towards me, "Sally told me."

I grabbed Constance by the shoulders, turned her around, and marched her out of my room.

"She also said to tell you a poem, but I can't remember it. I do remember that it ended with there's no tomorrow."

I slammed the door in her face and locked it.

"What does that mean?" Constance's muffled voice came through the door. "She's never said a poem before."

I ignored her and got down on my hands and knees to look under my bed. As I tried to locate my box of comics, the one with the magazines in it, something else caught my eye among the clutter. It was a small piece of silvery plastic about three inches long. I didn't recognize it at first, so I reached under the bed and pulled it out.

"What the hell," I said, holding up the little plastic knife that had been sharpened to a point. I recognized it as one of the toy utensils that came with my sister's play kitchen.

I walked back over to the door, unlocked it, and swung it open. I was going to confront my sister and ask her where the little knife had come from, but I changed my mind when I saw Say it Sally sitting on the floor across the hall from my room.

"I will feel…no sorrow…for you…there's no tomorrow," Sally said.

I kicked the doll down the hall, watching it fly through the air to land in the living room. I wasn't afraid of it. It was just a toy. If it wanted to keep threatening me, I was going to respond in kind.

"Have you seen Sally?" Constance asked, peeking her head out of her room.

"Nope," I replied. "If she knows what's good for her, she probably left," I added, returning to my room and shutting my door.

2:00 PM

"I found this under my bed." I held the toy knife in the palm of my hand so my mother could see it.

"So," she said. "I remember you doing something similar with one of your plastic army knives when you were younger."

"I only did that because you wouldn't let dad buy me a real one."

"Maybe she was just trying to make it more functional. You know how much she loves having tea parties and cutting up donuts like they are cake. I'm sure it's nothing."

"Nothing," I scoffed. "This thing is razor-sharp." I held it up like I would a real knife. "And why was it under my bed?"

"I'll talk to her," my mother said, pulling the knife out of my hand and setting it on the counter.

"Whatever." I threw my hands up and turned to leave. I knew Constance wouldn't get in trouble.

As I tried to walk out of the kitchen, something caught on my foot and almost sent me tumbling face-first into the corner of the granite countertop. If I hadn't flung my arms out and caught myself, I could have been killed.

"Are you going to talk to her about that too?" I said, kicking Sally across the floor. That stupid doll is what I had tripped over. "Every time I turn around, that ugly doll is in my way," I complained.

"I will talk to her," my mother said, walking over to retrieve Sally. "But if you kick or throw this doll, one more time…"

She pointed Sally at me as she gave her warning, and didn't have to finish what she was thinking. I knew what her favorite punishments were.

2:30 PM

"I'm sorry," Constance huffed from the doorway to my room.

"No, you're not," it was evident from her tone that she was only apologizing because my mother made her.

"You're right. I'm not, because I didn't do it."

"You didn't do what?" I wanted to find out what my mother had told her. She had a history of going easy on Constance

"I didn't make that knife, and I didn't leave Sally on the floor. I shouldn't have to apologize."

"Let me guess, Sally did it all by herself, right?"

"She did!" Constance yelled. "She was only trying help."

"Whatever." I got up and crossed the room to shut the door, "Apology not accepted, and for the last time, keep your doll away from me or else."

"Or else what?"

"Or else I'm going to pull off her arms and legs and feed them to the neighbor's dog. Now move so I can close the door."

"I'm telling mom."

"Go ahead," I said, shutting the door in her face.

I could hear her repeated cries of "Mom" as she ran down the hall to tattle on me. I didn't care.

4:00 PM

The sound of a piece of paper sliding under the bedroom door caught my attention. I got up from the desk and went over to pick it up. It was a handwritten note in red crayon that said: NO DAYS WILL FOLLOW FOR YOU THERE'S NO TOMORROW. I recognized my sister's handwriting.

I reached out and grabbed the handle to the door, intending to show my mother the note, but stopped myself. Knowing her, she would just dismiss it and tell me to grow up and stop acting like a toddler. It wasn't worth the hassle. I crumpled the note in my hand and tossed it into the wastebasket next to my desk. I had something else in mind to get even with my sister and Sally.

4:15 PM

When I saw Constance pass by my room on her way down the hall, I got up to see where she was going. I had opened my door, so I could keep tabs on her while I was waiting for the perfect time to enact my plan.

It's now or never. I crept down the hall and into Constance's room after I saw her step into the bathroom and close the door. While I was in her room, I took her jump rope off of her dresser, then walked over and grabbed Sally from her seat at the tea party table. Then I got to work.

When I finished, another idea occurred to me, so I ran down the hall to my room. Once I grabbed what I needed, I returned to Constance's room and added it as a final touch. *Perfect*, I admired my handiwork for a moment before leaving. I finished just in time too.

Constance walked out of the bathroom right as I walked back into my room.

I knew I was going to get in trouble for what I had done, but it was worth it.

4:25 PM

"MOM!"

I couldn't help but smile when I heard Constance yell, but my joy was short-lived. When her screams became sobs, I suddenly felt like the biggest jerk in the world. I was okay with making her mad, not with making her cry. From the way she was wailing, you'd think I actually killed her doll.

"What the hell is wrong with you?" My mother came into my room, holding Sally by the jump rope noose I had hung her with. Still taped to her dress was the altered note that now said: NO DAYS WILL FOLLOW FOR ~~YOU~~ ME THERE'S NO TOMORROW.

I couldn't look her in the eyes.

"Answer me! Why would you do something like this?" She raised the fist that was clutching the rope, making Sally sway.

"It was a joke," I replied, looking at the posters on my wall.

"This was not a joke." She removed the noose and note before tossing Sally onto my bed. "Go in there and apology to her." She pointed towards Constance's room.

I stood up and snatched the doll off my bed, which triggered her giggle.

"You'll be lucky if I don't tell your father about this when he gets back from his trip," my mother's voice carried down the hall as I knocked on my sister's door. She was watching me from the doorway.

"GO AWAY!" Constance yelled. "I HATE YOU!"

I turned and looked at my mother while gesturing at the door. How did she expect me to apologize to Constance if she was going to overreact like that? She just folded her arms over her chest and cocked her head to the side, letting me know I wasn't getting out of it.

"If you don't open the door, Sally's going to be lonely out here all by herself."

She didn't answer, but I could hear her get up off of her bed and walk across the room. When she opened the door, I held Sally out to her and apologized.

"I STILL HATE YOU!" Constance snatched the doll out of my hand and slammed the door in my face.

"Was that good enough?" I asked my mother as I returned to my room.

"Almost," she said, walking over to my desk and unplugging my laptop.

"What are you doing?" I complained. "I apologized just like you told me to."

"That wasn't your punishment, this is." She walked out of the room, carrying my laptop with her.

"When do I get it back?"

"Whenever I decide to give it back," she called out from the hallway.

6:00 PM

"What's for dinner?" I called from the couch.

I heard my mom in the kitchen and assumed she was getting ready to make us something to eat. Since she took my laptop away, I had spent the past hour watching television and was starting to get hungry.

"You're going to have to fend for yourself," she replied, leaning out of the kitchen. "I'm taking Constance to the movies."

"What?" I picked up the remote and paused the show I was watching. "Why does she get to go to the movies? That doesn't seem fair."

"It doesn't matter what you think. After the stunt you pulled, you're lucky I'm letting you watch TV."

"Can I at least have my laptop back before you leave?" I stood up and started to walk towards her as she turned around and went back into the kitchen. I made it a few steps before I tripped over something.

I was walking too fast to stop myself from falling, but I did manage to catch myself before planting my face into the carpet. When I looked back to see what I had tripped over, I wasn't surprised to see Constance's Say it Sally doll sticking out from beneath the couch.

"What was that?" The sudden clatter of me bumping into the end table as I fell brought my mother back into the room. "Are you ok?" she asked when she saw me getting up off of the floor.

"No, I'm not okay." I reached down and snatched Sally out from underneath the couch. "I'm tired of seeing this fucking doll every time I turn around. I swear it's trying to kill me."

"Adam! Language!" My mom yelled at me.

"If you don't want me to talk like that, then keep this fucking thing away from me." I threw the doll at her feet then stormed off to my room, slamming the door to make my point.

7:00 PM

"We're leaving now," my mother said, knocking on the bedroom door to get my attention.

I didn't answer.

"I left you some money on the counter if you want to order a pizza. We should be home sometime after nine." There was a brief pause before she spoke again. "Did you hear me, Adam?"

"I heard you," I replied, not bothering to put down the comic I was reading.

I waited until I heard the front door close before I got up and went into the kitchen to see how much money my mother had left me. I was surprised when I saw the twenty-dollar bill held in place by the cookie jar on the counter. It wasn't like her to leave me money when she went out. She must have decided to take pity on me after I tripped and almost killed myself in the living room.

I pulled the bill free and stuffed it into my pocket. I hadn't decided if I was hungry enough for a pizza or if I wanted to save the money for something else. My computer was the thing I wanted most of all at that moment, and so I went searching for it.

It wasn't anywhere in the kitchen. I didn't think it would be, but since I was already in the room, I figured I'd search it first. After that, I looked in the living room and the laundry room. I even checked the bathroom. When I didn't find it in my parent's bedroom, I started to think my mom might have taken the computer with her, but that wouldn't be like her. I'm sure it was somewhere in the house. I just needed to figure out where.

7:30 PM

I returned to my room when I couldn't find my computer. As I lay on my bed, staring at the ceiling, I tried to think like my mother.

Where would I hide it if I were her?

I already checked all of her regular hiding places, but she probably knew I would do that and found a new one. When she took it, she was mad at me because of what I did to Constance's Say it Sally doll.

She wouldn't.

I sat up as the perfect hiding place came to mind. The more I thought about it, the more it made sense. It was kind of brilliant actually.

I left my room and walked down the hall to Constance's room. "Very funny, mom," I said, swinging the door open to find my laptop on Constance's bed with Say it Sally sitting on top of it. Before I could walk across the room and grab the computer, the phone in the kitchen started ringing. The laptop wasn't going anywhere, so I went and answered the phone.

"Hello," I said.

"Hey, Adam, it's mom. Can you do me a favor a see if Constance left her doll at the house?" I would have sworn that she brought it with her, but it's not in the car."

"Yeah, it's here," I answered snidely, "Right where you left it, sitting on top of my laptop where you hid it in Constance's room."

"What are you talking about? I didn't hide your laptop in Constance's room. I put it under the sink in the kitchen. I would never hide anything of yours in her room."

"Well, that's not where I found it."

"I don't know what you're playing at Adam, but I don't have time for this. The movie is about to start," she said to me.

She must have covered the phone because when she spoke again, her voice sounded muffled and far away, but I could still understand what she was saying to Constance, "Adam said you left Sally in your room."

"I didn't leave her in my room. I brought her with us. I remember sitting her on the seat next to me and putting on her seatbelt," Constance's voice was much louder than my mother's.

"Well, that's where she is," she said to Constance. I could hear her remove her hand from the phone before she spoke again. In the background, Constance was yelling, trying to get my mother to believe that the doll was in the car. "I have to go," she said to me. "And stay out of Constance's room."

She didn't give me any time to reply before she hung up. I would gladly stay out of my sister's room, right after I got my laptop back.

The doll and computer were still on the bed when I walked back into Constance's room. Part of me expected them both to be gone after the day I'd been having.

"I will feel…no sorrow…for you…there's no tomorrow," Sally said as I leaned down and slid the computer out from underneath her.

"Fuck you," I replied, knocking the doll onto the floor with the back of my hand.

When Sally landed on the floor, something fell out of her dress. I leaned across the bed to get a better look at the object she had dropped. It was the little plastic knife that had been sharpened.

I stared at the toy knife, thinking that my little sister was a psycho for sharpening it and placing it in Sally's dress. *Why does she need a knife!* I seriously considered picking it up and shoving it through the forehead of that ugly little doll, but I knew that would make me look even crazier than Constance.

I decided to leave the doll and the knife where they fell and let my mother deal with it. I was about to grab my computer and go, but a sudden noise stopped me. It had sounded like someone had dropped a glass in the kitchen, but no one else was in the house with me.

I walked over to the doorway and leaned my head out enough to peek down the hall. When I saw a hand reaching through the broken pane of glass of the back door to unlock it, I knew I was in serious trouble.

Someone is breaking in! I quickly retreated into the safety of the room as I began to panic. I was alone in the house, and the only phone was in the kitchen. There was no way I could make it there and back without being seen.

I need to hide!

Constance's room wasn't very big, so there weren't many options. If the huge iron frame of her bed weren't blocking the window, I would have escaped that way, but there was no way to get to it without making a bunch of noise. I was running out of time and didn't know what else to do, so I crawled under the bed, pushing stuffed animals out of my way.

I positioned myself so that I could look out into the hallway from under the bed. I wanted to be able to track the intruder's movements as much as possible. If an opportunity to get out of the house arose, I wanted to be ready to take it, assuming I could overcome my fear and anxiety.

When I heard footsteps out in the hall, I turned my head towards the closet, wondering if it would have been better to hide there, but Sally blocked my view. Her stupid plastic grin was mocking the predicament I was in.

"I will feel…no sorrow…for you…there's no tomorrow," Sally's voice was deafening in the quiet confines of my hiding place.

No, no, no. I prayed the person walking down the hall hadn't heard the doll, but I wasn't that lucky. When I turned and looked back towards the doorway, I saw a pair of scuffed up work boots pointing in my direction.

"Jackpot," the man said, taking a step into the room.

I didn't know what he was talking about until I remembered I had left my laptop sitting on Constance's bed like an idiot.

"Aren't you a creepy little fucker," the intruder said, nudging Sally with the tip of his boot, causing her to roll over and face the ceiling. "Was that you that was talking?" He lifted his foot and placed the sole of his boot on the doll's head.

"I will feel…no sorrow…for you…there's no tomorrow," Sally said, but then she started laughing.

Every time she said that phrase to me, she didn't say or do anything else. The laugh was something new, and there was nothing funny about it. Hearing it gave me goosebumps.

"Fuck you," he said, stepping on Sally's soft plastic head, deforming it. But that didn't stop her from laughing. The sound must have bothered him as much as it bothered me because he pulled his leg back and kicked her under the bed and right into my face.

I couldn't stop myself from grunting when the hard plastic of Sally's arms connected with my cheek. I froze, hoping the sound wasn't loud enough to be heard.

"Looks like I found me a stowaway," the man's face came into view as he peered under the bed. He smiled, flashing his yellow teeth at me. "Get out here!" His smile disappeared as quickly as it had appeared.

Every instinct told me to run, so that's what I did. I grabbed Sally and slammed her into the man's face with as much force as I could muster. There was a loud popping sound as the doll connected with his nose. The stranger moved away, covering his nose with his hands. I used that opportunity to slide out from underneath the bed, hoping to make it to the door before he recovered. I didn't get very far.

"You shouldn't have done that," he punctuated his comment by cocking his gun. "Stand up," he commanded.

I did as he said, turning to face him while holding my hands up.

I must have given him one hell of a wallop. He was pinching his nose closed with one hand, trying to keep any more blood from leaking out of it. With his other hand, he pointed a small silver revolver at me.

"Get over here," he motioned at me with the gun.

I walked over and stood in front of him, trying to avoid eye contact with him.

"Turn around and get on your knees."

He's going to shoot me. My brief life flashed before my eyes. I thought of all of the things I wouldn't get to do, all of the people I'd never see again. I didn't want to die. Not like this.

"I'm…I'm sorry," I stammered. "Take anything you want…please don't shoot me." Tears streamed down my face as I turned around and started to get down on my knees.

"Does the little baby need his dolly," he mocked me in a childlike voice.

I looked down at Sally, lying on her back where she had fallen after I used her to smack the man in the face. It would figure that the last face I would see before I died would be hers. She was the reason this happened. I wouldn't have been home alone if the doll hadn't been fucking with me all day. She must have somehow known this was going to happen and set it all up.

Did she just wink at me? The tears in my eyes must have been playing tricks on me. Sally has never winked before. I wiped the back of my hand across my eyes then looked back down at the doll. She winked again. There was no denying it the second time.

As I stared at her, my face a mask of confusion, her head rolled to the side. *What the fuck is going on? What is she trying to tell me?* That is when I saw the little plastic knife clutched in her outstretched hand, the one sharpened one. That was when her plan became clear to me.

Sally wasn't trying to get me killed, at least not directly. Everything she had done was part of a carefully calculated plan to get my mother and sister out of the house. That was why she kept antagonizing me. She wanted to escalate things between Constance and me, knowing that my mom would take her out of the house, and they'd be safe.

I don't know how or why, but Sally knew someone was going to break into the house. She must have also known I'd be the one to confront him. Looking down at Sally, her head pointed towards her outstretched arm made me realize the knife was intended for me to use.

"Hurry up," the intruder pushed the barrel of the gun against the back of my head.

Once I was on my knees, I leaned forward, shielding Sally from the intruder's view as I retrieved the knife from her hand. When I leaned back, I picked her up and cradled her in my arm.

"I hope this works," I whispered into her hair.

"See you tomorrow," she replied.

"I hope that's not your doll," the intruder said.

"So, what if it is mine?" I tightened my grip on the toy knife, praying it was sharp enough.

"You're right. It doesn't matter." I could feel the tension in the air as he readied himself to pull the trigger.

"I'm sorry," I said.

"You should be," the intruder replied.

"I wasn't talking to you. I was talking to the doll." Before I finished talking, I whirled around, standing up in the process. I swung Sally out before me, using her body to knock the gun away as I lashed out with the toy knife.

The muzzle of the gun flashed at the same moment Sally collided with the intruder's hand. I felt the bullet burrow its way through my shoulder as it knocked me backward, but all of that happened after my knife nicked the soft flesh of the man's throat.

I didn't feel any pain until I hit the floor. It felt like someone had jammed a hot ice pick through my shoulder. The intensity of the pain was making it hard to breathe. I could feel my vision dim as I tried to calm myself down enough to leave the room.

It wasn't until I was able to get myself into a crawling position that I saw the intruder lying on the floor, gasping for air as he bled out from the hole I had made in his neck. When he saw me looking at him, he reached out his hand to me.

The sight of all that blood made me feel light-headed, or maybe it was all of the blood I had already lost. When I tried to stand, I couldn't keep my legs under me. I was able to take two steps towards the hall before I collapsed and let oblivion claim me.

THE NEXT DAY

When I opened my eyes, the bright and blurry surroundings were unfamiliar. I tried to sit up, but someone stopped me by placing a hand on my shoulder.

"Try to lie still," the nurse said. Her features were slowly coming into focus.

"Where am I?"

"You're in the hospital," she replied.

I was about to ask her what happened, but the memory of the previous night came flooding back before I could. The machine standing next to the bed started beeping faster, picking up my elevated heart rate.

"I was shot!" I said to her.

"Yes, you were. But you're okay now," the nurse said, placing her hand gently on my arm. "I'm going to go get the doctor. In the meantime, there's someone here to see you."

The nurse walked over to the door, opening it before waving someone over. I wasn't surprised when Constance walked in carrying Sally. My mother and father were a few steps behind her.

"I'm sorry," Constance said, hugging Sally.

"What for?"

"I'm sorry you got hurt." I could see tears forming in her eyes.

"It's not your fault," I said "Actually, if it wasn't for your doll, I might have gotten hurt a lot worse. Sally saved me."

"Sally saved you?"

"She did. And she saved you and mom."

WATER TREATMENT PLANT

"Welcome aboard. I'm Jim, the assistant supervisor." The burly man sitting in front of me extended his grease-stained hand across the desk.

"Alan," I replied, leaning forward to shake the offered hand.

"We're very excited to have you here, Alan. Now, before I give you a tour of the facility, I just need you to fill out some paperwork," Jim said, reaching over to grab a small stack of papers he had waiting for me. "It's mostly just basic employment forms, tax stuff, contact info, that sort of thing."

He handed the stack to me with one hand while he used the other to pull a pen out of a drawer. After I accepted the papers, he placed the pen on the desk and slid it over to me.

"I'm going to leave you to it," Jim said, gesturing at the papers with his chin as he got up and began to leave his office. "I've got a few things I need to check on before we begin the tour. If you need anything, just ask Carol." He pointed at his receptionist.

Once he left the office, I picked up the pen and began filling out the papers. It was the usual paperwork you'd expect to fill out when you start a new job, at least it was until I came to the last two forms. The first was a non-disclosure agreement, and the second was a complacency procedure agreement.

I know what a non-disclosure agreement is, I was just surprised to see that I needed to sign one to work at a water treatment plant. It was the complacency procedure agreement that had me confused. I had never heard of such a thing. I would have pulled out my phone and looked it up on Google, but they forced me to surrender my phone when I entered the plant. I got the impression security at the facility was very tight.

I needed the job, so there weren't many things that would keep me from signing the agreement. I just wanted to know what it was for before I signed it. After mulling it over in my head for a few moments, I decided to ask Carol about it.

"Excuse me, Carol," I said, picking up the form and walking over to her desk. "Can I ask you something?"

"Sure thing, hun," she replied, turning away from her computer to give me her full attention.

I dangled the form from my fingers so she could see it. "What is a complacency procedure?"

She sighed in annoyance, but not at me. "I take it Jim didn't go over the forms with you before running off and leaving you on your own."

I nodded my head.

"Typical," she said. "The complacency procedure is a special type of exit interview in case you ever decide to leave the company. You are going to learn a lot about how the plant operates while working here, and the owners don't want you to spill any trade secrets if you quit or get fired. The procedure is designed to ensure that doesn't happen. It's nothing to worry about. Everyone here has signed one. You won't be allowed to work here if you don't sign it."

She waited a moment while I processed everything she had told me before speaking again. "Does that answer your question?"

"Yeah, I guess it does, thanks," I said, turning and walking back into Jim's office, where I signed the form and waited for him to return.

"You all done?" Jim bellowed from behind me a few minutes later.

"Yep," I said, waiting for him to take his seat before handing him the forms.

He flipped through them quickly, stopping when he came to the complacency procedure form. I considered asking him about the procedure but decided against it. The form was signed. I was committed to the job at this point.

"Excellent," he said, standing up. "Now we can get started. Follow me."

Jim walked out of his office, the forms I had filled out clutched in his hands. I got up and followed him. As he walked by Carol's desk, he handed her my paperwork and asked her to file them.

"How much do you know about the facility?" Jim asked, holding a door marked *Authorized Personnel Only* open for me.

"Not much," I admitted, walking through the doorway. "I live over in August County, and a new water treatment plant in a neighboring county isn't exactly headline news."

"I guess it wouldn't be," Jim said, taking the lead down the corridor. "Truth be told, we tried our best to keep the plant out of the news when we took over water treatment duties for Howard County."

"Why is that?" I asked.

"Given the nature of the unique way the plant works, the people in charge wanted to draw as little attention to the facility as possible."

"Is that why you hire people from different counties?" When I applied, one of the requirements listed for the job was that I not reside in Howard County. According to the application, anyone from the county or that had visited it in the past three years was ineligible for employment.

You'd think they'd want to support the local economy by hiring people who live there, but I wasn't going to question it. I was just happy they were willing to give me, a guy with no experience in the water treatment industry, a chance to prove himself.

"That's one of the reasons," Jim smiled and then changed the subject. "This is our first stop," he said, leading me through one of the doors that lined the hallway.

The back wall of the room was filled from floor to ceiling with all sorts of meters and gages. Standing before the wall was an older gentleman dressed in coveralls and holding a clipboard.

"This is the monitoring station," Jim gestured at the wall with an open hand. "And this is Buddy," he said, placing a hand on the older man's shoulder.

"Alan," I said, reaching out and shaking Buddy's offered hand. He smiled and inclined his head in greeting.

"Buddy is our first line of defense against any potential malfunctions," Jim explained as Buddy went back to reading the meters and making notes on his clipboard. "Our filters can be temperamental at times, and it is Buddy's job to warn us before something like that gets out of hand. As a filter technician, Buddy is the most important person you will be working worth, so try and stay on his good side," he joked as we left the room and returned to the hallway.

"What were those oddly shaped gauges along the top of the wall," I asked Jim as we walked to our next destination. They didn't look like they could be real. They looked like something you'd see in a Dr. Suess book.

"Those are unique to our filtration system," Jim replied. "Once you see the filters, they will make a lot more sense."

I was about to ask another question about the dials when I was interrupted by a deep lowing sound coming from one of the exit doors we passed. I looked at Jim to gauge his reaction, but he didn't seem concerned about it and kept on walking, so I did the same.

My first thought was that a cow from the neighboring cattle ranch had wandered onto the property, but I didn't see how that was possible considering the treatment plant was surrounded by a chain-link fence topped with barbed wire. You could easily mistake the place for a prison.

My curiosity eventually got the better of me, "Was that a cow?" I asked, jabbing my thumb over my shoulder at the door.

"It was," Jim answered. "The county owns the ranch next door. It makes things a lot easier for us and helps keep people from asking too many questions about what we do here."

"Aren't you worried about the runoff from the ranch polluting the water?" If they weren't, they should be. I saw at least three or four hundred cows wandering around the large open field that bordered the plant when I drove by. That's a lot of animal waste that can easily make its way into the water system, especially since it was so close to the treatment facility.

"You could run raw sewage through this plant, and what would come out would be the cleanest drinking water in the country. I know this for a fact because we occasionally do it."

"What?" I blurted out.

Jim stopped and turned to face me. "Running this facility isn't cheap. Processing waste overflow from neighboring states helps us offset our operating costs. I know it sounds disgusting, but once you understand the process, it won't seem as shocking."

I had a million questions running through my mind, but I didn't ask any of them. I decided to wait until the filtration process had been explained to me before I said anything else.

"Here we are," Jim announced as we reached the end of the hall. Behind him was a large metal door. In the center of it was a wheel that had to be turned to unlock it, like the ones you'd find on a military ship. "Another security measure," Jim said, after seeing the puzzled look on my face. "From this point on, the facility is made entirely out of steel." He knocked on the wall. "The engineers used modern battleships as inspiration when designing the holding tanks for the plants."

"Plants?" I asked, "Is there more than one water treatment facility in the county?"

Jim didn't answer, he just smiled and said, "After you," as he pulled the heavy door open.

I stepped through the narrow opening and into a room lined with bright yellow environmental suits. On the far wall was another door like the one we had used to enter the room. A million more questions ran through my mind, but they all fled when I was startled by Jim slamming the door shut and spinning the wheel, locking us inside the tiny room.

"Grab a suit," he said, pulling one off of the wall and starting to put it on over his clothes. "We can't go any further without them."

I grabbed a suit and started to shrug into it. Once Jim finished putting his suit on, he came over and made sure that I had put mine on correctly.

"Your suit must remain waterproof at all times. I cannot stress this enough. If it ever tears while you are in one of the holding tanks, you need to get the hell out of there as quickly as possible," Jim's voice was muffled by the suit.

"Okay," I nodded. I was beginning to think taking this job was a bad idea. Now I was starting to understand why it paid so well.

"Now, before you can enter the holding tanks, you need to walk through the decontamination shower. You do that by walking through that door," Jim pointed to the door opposite the one we had entered. "Once you close the door, the showers will kick on as you proceed down the hall. It's all automated, so you don't have to do anything except walk. The system only allows one person in the shower at a time, so I will go first. When that light comes on," Jim pointed to a green bulb above the door, that means I've made it to the other side, and it is clear for you to enter. Any questions?" Jim asked as he unlocked the door.

I shook my head, despite the growing number of questions I wanted to ask.

"See you on the other side," he said, closing the door.

After Jim shut the door, the red light next to the green one lit up. I waited until it went off, and the green light came on before opening the door and stepping into the narrow hallway. Taking a deep breath, I shut the door behind me and began walking down the hall. Before I finished my first step, the showerheads in the ceiling came to life, dousing me with fluid.

I made my way to the opposite side, trying to keep a steady space. I didn't know what the shower was supposed to protect me from, and I didn't want to take any chances by rushing through it. When I reached the door at the end of the hall, the showers cut off. Before I could reach out and open the door, it swung open to reveal two people. One of them was Jim.

"This is Bill," Jim said, introducing the man beside him. "He's been working overtime while waiting for us to hire another filter tech."

"That's an understatement," Bill laughed. "I practically live here at the moment."

I stepped through the doorway into a wide-open space with a vaulted ceiling that must have been at least thirty feet high. In the center of the room were three large domed structures, each as big as a small house with large pipes coming out of the bottom of them.

I greeted Bill with a handshake, the bulky gloves of our suits making it awkward.

"Once you've completed your certification training, Bill will be your hands-on trainer," Jim explained to me. To Bill, he said, "Thanks, Bill. You can go prep the facilitator for filter one."

Bill turned to leave, but before he did, he placed his hand on my shoulder and said, "Don't worry man, the plant looks a lot worse than it is."

I didn't know how to respond to that, so I turned to Jim to see if he might elaborate on the comment. He didn't.

"Your suit has about forty-five minutes worth of air," Jim said, pointing to the small canister attached to my hip. "Fresh canisters are kept in those cabinets." He pointed to a small shelved unit off in the distance. "There is one in every corner of this room. It will be one of your responsibilities to ensure that those cabinets are fully stocked at all times and that all empty canisters are shipped out to be refilled."

I nodded to show that I understood.

"Are you ready to see the filter?" Jim asked.

"As ready as I'll ever be," I responded. At this point, I didn't know what to expect, but I was committed to seeing this through. I needed the job and couldn't afford to back out now.

I followed Jim over to a door in the closest domed structure. Painted upon the side of the dome were the letters F.I.L-T.E.R. below that was a large number 1.

Jim didn't say a word as he spun the metal wheel, unlocking the door. Once he had it open, he motioned for me to enter first.

I stepped through the doorway, what I saw defied belief. I was expecting a network of pools and pipes, along with a sophisticated filtration system. Instead, I saw a concrete room, in the center of which was a giant creature that vaguely resembled a deformed anemone, if an anemone could grow to be the size of a bus.

I turned and faced Jim, expecting him to start laughing at the joke he had just played on me, but he just held me with his gaze, obviously waiting to see if I would freak out or not.

"That's the filter?" I asked, pointing at it.

"It is," he replied. "To be more precise, it is a fungiform intelligent lifeform transdimensional environment regulator. Filter for short. I often refer to them as the water treatment plants since they sort of look like flowers."

"Intelligent? Are you saying that thing knows we are here?" I turned back around and leaned my head back to see if I could find anything that looked like a head or a face on top of it. "Can it understand what we say?"

"I'd say it is semi-intelligent," Jim replied. "It hasn't shown any indication it can understand us, but it does possess a cunning that rivals most predators."

"Is it safe to be this close to it?"

"As long as you have your suit on, you aren't in any danger. You could go up and touch it if you like."

"I'll pass," I said. "So, how does it filter the water?" I asked as curiosity started to replace my disbelief."

"It doesn't filter the water, it produces it," Jim answered.

"How?"

Before Jim could answer, Bill walked through the doorway leading a cow.

"Perfect timing," Jim said to Bill. To me, he said, "We think the filters are transdimensional creatures. That means they exist in two dimensions at once, ours, and another one. Our best guess is that the water it produces comes from this other dimension."

"How do you get it to produce water when you need it? It doesn't look like it is in the mood." The tentacles that surrounded its body seemed to be limp and inactive.

"That's what the cow is for. We call it a facilitator. Once the filter ingests the cow, it will come alive like a sprinkler and fill this room in a matter of hours."

As if on cue, the cow mooed when it was mentioned. The sound did not go unnoticed by the filter. Its tentacles came to life as it shifted its body towards the animal. The strange creature's excitement could be felt as a vibration in the air. Before the cow could respond to the threat, one of the filter's tentacles blasted it with a jet of water.

The cow turned to run but suddenly stopped. It stood there dripping wet, oblivious to the giant creature looming over it. Even when it turned its head and looked right at the filter, all it did was moo. When an opening formed in the filter's body, spilling forth a tangled mass of writhing tendrils to engulf the cow, it didn't struggle. It went to its death without putting up a fight.

A few moments after the cow was pulled into the filter, the tentacles atop its body began to swell and undulate before spurting forth a torrent of water, one after the other. It was impossible to avoid getting sprayed. I prayed my suit didn't have a hole in it. I saw what the water did to the cow.

"That's our cue to leave," Jim said, motioning towards the door.

I didn't need to be told twice. I was the first one out of the dome, followed by Jim, and then Bill, who closed the door and sealed it.

Before I could say anything, Jim held up his hand to stop me. "Let's get out of these suits and head back to my office. There is a lot to go over, and I'd rather not do it standing around in these uncomfortable suits."

I couldn't argue with that. I followed Jim back to the chemical shower. When it was my turn to walk through it, I stayed inside it longer than was necessary to ensure I was adequately decontaminated.

"Where did that thing come from?" I asked after Jim had taken a seat behind his desk.

"Well, that's a long story," he said, opening a drawer and pulling out a thick manual. He slapped it on his desk. "That's what this is for." He placed his hand on the book. "Everything you need to know about the filters, where they came from, and why they are here can be found in this book."

I picked up the book and read the title, *The Old One Accords*. Underneath the title was a string of gibberish that looked something like this: *ph'nglui mglw'nafh Cthulhu R'lyeh whah'nagl fhtagn*.

"Is this supposed to be some sort of training manual?" I asked.

"What if I told you that a race of ancient deities from beyond time and space had awoken and had been secretly subjugating the planet for years and that by the time the leaders of the world found out about it, it was already too late?" Jim's question sounded like the plot of a bad science fiction movie.

"Up until an hour ago, I would have assumed you were on drugs," I replied, "After what I've seen today, I'd give you the benefit of the doubt and hear you out before I decided if you were crazy or not."

"Well, it's true, but don't take my word for it. Read the book. It's all in there."

"What does any of that have to do with working here at the plant?"

"As part of the surrender agreement the government made with the Old Ones, every state had to give up one county to act as the seat of power for the Overseers A place where they could continue to manipulate the world without the world knowing it. The filters are for them. The water they produce keeps the local populace compliant and ignorant of the creatures that act as their friends and neighbors. It also keeps them from questioning things when someone happens to go missing if you know what I mean."

"No, I don't know what you mean. What are you talking about?" I leaned forward, placing my forearms on the edge of his desk.

"The overseers have a very particular diet," Jim paused to let his comment sink in. "Thankfully, they don't need to eat that often."

"You mean they eat…"

Jim nodded. "I find it's best not to dwell on it. I only mention it because I want you to know what's at stake if you decide to work here. That is why you have to read the manual. Once you're done reading it, you can become a certified acolyte, and you won't have to worry about what goes on in Howard County."

"Acolyte?"

"It's just a fancy title the Old Ones use to refer to those in their employ. Don't let that turn you off. We rarely use the term on the job."

"What if I decide the job isn't right for me?"

"Allow me to answer that." The voice that came from behind me made my skin crawl.

It was wet and phlegmy. The speaker spat the words out, clearly not used to speaking English or articulating words in general. I was too afraid to turn around, knowing the thing behind me wasn't human. It couldn't be.

"Of course, Overseer Or'azath," Jim said, standing to greet his boss.

After he spoke, Overseer Or'azath placed his hand on my shoulder. At least I thought it was a hand until I felt something cold and wet seep through my shirt. I froze, doing my best not to show my unease.

"Alan," he said, pausing as he leaned in close to my ear. "What is known cannot be forgotten. If you choose to leave, I'll have to hold you to the complacency agreement you signed." His breath smelled like a festering wound.

"What does that mean?" I asked, unable to keep the tremble out of my voice.

"It means, if you're not an acolyte for the company, you'll become Howard County's newest resident. At least you'll be a resident until your services are needed in other ways."

"Other ways?" I wasn't asking a question. I just happened to be thinking out loud, remembering what Jim had told me about the residents of Howard County.

"Yes, Alan. Other ways." Overseer Or'azath answered. "To put it bluntly, as your kind likes to say, if you're not with the company, you're with the cattle."

119

"Do you think this still works?" I asked, pulling the old rotary phone from the box in my parent's attic.

My friends and I had been asked by my parents to help them move a bunch of boxes from the garage to the attic after we helped unload the moving truck.

"Probably," Danny said. "But, you'll need to find a phone jack to plug it in." He grabbed the end of the phone's cord and held it up. "These new houses don't have them. Eli's probably got one at his house, though." He turned to look at Eli, who was rifling through one of the boxes.

"What?" Eli asked, lifting his head out of the box.

"Your house still has phone jacks, right?" Danny asked him while holding out the end of the phone cord for him to see.

"I think so, why?"

"Seth wants to see if that old phone still works."

"Why?" The question was directed at me. "It's just a phone. You already know how it works."

"But I've never used one of these," I held up the rotary phone, "Plus, it might be fun to make a prank call or two with it. Assuming it still works."

"I guess you can bring it with you when we head back to my house."

I set the phone aside while the three of us finished taking the boxes out of the garage. My mother didn't like to throw anything away. If she didn't need something any longer, instead of getting rid of it, she would pack it away.

"You never know when we might need it again," I once overheard my mother telling my father after he had asked why she didn't just throw something away.

"I bet she wouldn't even notice if we threw half of that crap out." My father said to me shortly after my mother had left the room that day. But he could never bring himself to get rid of any of it, which is why I was stuck hauling the boxes up to the attic as we moved into our new house.

Once we finished, I grabbed a change of clothes and my toothbrush while Eli and Danny waited for me outside. My parents wanted me out of the way while they got everything set up, so I was going to be staying with Eli for the next couple of days.

"Hold up," I said to my friends, leaving my stuff on the hood of Danny's car. Then I ran back into the house. A few minutes later, I returned carrying the old rotary phone. "I almost forgot this."

"I was hoping you would forget it," Eli said as the three of us got into the car.

A short time later, we were searching through Eli's house looking for a phone jack, but we couldn't find one.

"I thought we still had one in here," Eli looked around the kitchen, "I would have sworn it was right there next to the refrigerator." He pointed at the wall.

"Oh well, no big deal. It's like you said, it's just a phone." I don't know why I was so fascinated with the old phone. I guess I saw it as a novelty and wanted to be able to say that I had used one.

"Hey, Dad!" Eli suddenly yelled out.

"What?" His Dad yelled back from the other room.

"What happened to the phone jack that was in the kitchen?"

"Your mother got tired of looking at it. I got rid of it months ago. You'd know that if you were home more often."

Eli held out his middle finger towards the room where his dad sat. "I guess that's the end of that," he turned and said to me, dropping his hand back down to his side.

"Maybe not," Danny pointed out of the kitchen window.

Eli and I walked over, peering through the panes of glass and looking at the abandoned house that Danny was pointing at.

A rusty chainlink fence surrounded the house. No trespassing signs, their paint faded and flaking off, were affixed to the metal links every ten feet or so. A line of weeds tall enough to obscure the yard and the bottom half of the home acted as a second barrier to those who ignored the signs.

The house itself was unassuming. It was a clone of all of the other homes in the neighborhood. They were all rectangular boxes of cinderblocks with flat roofs that extended out over the side, creating a carport instead of a garage.

The only thing setting that house apart from the ones around it was its poor condition. The white paint that once coated its exterior walls had started flaking off long ago, allowing the natural color of the cinderblocks beneath to show through. All of the windows and doors were boarded over with large pieces of plywood. Each one of them adorned with the same no trespassing sign that hung from the fence.

The carport suffered the most damage. Its roof had collapsed a few years earlier, the weight of all of the water it had collected finally taking its toll, sending it crashing to the ground. The concrete drive was now littered with pieces of the moldy roof and a few stagnant pools that helped contribute to the growing mosquito population.

"You can't be serious," Eli scoffed at Danny's suggestion.

"Why not? That house has been empty for a couple of decades, right? It probably still has lots of phone jacks."

"It probably does, but I doubt they work," I said. "That house hasn't had power since the eighties."

Eli snickered at my comment. "You really don't know anything about old phones, do you?"

"No, I don't. Why is that so funny? I asked him.

"Landlines don't need electricity to function. They have a dedicated network of cables. As long as your phone isn't electronic and the house is still connected to the old phone line, you should be able to get a dial tone."

"It's not that important. We can forget about it."

"What's the matter, Seth? You're not chicken, are you?" Danny teased me.

"I'm not scared. It just seems like a lot of trouble to go through for a phone."

"Come on, Seth," Danny pled. "This is our last chance to go and see what's inside that old place. Remember how we used to always talk about becoming urban explorers? Well, now's our chance. With you moving across town and going to a new high school, this might be the last time we have an opportunity like this."

He did have a point. Once I returned home, the three of us would likely not have much time for each other, especially once school started. The idea of one last adventure with my friends did sound appealing.

I looked over at Eli. "What do you think?"

"I'm cool with it if you are," he answered.

"Fine," I relented. "But you have to carry this," I declared, grabbing the phone off of the counter and thrusting it into Danny's hands.

"How are we going to get in?" I asked a short time later. We had hopped over the fence and were wading through the weeds, walking around the outside of the house looking for a way inside. As far as I could tell, all of the windows and doors were securely boarded over.

"Through there." Danny pointed at the door that led into the house from the carport.

The board that once covered the entrance lay splintered on the ground. It must have been knocked loose when the carport collapsed.

We walked over to the door, carefully choosing our steps to avoid the jagged pieces of wood and rusty nails that lay scattered across the cement slab that was once the driveway.

Danny began to pull the remaining pieces of plywood away from the wall, exposing the door. Once it was free, he reached out and tried the knob, but it wouldn't turn. "Locked," he said, announcing the obvious.

"Did you seriously think it would be that easy," I asked.

"No, but I had to check." He turned to Eli, the biggest out of the three of us. "Why don't you try knocking." He stepped aside while pointing at the door. The comment was an inside joke between the three of us.

When we were younger, Danny and I locked Eli out of his bedroom while we raided his comic collection. He stepped out of the room to take a piss and was not happy to find himself locked out of his bedroom when he returned. When we wouldn't let him in, he began to jiggle the handle and throw his shoulder against the door.

His comic collection was his pride and joy, and he didn't want us messing with it. He was extremely pissed at us, but before we could put everything back and let him in, the door flew open, sending Eli stumbling into the room.

Danny being the smart ass that he is, looked over at Eli and said, "You could have just knocked."

We got in so much trouble and had to pay to have the door frame repaired. We also weren't allowed over at Eli's house for the rest of that summer.

Eli approached the door. He grabbed the knob and gave it a firm shake, testing the strength of the latch. Then he stepped back, lifted his leg, and kicked the door with the flat of his foot. The wood around the latched splintered into a dozen pieces as the door was forced open.

"Knock knock," Eli joked.

"After you," Danny swept his hand towards the door, indicating that I should enter the house first.

"Ladies first," was my retort.

"Pussies," Eli said, looking back at us as he walked through the doorway.

"Well, you did say ladies first," Danny laughed.

Eli didn't bother to turn around when he gave us a two-handed middle finger salute.

"I'm done carrying this," Danny pushed the phone into my chest as he followed Eli into the house.

I grabbed hold of the phone, took a quick look around to make sure no one was watching us then stepped into the house. As I expected, the carport door led into the kitchen just like all of the other homes in the neighborhood. When I walked into the room, Eli was examining a dust-covered breakfast table that still had place settings on it while Danny was opening the cabinets.

"The phone jack should be next to the fridge," Eli pointed at the old appliance.

I walked over to the counter, set the phone down, and began to unravel the cord while I searched the wall for the jack. It was pretty easy to find. It looked like a modified outlet for a plug. My first attempt to connect the cord failed. The plastic piece on the end of it fell out of the wall the moment I pulled my hand away.

"You have to turn it so that the little plastic knob clicks into place," Eli said after watching me pick up the end of the cord and stare at it for a second.

I did as he suggested and felt the cord snap into place.

"I hope that thing works because I'm not getting any service here." Danny was slowly turning in a circle holding his phone out, searching for a signal.

"Only one way to find out." I lifted the receiver and held it up to my ear.

"The end with the cord goes down by your mouth." My inexperience with the phone was becoming a source of amusement for Eli.

I turned the phone around and listened, but I didn't hear anything. "How do I know if it works?" I turned and asked Eli.

"You should hear a dial tone," he answered.

"I don't hear anything."

"Why don't you try dialing a number?" Danny suggested.

"Who should I call?"

"Call 911 and tell them you lost your brain."

"I'm not calling 911. Can't they trace the number?"

"Not if you hang up fast enough," Eli said.

I had to admit that prank calling 911 did have a certain appeal to it. If this was going to be the last night of fun the three of us were going to have together, I might as well make it memorable.

"Okay, I'll do it."

"What a rebel," Danny mocked me.

"Just make sure you dial the numbers backward. That's how those old rotary phones work." Eli explained.

"Seriously?" I asked.

Eli looked over at Danny.

"Uh…yeah, seriously. That is why people don't use those phones any longer. It was confusing a lot of people." Danny said.

I looked from Danny to Eli as I started to dial the number. When I finished, the two of them started laughing.

"Assholes," I said, pulling the phone away from my ear. I had suspected they might be playing a joke on me but figured it was no big deal. It was only three numbers, and the call probably wasn't going to go through anyway. I was about to hang up and redial the number but stopped when I heard someone speaking through the receiver.

"Hello," I said, holding the phone up to my ear.

"119, what is your preferred emergency?" the woman on the other end of the line repeated herself.

"Holy shit, I can't believe it worked?" Danny said, walking over to stand next to me so he could listen in on the call.

"What did they say?" Eli asked.

I placed my hand over the receiver, "She asked me what my preferred emergency was."

"What kind of question is that?" Danny blurted out. "If I had a preferred emergency, it would be that there are too many girls in my life," he laughed.

"Your emergency has been logged and will begin shortly," the women on the phone said. "Thank you for calling 119 emergency services." After she finished speaking, the call was disconnected.

"What happened?" Eli asked, seeing the look of confusion on my face.

"She said our emergency has been logged and will begin shortly." I placed the receiver back in its cradle on top of the phone while looking at my friends.

"She must have heard you," Eli said to Danny.

"You say that like it's a bad thing," Danny responded. "Can you think of a better emergency than having too many girls?"

"No, I can't." Eli shook his head.

"Then what's the problem with it?"

"It's just not a believable emergency." Eli began to smile. "No one would ever believe that you would ever have too many girls. The only emergency you are likely to have involving girls is that you can't find one that likes you."

"Fuck you," Danny said while raising his middle finger.

"It has to be a joke, right?" I interrupted them before their war of words could escalate. "The operator must have known I had misdialed the number and decided to mess with me."

"Maybe," Danny said, shrugging his shoulder. "Who cares? It's not like they had time to trace the call and find out where we are. Let's forget about the phone and check out the rest of the house."

"Maybe we should leave," I suggested.

"Don't be like that," Danny said. "I helped you find a way to play with your phone. You could at least stick around and explore with me."

I looked over at Eli as Danny walked out of the kitchen and into the living room before turning and waiting for us to follow.

"I've got nothing better to do," he said, walking by me to join Danny. "And I didn't come here just so you could use your phone. I think we should check out the rest of the house before we leave."

I started to walk out of the kitchen but stopped when I noticed the door to the refrigerator was slightly ajar. I would have sworn it was closed when I first entered the kitchen.

I reached out and used the tips of my fingers to swing the door fully open.

"What…the…hell?" It came out as a whisper while I leaned down to get a closer look at the contents of the refrigerator.

"What?" Eli and Danny said in unison.

I grabbed one of the mason jars that was sitting on the topmost rusty shelf and held it up for them to see. It was covered in dust and filled with a dark amber solution. Picking it up caused the remains of what appeared to be a flower blossom to rise off of the bottom of the jar and float through the liquid.

"It looks like piss," I heard Danny say as I set the jar on the table.

I reached in and grabbed two more jars, one in each hand, and set them on the table next to the first jar as Eli and Danny returned to the kitchen to get a closer look at them. "There are dozens of them in here," I said, stepping out of the way so they could see the shelves full of jars.

"Don't open it!" Eli cried out as Danny picked up one of the jars and unscrewed the lid.

I could smell the contents the moment he removed the lid. It had a scent like rancid ammonia. The fumes were so strong that my nose began to burn. It was as if someone had used a strong cleaning product to clean up rotten meat, but all they wound up doing was combining the smells.

"Ew, I think this might be real piss," Danny scrunched up his face in disgust as he quickly screwed the lid back on the jar and set it back on the table.

"If that is piss, I think the person it came from needs to see a doctor. That does not smell healthy." I waved my hand in front of my face while I backed away from the table.

"I can't take this," Eli said, covering his nose with his shirt while fleeing the kitchen. Danny and I followed closely behind him. Even though the jar was only open for a couple of seconds, the lingering smell was still quite strong in the air.

"What the hell, man" Eli pushed Danny as we gathered in the living room. "I told you not to open it."

"Sorry," he replied sheepishly. "I thought it might be alcohol."

"So what if it was?" Eli argued, "Do you make it a habit of drinking strange liquor you find in abandoned houses?"

"I wasn't going to drink it," Danny said. "I'm not that stupid. I thought we might be able to sell it."

"Who would buy something like that?" I asked.

"I don't know," he shrugged his shoulders, "maybe the winos downtown or one of those idiots on the football team. It doesn't matter now. No one is going to buy that horse piss." He jerked his thumb over his shoulder towards the kitchen.

Before Eli or I could respond to the stupidity of Danny's idea, we were interrupted by a series of loud bangs emanating from the hallway on the other side of the living room. The three of us looked at each other before turning our attention to the archway that led to the dimly lit hall.

"What the fuck was that?" Eli hissed his voice tense from the fear that was taking root in his mind.

"It sounded like someone banging on one of the bedroom doors," I answered with a whisper.

"Maybe we should leave," Eli suggested. "Whoever put those jars in the fridge might still be here, and they might not be happy to find we were messing with them."

"Shh...I think I hear someone." Danny, who was closest to the hallway, waved his hand to shush us while he crept towards the opening. As he walked, he cocked his head to the side, waiting for the sound to return.

Then I heard it, the sound was muffled, but I was convinced it sounded likely someone yelling for help.

"You heard that, right?" Danny turned and asked us.

"Yeah," Eli and I both responded.

Right after we spoke, the pounding resumed, causing me to flinch at the unexpected noise. Once it subsided, the pleas for help began anew.

"We have to do something," Danny said right before he disappeared down the hallway.

Eli and I exchanged a look, each of us waiting to see what the other would do, neither one willing to be the first to act. Our standoff was short-lived, though.

We were prodded into action when Danny ran back into the living room, yelling, "Someone is locked in the closet!"

"What?" I heard what he said, but my brain was trying to dismiss the idea as a joke or a misunderstanding.

Danny gave me an annoyed look, "Someone is locked in the hall closet," he answered, pointing down the hallway.

"What?" I repeated. I know I must have looked and sounded like an idiot, but I didn't know what else to say. Everything that had happened in the house so far had taken on a dream-like quality.

"For fuck's sake, snap out of it and come help me unlock the door," Danny rushed across the room, making his way behind us, so he could push us towards the hallway as he spoke. That snapped Eli and me out of our trance as the three of us walked down the hall.

The closer we got to the closet, the clearer the pleas for help became. The voice was that of a young lady.

"We're going to get you out of there," Danny assured the frightened woman.

"Thank you," was the muffled reply.

"Who does something like this?" Eli commented after seeing the planks of wood nailed across the frame of the closet door, barricading it shut.

"Let's worry about that after we get her out," Danny said, stepping to the side of the door and planting his fingers along the edge of one of the boards. "Help me pull these off," he nodded at the door.

The three of us worked together, prying the planks of wood off of the wall, one by one, all eight of them. By the time we pulled the last one free, the joints of my fingers were aching, as were the muscles in my forearms.

"Watch out," Danny said, pushing Eli and me to the side with one hand as he stood in front of the closet door and reached out for the doorknob with the other.

When he swung the door open, I was expecting to see a woman standing in the middle of the closet. Instead, there was a flight of stairs leading down into the darkness under the house.

"Do any of the other houses in the neighborhood have basements?" I leaned in and whispered into Eli's ear.

"Not that I know of," Eli answered, "This is a closet in my house."

"It was a closet in my old house as well," I said. "I didn't think these old homes could have basements, not with crawlspaces underneath them."

"You can come out now," Danny called out from the top of the steps, calling our attention back to the closet that wasn't a closet.

The three of us watched as a barefoot girl, not much older looking than us, stepped into the dim pool of light shining at the bottom of the stairs. She had long blonde hair and was dressed in a dirty white nightgown that came down to her knees.

"Holy shit," Danny whispered, turning to look back at Eli and I as two more girls, stepped into the light. "They're triplets," he said, stating the obvious.

The girls smiled as they ascended the stairs, one at a time.

Danny began to walk backward as they neared the top, not stopping until his back bumped against the wall behind him. I didn't want to crowd them, so I retreated a few steps towards the living room. Eli saw me step back and decided to do the same, but he moved further down the hall towards the bedrooms.

"Thank you," the first girl said, looking at Danny as she stepped out into the hall. He just stared awkwardly at her, a nervous grin on his face.

The other two girls, who I assumed were her sisters, followed closely behind her. Once they were out of the doorway, they spread out in the hall, so they were standing shoulder to shoulder.

"And you," the girl looked over at Eli and then at me as she spoke, "Thank you for helping us."

I nodded my head, accepting her gratitude.

"Who locked you down there?" Danny had finally snapped out of his trance.

"I don't know," the middle girl answered, returning her attention to Danny. "I don't even know how we got here."

"What do you remember?" I asked, folding my arms over my chest.

All three girls turned to look at me, but it was the middle one that answered again, "Waking up on the cold floor of the basement and then hearing the three of you talking."

"You can't remember anything before that?"

She shook her head.

"What about your name, do you remember that?"

"Yes," she answered after a brief pause, "I'm Ena." As she spoke, she placed her left hand on her chest. "This is Dio." She moved her hand to the shoulder of the girl standing to her left, "And this is Tria." She placed her right hand upon the shoulder of the girl standing to her right.

"I'm Danny," Danny gestured at himself. "That is Eli," he pointed to his right. Eli lifted his chin in greeting. "And that is Seth," he said, redirecting his finger to point at me. I fanned my fingers from where they sat on my forearm, acknowledging the introduction.

"I need to go to the bathroom," Dio, the girl closest to Eli said, fixing him with her bright blue eyes. She clutched her arms against her stomach, signaling her urgency.

"uh.." Eli stammered and began to blush while looking at the floor.

She smiled, amused at his display of discomfort. "Do you know where the bathroom is?"

"Yeah...yeah, it's right here," he said, stepping across the hall to push open the bathroom door.

"There's no toilet," Dio said after peeking her head through the doorway.

"That's weird," Eli replied, walking by her to enter the bathroom and see for himself. "I guess someone must have taken it."

"I really have to go," I heard Dio whisper to Eli when he walked back out into the hall.

"There's another bathroom in the master bedroom if you want to check back there," Eli suggested, pointing to the door at the end of the hall.

"Could you come with me?" she asked him. "I don't want to go by myself, not after being trapped down there." She looked over at the stairs that led down into the basement.

"Uh...yeah...sure," he said, casting a quick look back at Danny and me before walking down the hall, Dio a step behind him.

"We should probably call the police," I said while pulling my phone out of my back pocket.

"Good luck with that," Danny said, "I haven't had service since we got here."

I looked down at my phone and confirmed what Danny had said. My phone didn't have any service either.

"I could try the phone in the kitchen," I suggested, sliding my phone back into my pocket. "It was able to connect. Maybe I could use it to call 911 for real this time."

"Are you serious?" Danny turned his attention back to Ena. You don't remember how you got down there?"

Ena shook her head.

"Was there anything else down there with you?" he asked.

"Just a bunch of old boxes," Ena answered. "Why?"

"Maybe there's a clue to what happened to you in one of those boxes," Danny suggested to Ena before turning to me and saying, "I think you should hold off on calling the police. We are technically trespassing and could still get in trouble."

That was bullshit. I knew he wanted to see if there was anything worth taking from the basement.

"Whatever," I snapped at him as he started to walk down the stairs. "Just hurry up. I want to get out of here."

"I'll go with you," Ena said. "Maybe I'll remember something."

That left me alone in the hallway with Tria. When she looked over at me, I offered her a thin-lipped smile before quickly looking away. I suddenly felt very awkward being in the company of an attractive girl.

"Do you live around here?" I asked, immediately regretting the stupid question. I was trying to break the uncomfortable silence between us but only succeeded in making myself look like an idiot.

"No," she politely answered.

An apology was about to escape my lips, but it was forgotten when a series of thumps echoed down the hall. The sound came from the master bedroom where Eli and Dio had gone to find the other bathroom.

"Eli?" I called out, taking a few steps down the hall. When I didn't get a response, I took a few more steps and called out his name again. "Did you hear that?" I turned and asked Tria.

"Hear what?" was her response. There is no way the noise could have escaped her notice, but I wasn't going to press the issue. Instead, I continued down the hall.

When I made it to the end of the hall, I reached out and pushed the door to the master bedroom all the way open, so I could survey the room without having to enter it.

There was nothing to see, so I made my way across the room, one step at a time until I stood in the doorway of the master bathroom.

"Eli?" I said, struggling to make sense of the insane scene laid out before me.

Lying dead on the floor was Eli. His lifeless body was a desiccated husk seemingly drained of all liquid like a mummy. That wasn't the crazy part. Not by a long shot. What my mind was refusing to accept was the sight of Dio straddling Eli and grinding her pelvis against his, the both of them naked from the waist down.

As I watched, Dio began to moan as she climaxed, but that wasn't the end of the insanity. As she writhed atop Eli's body, her moans of pleasure quickly became groans of pain. The source of her agony was surely the way her body began to bend and distort in impossible ways.

I was frozen in place, unable to move and unable to look away as Dio's body began to split in two.

"Looks like another sister is about to be born," Tria said from beside me. I jumped at the sound of her voice. She had snuck up on me while my attention was on the grisly scene unfolding before me.

I whipped my head to the side, breaking free from the paralytic fear that had grabbed hold of me. Tria looked back at me and smiled, but not in a friendly way. The smile told me that I was next.

"Danny!" I yelled as I ran out of the room and down the hall.

I stopped when I reached the doorway of the basement, calling out his name again. But he didn't answer.

I took a step down the stairs but stopped when I saw two girls walk out of the darkness, both completely naked and covered in a sheen of sweat.

"Where's Danny?" I yelled, already knowing the answer.

"He died happy, just like Eli did," Tria said, walking down the hall towards me. "Happier than they ever could have imagined." She stopped a few feet away from me and reached out her hand towards me. "Let me make you happy, Seth."

I backed down the hall away from her. She followed, matching me step for step as I made my way through the living room and towards the door in the kitchen. The one Danny, Eli, and I had used to break in.

When I felt I was close enough to make a break for it, I turned and ran for the door, but Tria had anticipated my move and made it to the door a moment before I did.

"You can't leave," she said, reaching out and stroking my cheek with the back of her hand.

I backed away from her touch, bumping into the kitchen table as I tried to escape. The impact caused something to fall over and start rolling across the tabletop towards me.

I glanced behind me and saw the jars I had pulled out of the refrigerator still sitting on the table, one of them on its side, making its way to the edge of the table.

I turned around, grabbing the jar before it could fall, and began to unscrew the lid.

"There is no use fighting it," Tria said, pressing her pelvis against my backside while grabbing hold of my hips.

"I'm gay," I said, twisting out of her grasp then flinging the contents of the jar into her face.

The smell of the liquid hit me like a slap in the face. It was so foul and overpowering that I immediately fell to my knees and started retching. It didn't help that some of the contents of the jar splashed onto me when I threw it.

Even though my body's reaction to the smell was quick and violent, the effect the liquid had on Tria was much worse.

"What have you done?" she screamed at me while desperately trying to wipe the liquid off.

I could see little wisps of smoke rising from her body where the liquid had made contact with her skin. That was right before her eyes rolled into the back of her head, and she fell to the floor, convulsing.

I got up and backed away from her, examining the spots where the liquid had splashed onto my arms. I was expecting it to have the same poisonous effect on me, but nothing happened. The liquid did not affect me except to make me feel nauseous.

"You shouldn't have done that, Seth," I couldn't tell who the speaker was, but it had to be Ena or Dio, the other two girls standing beside them didn't know my name.

"We're done here," I said, walking around the table so that it was between the group of unclothed girls and me. To make sure they got my point, I reached out and picked up one of the jars remaining on the table.

The four of them walked forward, two of them started to walk around the left side of the table while the other two walked around the right.

Taking a deep breath to ward off the smell, I quickly unscrewed the lid of the jar and cocked my arm in a threatening gesture. "Back off!" I commanded. "You know what will happen if this touches you."

"You can't possibly get all four of us with that one little jar," Ena or Dio taunted me, thinking they could overwhelm me because they outnumbered me.

"I don't need to hit all four of you, just two," I taunted back. It was true. Since they were split into two groups, I only needed to throw the liquid on two of them to escape the kitchen, but that wasn't my plan.

"Which of you feels like dying?" I said, glancing down at the contorted body of Tria to make my point. "It looks like a painful way to die."

"Okay, you win," one of the girls spoke. "You are free to go," she said, motioning for the other girls to clear a path to the door.

"That's not good enough," I said.

"What more do you want?"

"I want you to return to the basement."

The girls exchanged glances, before one of them spoke, "Fine," she said.

As one, they turned and made their way across the living room and down the hall. Before I followed them, I grabbed the remaining jar from the table.

As they descended the stairs, I waited in the doorway until they were all in the basement. Then I took the open jar and splashed its contents all over the stairs. I did the same thing with the second jar. I didn't stop there. I wanted to make sure they stayed put, so I went to the refrigerator and started grabbing jars and lining them up on the top steps without their lids.

Once I was satisfied that they wouldn't escape, I shut the door and returned to the kitchen to call the police on the old rotary phone. As I reached out to lift the receiver from the cradle, the phone rang.

I picked it up and held it to my ear, "Hello," I said.

"This concludes your emergency. Please hold for a brief survey." It was the same voice that had answered the phone earlier and asked me what my preferred emergency was.

VIRAL VIDEO

"How much is this TV?" I called out, trying to get the attention of the cashier sitting behind the counter of the thrift shop.

"There should be a price tag on it," she replied, not bothering to take her eyes off of her phone. "It's usually taped to the back with the remote."

I looked again but still didn't see one. All of the other television sets on display had price tags except for the one I was interested in. "I don't see one."

The cashier exhaled noisily. "Hold on," she said, setting her phone down before walking around the counter to help me.

I stepped out of the way as she approached and watched as she lifted the small flat-screen television, angling it in every direction as she searched for the price tag. When she couldn't find it, she dropped it back on the shelf. "Ten bucks," she said.

"Really?" I was surprised it was so cheap. All of the other televisions they had were priced at least double that. "Don't you have to check with the owner?" I knew she was just a minimum wage slave like myself and didn't want to get my hopes up.

"If it doesn't have a price tag, I get to choose the price," she said, starting to walk back to the counter. "Ten bucks. Take it or leave it."

"Oh, I'm definitely going to take it," I mumbled to myself, picking the set up off of the shelf and carrying it over to the counter. As a starving college student trying to get by on a minimum wage retail job, I had put off getting a television for as long as I could. I'd be stupid not to seize the opportunity while it presented itself. I looked forward to being able to watch my favorite shows on something other than the tiny screen of my phone.

I paid for the set and quickly left, eager to get it home.

***

"You better work," I said to the television screen, after making sure I had connected all of the wires correctly. *Moment of truth*, I pressed the power button on the remote, but nothing happened. "Seriously," I sighed. I pressed the button several times and once even kept it pressed for several seconds, but the screen never lit up.

"Figures," I said, tossing the remote onto the TV stand. When it landed, the battery cover flew off the back and fell to the floor. "Way to go, Einstein," I scolded myself upon noticing the empty battery compartment.

"Let's try this again," I said, standing before the television holding the remote with its fresh set of batteries.

"Yes!" I cried out as the television came to life and began blaring the sound of white noise to go with the static on the screen. I quickly flipped through the different inputs until I found one that showed a menu. A menu that displayed several different streaming apps already loaded onto the set.

I figured I was going to have to buy a Roku or something similar before I could watch TV, but I lucked out. My new television was a smart TV with built-in wifi. The thrift shop could have easily charged a lot more for the set if they had bothered to check it. If I were the owner of that shop, I'd fire the cashier before she gave anything else away.

Once the television was connected to the internet, I settled into the couch, trying to decide which app I wanted to use first. They all had free trials, so it was just a matter of choosing the one with the best collection of shows.

Reading reviews for the different apps on my phone was starting to get tedious and wasn't helping me make up my mind, so I just picked the one that was listed first in the row. With all of the different shows each platform was releasing every month, there had to be something worth watching on it.

Surprisingly there wasn't much, which was disappointing, but I did find an old science fiction series I had wanted to watch a few years ago. It wasn't very popular when it first came out, but it was better than watching pirated episodes of newer shows on my phone.

As expected, the show was good, but not great. I watched the first two episodes without interruption and was about to start the third when an advertisement started paying. *I thought this was supposed to be commercial-*

free. I guess that wasn't the case for the free trial I had, at least that is what I assumed as the commercial began to play.

I sat impatiently waiting for the ad to end, but it just kept going and going. That is when I realized I wasn't watching a typical commercial. It was an infomercial. One of those thirty-minute ads cable channels usually broadcast in the middle of the night. There was no way I was going to sit through an ad that was almost as long as the show I was watching. It wasn't that good.

Deciding I had watched enough TV for the time being, I picked up the remote and turned off the set.

When I got up to leave the room, I heard a click followed by the hum of the television turning on. I looked down at the remote, wondering if the power button had accidentally been pressed when I tossed it onto the couch.

I walked over to the set, intending to press the manual power button to turn it off, but I stopped when I realized the same infomercial was playing. That wasn't the strange part. What I found odd was that it had started over from the very beginning. I thought the television was supposed to reset itself when it was turned off and return to the main screen, the one that displays all of the apps.

"No, I don't want to buy your *top of the line* knife set," I said to the TV, pressing the power button and turning it off.

That was what the infomercial was trying to sell me, a knife set. I don't cook, and I get by fine with the ancient utensil set my parents gave me when I moved out. A new knife set was the last thing I needed.

I thought I had solved my problem by manually turning off the TV, but I hadn't. When I turned around and tried to walk away, the television turned itself back on, and the infomercial began to play from the beginning again.

"Whatever," I said, waving my hand dismissively over my shoulder. *Maybe if I let it play until it was over, it would stop restarting itself, and I could get back to watching the shows I wanted to watch.*

I walked into the kitchen and decided to make myself a sandwich. I took my time getting out everything I needed and then took my time making it. When I was done and had put everything back where it belonged, I noticed the apartment was quiet.

The commercial must be over.

"Finally," I said, picking up the sandwich and carrying it into the living room.

I was looking forward to getting back into my show, but that wasn't going to be happening any time soon. When I walked back into the room and looked at the TV screen, the picture was frozen, like someone had paused it, but I didn't do that. I left it playing when I walked out of the room.

Before I could grab the remote and turn the television off, for the third time, the ad started playing again. I know how absurd it sounds, but I think it had somehow paused itself when I left the room and was waiting for me to return before it started playing again.

I didn't know if it was the app I was watching or the television that had caused the ad to keep playing, and I didn't care. I'd had enough of the TV acting weird. I didn't know what was wrong with it and I didn't care. It was going back to the store.

***

Thankfully, when I got back to the thrift store, the girl that had sold me the television wasn't there. In her place was the owner.

"You bought this here?" the owner asked, turning the set around so he could get a better look at it.

"I did," I replied, pulling the receipt out of my pocket and showing it to him.

"I don't remember having a set like this," he said, pushing his glasses up the bridge of his nose so he could read the receipt.

"The girl that was here this morning sold it to me."

"That explains the price," he said. "That was my niece. She helps out around the place sometimes and apparently can't be bothered to look up the prices like I showed her." He walked over to the cash register and hit a button that opened the till. "Is there anything wrong with it?" he asked.

"I'm not exactly sure," I replied. "It worked fine at first, but then it just kept playing this infomercial over and over and wouldn't let me watch anything else."

"That's odd," he said, handing me my refund. "I can't say I've ever heard of a TV doing that before. I thought they were supposed to be smart."

"That's what I thought."

"Sorry, it didn't work out. If you like, I can give you a discount on one of those other sets." He pointed to the shelves of electronics at the back of the store.

"Okay," I said. "I'll take another look at them."

I turned and started walking to the back of the store while the owner picked up the TV I had returned and carried it off through a curtained doorway. The moment he was out of sight, all of the television sets on the wall turned on and began to play the same infomercial that my television was playing.

"It slices! It dices!" the sales pitch sounded like an echo coming from all of the TVs at once.

That's impossible, I thought, as everything seemed to take on a dreamlike quality. Either I had entered the *Twilight Zone*, or someone was playing an elaborate prank on me.

"Find one you like?" the owner asked.

I whirled around and confronted him, "Is this some sort of joke?" I jabbed my thumb over my shoulder.

"I'm sorry, son, but I don't follow. Is what a joke?" The confused look on his face seemed genuine.

"The ad, the one playing on the televisions right now, it's the same one that kept playing on the one I returned." I turned to point at the screens to show him, but they were all blank.

The owner eyed me, clearly assessing my mental state.

"I'm not crazy," I snapped at him. "All of your TV's were just playing an ad for a knife set. It was the same ad that kept playing on the one I had bought."

"That's not possible," he said, "Those TV's aren't connected to WIFI or cable. They can't play anything but static."

"I know what I saw," I said with an exasperated sigh.

"I believe you," he said, but it was clear he didn't. He was just trying to placate me. I could tell he was ready for me to leave. "I'll take a closer look at the one you returned and see if I can find out what's wrong with it."

"Whatever," I said, waving my hand dismissively as I headed for the exit. "It's your problem now."

When I got back to my car, I pulled my phone out of my back pocket and threw it onto the passenger seat. I was annoyed, angry, and confused. What had started as a great day had turned into a circus of shit because of that fucking television.

I reached out and grabbed the steering wheel in a two-fisted grip, trying to calm myself down.

"It's over," I said, trying to calm myself. "The TV is gone, and you can get on with your life and forget about it." I took a deep breath, started the car, and left.

"It slices, it dices," the announcer's voice called out from the speaker of my phone before I could even leave the parking lot of the thrift store. I slammed on the brakes and looked over at the phone. It was playing that stupid fucking commercial.

I picked up the phone and tried to get it to stop. When that didn't work, I tried to turn it off. I wasn't able to do that either. I was about to throw it into the glove compartment but changed my mind. The commercial was going to keep playing no matter what I did, and it wasn't going to let me avoid it. After what had happened so far, I was pretty confident about that. The only way to get the commercial to stop was to watch it. At least I hoped that was the case.

I pulled into the nearest parking spot and propped my phone up on the steering wheel so I could watch. The commercial was exactly what you'd expect it to be, dull and full of false excitement about the knife set. The thing I found odd about the commercial, besides the fact that it seemed to be haunting me, was that it never showed the face of the person wielding the knives. The entire infomercial was one long close up of some guy using the knives and other sharp instruments to cut various odd objects while an announcer gave a voiceover of what was happening.

"How would you like to own your very own set of these amazing knives?" the announcer asked.

"Finally," I said. I knew the commercial must be ending soon since it had moved on to the sales pitch.

"These amazing knives can be yours for free," the announcer said.

"Free?" I scoffed, knowing there was always a catch.

"That's right, free," the announcer said as if he were replying to my skepticism. "The first one hundred customers that respond to this ad will be given a full set of knives for free in exchange for an honest review on our website. What are you waiting for? Pick up your phone and call now!"

Once the commercial ended, the screen of my phone went black. I stared at it for a while, expecting the ad to start playing again at any moment, but it didn't. Feeling like my ordeal might be over, I reached out and started the car, keeping my eyes on the blank screen the entire time. When I was sure the ad wasn't going to start playing again, I tossed the phone back onto the empty passenger seat and drove home.

On the drive home, I was starting to feel hopeful that I would never have to watch that annoying ad again. That feeling of freedom continued to take root long after I got home. It had been almost an hour since the video took over my phone, and it hadn't reappeared since. I thought I was free, but I didn't realize how wrong I was until I sat down on the toilet and tried to play a game while I answered nature's call.

After pressing the icon that would start my game, I expected the little cartoon logo to appear and the game to start, but that isn't what happened. Instead, the screen went black then displayed the Butcher Brand Knife logo as a familiar announcer's voice began speaking.

"I can't even take a shit in peace," I said, placing the phone on the bathroom counter with the screen facing down. That didn't stop it from playing, though. I could still hear the ad as it played, and no matter how many times I pushed the button, the volume never changed.

For the rest of that afternoon, the ad continued to play every hour if I was within earshot of my phone. It eventually got to the point where I was going to bang my head against the wall in an attempt to knock myself out if I had to listen to that announcer's voice one more time.

"Call now!"

"Oh, I'm going to call," I said to the announcer, picking up the phone and dialing the number flashing on the bottom of the screen. I had heard it so many times I probably could have dialed it without looking.

"Congratulations, lucky caller number one hundred!" It was a recorded message in the voice of the announcer.

I tried pushing zero, hoping it would take me to an operator so I could talk to a live person, but the recorded message just kept playing.

"To claim your free set of Butcher Brand Knives, all you have to do is leave your name and address at the beep."

I hung up the phone and set it on the counter. The second I pulled my hand away, the ad began playing again.

"Goddamn it!" I picked the phone back up. "You win, I'll order your stupid knife set if you will just stop playing that fucking commercial!" I yelled at the screen.

The ad stopped playing. Appearing in its place was the telephone keypad. I dialed the number.

"Congratulations, lucky caller number one hundred!"

"Yay, lucky me," I said, my words dripping with sarcasm. I bet everyone that called was lucky number one hundred.

I waited for the beep, stated my name and address, and then hung up the phone.

Thankfully, ordering the free knife set stopped the infomercial. At first, I didn't believe it had stopped. I expected my phone to start playing the ad at any moment, but after a few days of nothing happening, I allowed myself to relax

After returning to my regular routine, I was able to forget about the infomercial for a couple of weeks. I was even considering purchasing another used television, this time from a friend, but I changed my mind when I saw the package waiting for me next to the door of my apartment.

I unlocked the door and carried the box into the apartment. It was easy to tell what was inside it. The Butcher Brand Knives logo was featured prominently all over it.

After removing the tape and pulling back the flaps of cardboard, the first thing I saw was a type-written note reminding me to review the product, which I had agreed to as part of their free promotion. Included with the note was a website address.

I wasn't planning on using the knives. I was going to see if I could sell them on eBay, but I was still going to leave a review to fulfill my end of the agreement.

Once I cleared out all of the packing material, all that remained was a black canvas knife case. It was the kind of case where you slide the knives into little pockets and roll them up for easy transportation and storage.

I untied the case and unrolled it. There were ten knives in the set, I recognized most of them from the commercial, but there were a couple of them that I didn't recall seeing. One looked like an oversized scalpel, and the other looked like a miniature hand saw. I wasn't a chef and couldn't say for sure, but the scalpel and saw looked more like medical tools than cooking utensils. I didn't care, though, because I wasn't planning on keeping them.

I pulled out my phone and snapped a few quick pictures of the set to use when I put them up for auction. After that, I rolled the knives up and put them back in the box.

Since I already had my phone out, I decided to go ahead and write a quick review and get that obligation out of the way. When I entered the address of the website printed on the slip of paper, I was taken to an online form where I was prompted to enter my review. This is what I wrote:

```
This is the best set of knives I have ever
owned! I just wish the advertising was a lit-
tle less aggressive.
```

I hit enter, but instead of the review being accepted by the site, I got an error message that said:

We're sorry. We can't accept your review until you have had the pleasure of trying the Butcher Brand knife set for yourself.

I tried writing another review but got the same error message.

"Oh well," I said. I tried to write a review. It's not my fault they didn't accept it. That was on them, not on me. I wasn't going to be keeping the knife set long enough to use it.

I closed the browsing app and was about to press my finger on the eBay app, but I never got the chance. Instead, another video took control of my phone and began playing.

"Now that you've received your Butcher Brand Knife set," the familiar announcer said, "It's time to learn how to use them."

"The fuck it is," I said, shoving the phone into the nearest drawer and slamming it shut.

I waited a few minutes before reaching out and easing the drawer open. I couldn't live without my phone and knew there was no way to get this new video to stop playing without watching it. That didn't mean I had to be happy about it.

The moment my phone came into view, the video, which had paused itself when I shut the drawer, started playing again.

"Motherfucker!" I yelled, slamming the drawer shut with each syllable of the word.

It was a momentary loss of control brought about by all of the frustration I felt from the first video returning all at once. I felt sorry for the drawer, but I needed to take my anger out on something.

After taking a few deep breaths, I eased the drawer back open and pulled out my phone. "Let's get this over with," I said, carrying the phone over to the couch so that I would at least be comfortable while being forced to watch the new infomercial.

"Our first video demonstration will be for the scalpel," the announcer said after giving an overview of all of the knives in the set.

"Great," I moaned.

If this was the first video, that meant I had nine more videos to watch, one for each knife.

"The scalpel is the perfect subdual knife. Its small size allows you to hide it in the palm of your hand while its sharp blade can cut deep with the flick of your wrist."

"What?" I said to the phone. What I had thought was a set of cooking knives was quickly turning into something much worse.

"To use the scalpel effectively, you'll first need to learn a little bit about anatomy, specifically where all of the major arteries are."

I started involuntarily shaking my head as the person demonstrating the knife showed me where the carotid artery was on a real person. I've seen enough horror movies to know when something looks staged, and there was nothing staged about what I was seeing. The man in the video had killed a woman as part of the scalpel demonstration.

Blood poured out of the tiny slit made by the scalpel as the woman fell forward, clutching her throat. The scene made me sick, even more so because there was something familiar looking about the murdered woman. I couldn't shake the idea that I had seen her before, but I couldn't get a good enough look at her face to identify her.

The bile started rising in the back of my throat right before I began to dry heave. But the demonstration wasn't over.

"While not as easy to reach as the carotid artery, the femoral artery is just as deadly." The announcer sounded like he was doing a voice-over for some medical show on the Discovery Channel instead of the snuff film he was narrating.

I threw the phone across the room and stormed out of my apartment. I didn't know where I was going. I just knew that I needed to get away from everything that was happening.

I ended up at a little coffee shop a short walk from my apartment. It was always busy, and I figured being surrounded by people might keep the videos away, at least for a little while.

Waiting in line to place my order allowed me to watch the news on the television the shop had mounted on the wall. It was a relief to be able to watch something without worrying about the videos intruding. I was convinced they were for my eyes only. As long as someone else was watching with me, I didn't think they'd appear. But I quickly learned that being in public didn't keep them from finding me.

When the lady in front of me began to order her coffee, she lowered her right arm to her side. Clutched in her hand, with the screen facing me, was her phone. I only glanced down at it for a second, but that was all it took. The screen lit up and immediately started playing the scalpel tutorial video, the volume just low enough for me to hear.

"Did you say something?" the lady turned around, her brow furrowed in annoyance at being interrupted while she was trying to place her order.

"No," I shook my head. "I think it's your phone," I pointed at her hand.

By the time she looked down, the video had cut off. She scoffed at me, then turned back around and completed her order.

I closed my eyes so I couldn't see her phone again, but all that did was allow my mind to conjure forth the disturbing images I had seen in the video. With those images came a feeling of claustrophobia. I felt like I was trapped, and everyone was staring at me. I could feel the sweat starting to bead up on my forehead. I had to leave.

"What a weirdo," I heard the lady say to the cashier as I gave up my place in line and rushed out of the coffee shop.

I walked down the street, trying to keep myself from thinking about the video. When I passed by the bank, I made the mistake of glancing over at the ATM, like the lady's phone in the coffee shop, the screen came to life and started playing the video.

I grabbed the arm of a man that was passing by in the opposite direction, "Do you see that?" I asked, pointing at the ATM like a madman.

"Get your fucking hands off me, creep!" He pushed me hard enough to make me stumble back a few steps before tripping over my feet and falling on my ass.

I suddenly felt very vulnerable and exposed. Everyone else on the street was starting to stare at me. Not knowing what else to do, I picked myself up and ran back to my apartment.

The ad could play whenever it wanted as long as there was a screen around, and these days there were screens everywhere. I was never going to be able to escape them. I wouldn't be able to do my job or my homework without them. I didn't have a choice. I was going to have to watch the videos if I wanted to get my life back.

When I returned to my apartment, I stared at the phone lying on the floor where I left it. Thoughts of what I had seen in the most recent video raced through my mind. If I was going to watch the tutorial videos, I had to do it now. As much as I didn't want to, I didn't have a choice. Thankfully, I didn't have any classes and wasn't scheduled to work.

I walked over and picked up the phone, keeping the screen turned away from me. I didn't want the video to start playing until I had time to prepare myself. I sat down on the couch, took a couple of deep breaths, and turned the phone around. The video started playing immediately.

Watching the scene where the man on the video slices his victim's throat was still tough to watch, but not as bad as it was the first time. I squinted, trying to distort my vision as the killer moved on to a new victim for his femoral artery demonstration, but it wasn't as bad as I thought it would be.

In total, the video took about thirty minutes and just covered the major arteries in the arms, legs, and neck. When it finished, I took a break and went to the kitchen to get something to drink. While I was in there, I pulled the knife set out of the box and unrolled it. I reached out and slipped the scalpel out of its sheaf, running my finger along its blade. A thin line of blood welled up where the sharpened edge touched my skin.

I put the scalpel back then went and bandaged my finger before returning to the couch. The moment I picked up my phone, the next video began.

"Once you have subdued your victim, you are going to need to dismember them quickly for easy transportation and storage, that's what the bone saw is for, but keep your scalpel handy as well you're going to need it," the announcer said.

Of all the videos I had to watch, that one was probably the worst, especially the part where they demonstrate how to properly crack through the ribs and remove all of the soft organs from the abdomen. I had to stop it several times to keep myself from getting sick.

When that video ended, I took a break and decided to take a shower. All of the blood and gore I had witnessed had left me feeling unclean. I was hoping the hot water would help wash the creepy feeling away, but it didn't work. No matter how hot I made the water or how much soap I used, I couldn't wash it away. I also couldn't erase the tortuous images that were seared into my brain.

Unsurprisingly, I wasn't hungry even though I hadn't eaten anything since breakfast. The way I was feeling, I didn't think I'd be able to eat anything for a week. I did grab myself a soda from the fridge before I sat down and continued watching. The sweetness of the carbonated drink helped settle my queasy stomach.

The remaining videos were a breeze to watch and thankfully covered several knives per demonstration. The pieces of meat they were cutting up could easily have been pork or beef; at least that is what I kept telling myself to make getting through them easier.

"That concludes our video demonstrations. Thank you for watching," the announcer said as the screen faded to black.

"As if I had a choice," I scoffed.

Relieved that I had managed to make it through all of the videos, I decided to call it a night. I could feel a headache coming on, plus I had to get up early for classes the next day.

On my way to the bedroom, I stopped in the kitchen to grab some aspirin. While I filled up a glass of water, I looked over at the knife set still unrolled on the counter. Flashes of the videos played in mind as I looked at the shiny blades gleaming in the kitchen light.

I closed my eyes, trying to erase the images, but it didn't work. They only became more vivid in the darkness.

Not wanting to be reminded of the videos anymore, I rolled up the knife set so I could put it back in the box. Doing that exposed the little slip of paper reminding me to write a review.

When I tried to write a review earlier, I got an error message telling me that I needed to try the knives first. Right after that, the demonstration videos started. I wasn't about to make that mistake again. However, I felt like I was in a *damned if I do, damned if I don't* situation. If I wrote a review without trying the knives, there is a good chance it would start the cycle of videos over again. Likewise, if I didn't write the review, that could also trigger the videos to keep playing until it forced me to write the review. The only solution my tired mind could come up was to use the knives.

I opened the refrigerator and tried to find something I could use the knives on. My only choices were a block of moldy cheese, some hot dogs, and an onion. I pulled all three out and placed them on the counter. If I used the knives to cut all three things, I would have technically used them, which I was hoping was enough to satisfy the review system. There was no way I was going to use the knives the way they showed me in the videos. The hot dogs would have to suffice as a meat product if that was one of the requirements.

One by one, I used each knife on the cheese, the hot dogs, and then the onion. When I finished, I threw the cut up pieces of food in the trash and tossed the knives in the sink.

"I hope that worked," I said, picking up my phone and entering the website address to submit my review.

I wrote a slightly longer review than my first attempt, making sure to mention each knife. I was hoping that by adding more information to my review, it would increase the chances of the site accepting it

Here we go, I thought, pressing the accept button on the bottom of the screen. A second later, I got the same error message I had gotten earlier:

We're sorry. We can't accept your review until you have had the pleasure of trying the Butcher Brand knife set for yourself.

My face turned red as I clenched every muscle in my body. I was beyond mad at that point. I looked down when I heard something snap, smiling when I saw the large crack appear in my phone case. I squeezed the phone even harder, cracking it further when the video started.

"Now that you've received your Butcher Brand Knives," the announcer started, but I didn't let him finish.

After placing my phone on the counter, I grabbed a dirty pot from the sink and began to pound the obnoxious device to pieces. I didn't stop until the phone was an unrecognizable mess scattered across the countertop. Even then, I didn't stop smashing the pieces until I had spent my rage.

Feeling a bit better after releasing my pent up anger, I gathered up the bits of glass and plastic and tossed them in the trash. Then I gathered up all of the knives, wrapped them back up in their case, and threw that in the garbage as well.

"You can't force me to use your knives if I no longer own them," I said, taking the bag out of the trash can and carrying it to the dumpster behind the apartment building.

I took a quick shower when I got back inside and then went to bed. I was so exhausted and mentally drained from all of the shit that happened that I fell asleep quickly. But even in sleep, I wasn't allowed any peace. The videos played through my dreams in sequential order. What made them worse than the videos I had already seen, besides being unable to wake up, was that I was the person demonstrating the knives.

I woke up the next morning feeling sick to my stomach. The dreams were so vivid and so real. I could still feel the handle of the last knife I held, and the slick wetness of the muscle I was cutting. The most sickening thing of all is that I finally recognized the person that was murdered in the first demonstration video. It was the girl from the thrift store, the one who sold me the television that started this whole nightmare.

I decided to skip classes for the day. I wasn't in the right frame of mind to learn anything, and I was pretty sure I wouldn't be able to avoid any kind of screens while I was there.

I quickly realized that being alone in my apartment with no phone and no television was not any better than being trapped at school surrounded by blank screens. With nothing but my thoughts to keep me occupied, I was quickly becoming a nervous wreck. Every other thought that popped into my head was about those crazy videos.

To keep myself occupied, I spent the rest of the morning cleaning the apartment. I vacuumed the floors, scrubbed the bathroom and kitchen from top to bottom, I even washed the windows inside and out. The distraction worked for a while, but then I wore myself out and had to take a break. The moment I sat on the couch and closed my eyes, the images returned.

"I have to get out of here." I put my shoes on and decided to venture outside for some fresh air. I didn't get very far before I heard someone calling out my name.

"Hey, Mr. Dupree," the manager of the apartment complex was walking back towards her office when she called out to me.

I stopped and waited for her to catch up.

"I was wondering if I could speak to you for a moment?" she asked.

"About what?" I had no idea what she wanted to talk to me about. I wasn't a loud or dirty tenant, and I always paid my rent on time.

"I don't know if you've heard, but the complex is changing owners, and there are a few things I wanted to go over with you before that happens."

"Okay," I said.

"Let's go into the office," she said, motioning towards the small building across the lawn.

I looked off in the distance then back towards the office, trying to think of a way to avoid going into the building, which I knew had several computers and a large wall-mounted flat-screen television in the waiting area.

"Are you busy?" she asked, noting my hesitation.

I wanted to say yes, but I couldn't force the words out. Instead, I said, "No."

"Great! This will only take a moment."

I followed the manager into the office and took a seat on the opposite side of her desk.

She talked as she typed on the keyboard in front of her. "As I mentioned, the complex is being sold. Once the sale goes through, the new owners are planning on raising the rent on several of the units. Unfortunately, yours is one of the units that will be affected."

"Raising it how much?" I asked.

"Two-hundred a month," she replied.

"Two-hundred! I can't afford that," I complained.

"I understand, and that is why I wanted to talk to you before it was too late. I have a few smaller units I am holding onto for those tenants that can't afford the increase." She turned her computer screen around so I could see it. "This is a map of the complex. The units I have available are marked in green."

When she turned the screen around, I didn't see a map of the complex. Instead, the first demonstration video started to play, the one about the scalpel. But it was slightly different this time. Besides playing without sound, the victim in the video wasn't the girl from the thrift store. This time it was the apartment manager. I could tell because the woman in the video was wearing the same gaudy flower print dress the manager was currently wearing.

"If you like, we can go and take a tour of the units before you decide," she offered.

I turned the computer screen around as the video version of the manager fell to the ground bleeding out, but it cut off and returned to showing a map of the complex before the manager could see it.

"That's not necessary. I'll take the one that is closest to my current apartment."

"Are you sure?"

"Yeah, it's no problem," I said, rising from my chair.

"Great! I'll draft up a new rental agreement and give you a call when it's ready."

"Sounds good," I said, not bothering to tell her I was currently without a phone. That reminded me that I needed to find a way to call work and let them know I wasn't coming in. Something I had decided while the altered video played in front of me. "Do you have a phone I can use? I left mine in my apartment." I lied.

"There is a courtesy phone in the lobby," she pointed to the archway that led to the waiting room.

"Thanks." I turned and walked through the archway and over to the little table where the old push-button phone was sitting. The moment I sat down, the wall-mounted television began replaying the altered scalpel demonstration video. In place of the announcer, there were subtitles.

I turned away from the screen and focused my attention on the phone while I called my boss and told him I wasn't feeling well. Once that was out of the way, I left the office and started walking back to my apartment. I had gotten enough *fresh air* for one day.

"You have got to be kidding me," I said, turning the corner and seeing a familiar little box sitting in front of my apartment door.

Instead of picking the box up, I unlocked the door and kicked it into the apartment. Then I kicked it three more times, yelling

"Leave...me...alone," one word per kick. The final kick busted the box open, sending the knife case rolling across the floor where it eventually unraveled, freeing all of the knives.

***

"Is that when you killed the girl from the thrift store?" The detective sitting across from me asked. Up until that point, he had remained silent while I told him my story.

"No," I answered. "That was Monday. I didn't kill her until Wednesday."

"What happened between Monday and Wednesday that finally pushed you over the edge?" It was apparent from his question that he didn't believe my story about the videos.

"I couldn't take it any longer. I wasn't able to shut my eyes for two seconds without seeing those videos."

"Is that when you started taking the alertness aids and energy supplements to stay awake?"

"Yes. But they didn't help."

My mind drifted back to that final night. The night the hallucinations started. It was like my eyes were projecting the videos in front of me, allowing them to play like a holographic movie. By Wednesday morning, I was ready to do anything to make it stop.

The detective eyed me for a minute before turning off the recorder he was using to tape my confession.

"I think you're full of shit," he finally said. "There is no such company as Butcher Brand Knives. You claim you left the knife set at the scene, but no knife set was recovered. We've gone through your phone records and found no history of you visiting the website address you gave us. You know what I think?" he asked, fixing me with his cold hard eyes.

I knew better than to reply. I just stared back, waiting for him to answer the question himself.

"I think you're trying to avoid the death penalty by pleading insanity. Well, I've got news for you, that's not going to happen. Not if I have anything to say about it. I am going to make sure you fry for what you did to that poor girl."

"I can prove it," I whispered.

"What's that?" he leaned forward.

"I said, I can prove it, all of it, but to do that, I'd have to show you first-hand how it happened."

"How do you plan on doing that? We already tried to corroborate your story. What can you show me that we haven't been able to find out for ourselves?"

"Can I borrow your phone?" I reached my hand across the table, palm up.

"Why?"

"I need it to show you the website."

"You better not be wasting my time." He pulled the phone out of his jacket pocket and placed it in my hand.

I held the phone up so he couldn't see the screen as I entered the website address for Butcher Brand Knives. Instead of being taken to the review screen like I initially was, I was greeted with a different message. This is what it said:

Thank you for using Butcher Brand Knives, your review has been accepted. Press here to refer a friend.

The first thing I did after killing the thrift store clerk was to use her phone to write a review. That was when the site first prompted me to refer a friend. At the time, I didn't want to force this curse on anyone else, but the detective had helped to change my mind.

"What's your first name Detective West?" I asked with a smile.

ONE EYE OPEN

The soft tickle of something crawling down my cheek roused me from sleep. Half-awake, I brushed at it with the back of my hand. *There's something on my face,* someone said. When I realized that someone was me, I sat up and began frantically brushing off every inch of my head. While running my hand across my forehead, I noticed something odd about my face. The left side felt different than the right.

Something's missing!

At first, I thought my mind was playing tricks on me. Similar things have happened to me before when I've been startled awake. I'm a deep sleeper, and if I don't wake naturally, I tend to get confused.

I once woke up a couple of years ago and thought I was missing an arm. My parents were not happy about being dragged out of bed when I yelled out. They quickly showed me that my arm wasn't missing, but I didn't believe them. I couldn't feel it moving even though my mom lifted my arm and showed me the wiggling fingers of my hand. They had to sedate me to get me to calm down. Unsurprisingly to everyone but me, my arm was there when I woke up the next morning, working as it should. I was so relieved. My father said I must have slept on it wrong, making it go numb.

Slowly, I reached back up and ran my hands down both sides of my face at the same time. I was expecting the two halves to feel normal, but the hole I felt on the left side of my face was still there.

This isn't a dream!

Where my left eye should be was nothing but an empty socket.

My pulse quickened, and I started breathing rapidly. I was beginning to hyperventilate, feeling lightheaded and dizzy.

"It's just a dream. It has to be," I said, exploring the depth of the orbit with my finger while wondering how I could lose an eye and not feel a thing. "I'll wake up any moment, and everything will be fine," I whispered. Even though I was fully awake, I was still trying to convince myself it wasn't real.

I tossed the covers to the side, stumbled out of bed, and ran to the bathroom across the hall. Before I turned on the light, I leaned on the counter and took several deep breaths, trying to calm myself down. Once I finally got the courage to turn on the light and look at myself in the mirror, the reflection staring back at me confirmed my fears. My left eye was gone. Even my eyelids were missing. There was nothing but a hole where my eye should have been.

I stared into the hole for a few minutes, angling my head so that the bathroom light shined directly into it. The socket looked like it had been empty a lot longer than a few hours. It was completely dry and lined with skin. *How is that possible?* The eye was there when I went to bed. If something had happened to it, there should be evidence of some sort. It should hurt. There should be blood. There should be something besides an empty hole that looked like it had never contained an eye.

I should wake my mom. Now that I had confirmed that I wasn't dreaming and that my eye was not where it was supposed to be, I wouldn't feel bad for waking her up.

I took a deep breath, intending to call out for my mom, but I didn't get the chance. Something skittered past the doorway, distracting me.

Having only one eye kept me from getting a good look at whatever it was. All I could tell was that it was small, about the size of a mouse, and that it had several legs like an insect. *That was a big fucking bug.*

I leaned out of the bathroom, reaching for the hall light on the wall. After flicking it on, I stepped out into the hall just in time to see the creature turn the corner and run into the living room.

"What the fuck?" I whispered.

I thought waking up without an eye was insane, but the thing I saw running down the hall was way more insane.

When I stepped out into the hall, I was able to get a good look at the creature as it fled. It couldn't possibly be real, which made me start to rethink the idea of being trapped inside an extremely vivid nightmare. How else could I explain the sight of an eyeball running down the hall, using its blood vessels and nerve endings as legs?

I didn't move. I just stood out in the hall, staring at the point where the eye turned the corner, my mouth hanging open, questioning my sanity.

My mind started making excuses. *It was just a really big spider. The shock of losing your eye has you on edge. The light and shadows must be distorting your vision. You're not used to viewing the world with one eye.*

The excuses stopped when the eye reappeared at the end of the hall.

It skittered around the corner then stopped, lifting itself on ropey tendrils of flesh as if to get a better look at me. I took a step back when it blinked, reaching my hand up to the empty socket. I was positive that it was my eye. How could it not be?

Mom! My mother would know what to do! I started to call out for her, but the actions of the eye stopped me. It started moving its gelatinous orb of a body back and forth. If I had to guess, I would say it was telling me no. It didn't want me to call my mom, but why?

I took a step towards the eye, waiting to see how it would react. It turned around and started walking back towards the living room. The way it moved gave me the creeps. It reminded me of an octopus if the octopus were able to walk on its legs like a spider.

After taking a few steps, the eye stopped and turned around. I got the impression it wanted me to follow it and was waiting for me to catch up.

I took a step and then another. The eye continued moving forward while I followed. It led me across the living room and through the kitchen, stopping when it came to the coat closet.

I looked down at the eye. It looked up at me then back at the closet door.

"This is insane," I said, grabbing the handle of the closet door and easing it open.

The eye rushed inside as soon as the opening was wide enough.

"It's just a closet," I said, standing in the doorway. "There's nothing in here but a bunch of coats and shoes."

"Who are you talking to, honey?" My mother's voice, along with the sudden brightness of the kitchen light, startled me. "It's the middle of the night?"

"I'm just talking to myself," I replied, watching the eye scamper into one of my old sneakers. As I turned to face my mother, I kept my head down so she couldn't see my face.

"What's wrong? Why were you standing in front of the closet?" she asked, knowing something was off from my odd posture.

I slowly raised my head. She placed her hand over her mouth when she saw my missing eye.

"Where's your eye?" she asked. She recovered quickly from the shock and walked over to me, holding my head so she could examine the empty socket.

I pointed my thumb over my shoulder.

"Your eye is in the closet?"

I nodded. I didn't expect her to believe me so readily. The fact that she was able to keep her calm when presented with my bizarre situation felt off to me. I expected her to freak out. But as I thought about it, it started to make sense. She was a doctor. I'm sure she's seen some crazy stuff. The real test of her resolve would come when she saw the ambulatory eye.

I stepped out of the way so she could walk into the closet.

She leaned into the closet, slowly moving her head from side to side as she scanned the interior for the eye. "I don't see it," she finally said.

"It's hiding in my sneaker."

"How did it get in the closet?" she asked, squatting down in front of the row of shoes.

"I opened the door for it."

"How long has it been detached from the socket?"

"You don't seem surprised by this," I confronted her. "Why?"

"I will explain everything, I promise, but I need to put the eye back in the socket before it's too late. The longer it is away from you, the harder it will be to reattach. Now I need to know how long it's been out on its own."

I ran my hand through my hair, trying to think about how much time had passed. "It couldn't have been more than fifteen or twenty minutes, thirty at most."

"Get me one of the empty mason jars from the pantry."

I did as she asked, removing the lid before handing it to her. Then I leaned against the door frame and watched as my mother scooped up the shoe, flipped it over, and knocked the eye into the jar.

The eye tried to climb out, but my mother quickly put the lid back on the jar and then held it out to me. "Hold this," she said.

I took the jar, holding it up before my face. "What are you?" I whispered to the imprisoned eye. It stopped its frantic attempts to escape and stared at me, blinking when I did.

"We need to go to the clinic," my mother said, brushing past me as she left the closet. The clinic she was referring to was the infertility clinic my parents owned.

"Should we call dad?" I asked. He was away at a conference and was not scheduled to be back for a few more days.

"There's nothing he can do to help us right now." She placed her hands on the sides of my shoulders. "We'll call him and tell him everything tomorrow, okay?"

"Okay," I said, nodding my head.

"I can fix this," she said, cupping my chin with her left hand while holding the gaze of my eye.

"Okay," I repeated.

"Go get dressed and wait for me in the car," she said, turning and walking towards the hall. "I'll be there in a minute."

I took the jar with me to my room and set it on the nightstand while I got dressed. The eye watched me the entire time I was getting ready, always keeping me in its line of sight no matter where I was in the room.

On my way to the garage, I grabbed my sneakers and put them on after getting into the car. My mother arrived a few moments later.

A million questions ran through my mind as we pulled out of the driveway, but there was one I kept thinking about as I watched the eye sitting in the jar. *Why the closet?*

"Why did it lead me to the closet?" I turned my head so I could look at my mother.

"What?" she asked, keeping her eyes on the road.

"Why did the eye lead me to the closet? What was it trying to show me?"

"I don't know, honey."

"How are you going to put it back?" I changed the subject. "Won't it just crawl back out again?" I avoided asking the one question I wasn't sure I wanted an answer to, which was, *why the hell did my eye crawl out of my skull?*

"Everything will be fine," she took her hand off of the wheel and placed it on my cheek. "Don't worry about it." A few seconds later, she said, "Why don't you turn on the radio?"

That was her way of telling me she didn't want to talk about it. I wasn't in the mood to listen to music, so I spent the rest of the ride staring silently out of the window.

When we got to the clinic, my mom pulled around back and parked right next to the rear entrance. I got out of the car and stood next to the door while she unlocked it. Once we were inside, I followed her into one of the exam rooms.

"Lie down on the table," she said, putting on a lab coat and grabbing a pair of sterile gloves.

I set the jar on the counter before hopping onto the table.

"Are you going to tell me why this is happening to me?" I finally got up the courage to ask.

"I will after we're done here. Now lie back." She put her hand on my chest and gently pushed until I was lying flat.

A loud knock on the exam room door caused me to flinch. I wasn't expecting anyone else to be at the clinic. My mother walked over to the door and opened it, letting a young man wearing light blue scrubs into the room.

"Sorry, Dr. Lyle, I got here as soon as I could," the man said.

"Who's he?" I asked.

"It's okay, Travis, we just got here ourselves," she said to the man. To me, she said, "This is Travis, he is one of our nurses. Since your father isn't here, I asked him to come in and help."

"Fascinating," Travis said, picking up the jar that held the eye.

I smiled when the eye kept turning away from Travis as he tried to get a good look at it. *I guess he doesn't like you either.* I know I was being unfair to the guy, but I couldn't shake the feeling that he shouldn't be there.

"What's that?" I asked, propping myself up on my elbows when I saw the syringe in my mother's hand.

"It's an anesthetic," she replied, holding the syringe up and pressing the plunger to release the trapped air.

While my mother readied the needle, Travis put on a pair of gloves and began cleaning a spot on my arm, just below the shoulder, with an alcohol wipe.

"Is that really necessary?"

"It will help you calm down, honey. I can't have you squirming around while I put your eye back."

"I don't know," I said, something didn't feel right about all of this.

"You don't trust your own mother?"

"I do, it's just...," I couldn't finish the thought. I didn't want to tell her the truth, which was something felt wrong to me. It's like every cell in my body was screaming at me to run.

"You'll be fine," she said, holding the sleeve of my shirt up and centering the needle over the muscle of my arm.

I raised my gaze from the needle to my mother's face. When our eyes met, she turned her head away and injected the contents of the syringe into my arm.

"See, that wasn't so bad, was it?" she said, lowering my sleeve.

The effects of the drug were quick. Within a minute, I was feeling light-headed. My thoughts became muddy as my limbs grew heavy. *Where…am… I?* That was the last thought I had before giving in to the oblivion washing over me.

***

BEEP! BEEP! BEEP!

The sound of an alarm going off dragged me out of sleep. I reached out, feeling along the top of the nightstand for my phone so I could turn the annoying thing off and go back to sleep.

"Shit," I mumbled when I heard the phone fall to the floor.

I threw the covers off and sat up, swinging my legs out of bed. Bits and pieces of the dream I was having retreating into my subconscious as I came awake.

"Shut up!" I said to the phone, picking it up and pressing the button that would silence it before tossing it back on the nightstand.

"Great," I said, running my hands down my face, "I think I'm getting a headache."

I got up and went into the bathroom to grab some aspirin. As I opened the bottle, I looked up at my reflection in the mirror and gasped. For a moment, I thought I was missing my left eye. There was nothing but an empty socket where the eye should be.

What the hell!

I clenched my eyes shut. The image I saw in the mirror looked so real, but it couldn't be.

When I opened my eyes, I sighed in relief. They were both where they were supposed to be.

The sound of my mother's voice carried through the house, but I was too far away to make out what she was saying. Being the nosy kid that I was, I crept down the hall so I could hear what she was talking about.

"No, you don't need to come home early," I heard her say. "I've already taken care of it."

She must be talking to dad.

Immediately after that thought, the image of my mother holding a syringe flashed before my eyes. It had a dreamlike quality, like a lost memory resurfacing, but the feeling was gone as soon as it appeared.

"He's fine. He's sleeping," my mother said, obviously talking about me. "Yes, I put the sample with the rest, stop worrying about it."

My world started spinning. Images of something that looked like a cross between a spider and an eye crawled through my mind. I had to place my hand on the wall to steady myself. The sound alerted my mother to my presence.

"I have to go," she said, quickly hanging up the phone. "Everything okay, honey?" she asked, seeing me leaning against the wall.

"Yeah," I said, dragging my feet towards the breakfast nook where she was sitting. "I just have a headache.

"Did you take something for it?" The way she gazed at me made me feel like a specimen under a microscope.

I nodded.

"I have to go into the clinic for a few hours," she said, picking up her phone and putting it into her purse. "Will you be okay here by yourself?"

"Yeah, why wouldn't I be?" her question seemed odd. I wasn't a little kid. She frequently left me home alone.

When she pulled out her car keys and walked by me on her way to the garage, another image popped into my mind. It was of the exterior of the clinic, but it was dark out. It felt weird because I don't recall having ever been at the clinic at night.

"Maybe you should go back to bed," she suggested, scrutinizing me again.

"I'm fine," I snapped.

"Okay," She lifted her hands with the palms out in mock surrender, then reached out and opened the garage door. "Call me if you need anything," she said, walking out of the house.

After she left, I stared at the garage door, wondering why I couldn't shake the weird feeling that I had forgotten something important. I stood like that for several moments before I was able to pull myself out of my thoughts and walk away.

The feeling left me with a dry feeling in my mouth, so I grabbed a soda on my way back through the kitchen. When I closed the refrigerator door, I caught sight of the closet around the corner. Seeing the door reminded me of sneakers for some reason.

I popped open my soda and took a sip while I walked over to the closet. "It's just a closet," I said to myself. "There's nothing in here but a bunch of coats and shoes."

Why did I say that, and why did it sound so familiar?

I opened the door as wide as it would go and stepped back so I could see everything in the closet. There was a row of old shoes lined up on the floor, mostly belonging to my dad and me. There was one pair in particular that my gaze kept returning to. It was a really old pair of mine that should have been thrown out a long time ago.

Above the shoes, hanging from the rack, were several jackets. None of them seemed unusual to me. On the shelf above the jackets were several shoeboxes filled with random junk that my parents weren't willing to throw out.

I lingered in the doorway of the closet, trying to figure out why I had an overwhelming sense of déjà vu. I couldn't remember the last time I had gone into the closet, and yet I felt like I had recently been in it.

I was about to shut the closet door when I noticed a thin line in the ceiling.

What is that?

My first thought was that someone had drawn the line up there with a marker, but on closer inspection, I realized I was looking at the opening to a crawlspace. The panel covering the opening was slightly askew, leaving a tiny gap that was barely visible as a line. Whoever had opened it last didn't put it back correctly.

Why have I never noticed that before?

Curious to see what was up there, I went out to the garage and grabbed my father's step stool. After putting it into position, I climbed up and slid the panel to the side. The opening was much larger than I initially suspected. Two people could have easily stood shoulder to shoulder within it and still have plenty of room to maneuver around.

Warning Biohazard, I read the label on the case that was sitting about a foot away from the opening. It was about two feet wide and three feet long. The body of it was made out of a thick white plastic while the edges were trimmed with metal. Above the handle was a keypad with a little digital screen.

Why would my parents hide this in the closet?

When I reached out and put my hand on the case, I had a strange feeling. It was hard to explain. It was sort of like déjà vu, but not in the sense that I felt like I was reliving a moment. Something about the case felt familiar to me even though I was sure I had never seen it before.

I grabbed the handle of the case and pulled it through the opening. It was much heavier than I anticipated, throwing my balance off as the full weight of it came sliding towards me. It almost knocked me off the stepstool. Luckily, I was able to stop it from sliding any further by bracing it against my shoulder. That allowed me to grab the other handle and distribute the weight better as I climbed down off the stool.

The passcode programmed into the lock was a six-digit number. After setting the case on the kitchen table, the first number I tried was my mother's birthday. I didn't think it would work, but I had to start somewhere. I tried my father's birthday next. It still didn't open. To be thorough, I decided to try my birthday before moving on to other significant dates.

I can't believe that worked!

The second I punched in the last number of my birthday, there was a click, and then the sound of air rushing out as the latches of the case unlocked.

"Let's see what my parents are hiding?" I said, easing the case open.

There were several specimen jars nestled in the case, each of them containing a different body part. The largest jar had an entire arm in it, but that's not the one that caught my attention. The one I was drawn to was the one with an eye in it. I pulled the jar out and held it up to get a better look at it. There was a label on the top of it, with a handwritten date on it. The date was yesterday.

That's my eye!

Suddenly, all of the images that had flashed through my mind since I woke up began to make sense. They were buried memories trying to resurface. But they weren't buried any longer. Seeing my eye in the jar brought them all back.

She drugged me. Whatever she gave me at the clinic must have made me forget what happened.

I don't understand what's going on. Looking at the various body parts made me feel light-headed and confused. *Are these all pieces of me? They must be, but how?* I set the jar on the table and lifted my hands before me, looking for any mark or scar that could explain what I was seeing.

"Jason," the sound of my mother's voice made me jump. "We need to talk."

I turned to face her, trying to shield the case from view, "What are you doing here?"

"I got an alert that someone was trying to open the case." She held up her phone.

I stepped to the side so she could see that I had opened it.

"I never wanted any of this to happen to you," she said, approaching the table.

"Is this what I think it is?" I asked, picking up the jar with the eye in it.

"It is," she replied, taking the jar from my hand. "These all belong to you." She placed the jar back in the case. "Remember that night, a few years back, when you woke up and thought your arm had fallen off?" She reached out and ran her fingers down the glass container that held the arm.

I nodded.

"That was the night it started."

"The night what started?"

"That was when you started..." she fluttered her hands as she tried to think of the right words to say, "...started shedding body parts."

"How is that even possible?" I asked.

Nobody sheds body parts, especially not parts that can move around on their own. It was time for my mother to tell me the truth.

She took a deep breath and looked off into the distance, collecting her thoughts.

"No more lies," I said, making sure she wasn't trying to figure out another way to sedate me and make me forget.

"No more lies," she agreed, pulling out a chair and sitting down.

I decided to remain standing.

"I was so happy when you were born," she began, "I never thought I'd have to face losing you at such a young age." When she looked at me, I could see tears in her eyes. "I've never felt so helpless in my entire life. There I was, a doctor, and there was nothing I could do to save you."

"What was wrong with me?"

"Cancer," she said, wiping her eyes with the backs of her hands. "You had a malignant rhabdoid tumor on one of your kidneys. By the time the doctors found it, it had already metastasized to your liver and parts of your small intestine. At the rate it was spreading, they gave you less than six months to live."

"Why don't I remember any of this?"

"You weren't even a year old yet."

"What does the cancer have to do with these?" I picked up one of the other jars and examined the contents. In it was a collection of fingers shoved together like pickles.

"The doctors refused to treat you. They were afraid the treatments would only shorten what little time you had left," she paused for a moment. "You have to understand how desperate I was. You were my world. I couldn't lose you."

"Just tell me what happened already!" I slammed the jar I was holding onto the table. I didn't mean to snap. I just wanted her to spit it out. She could justify her actions after she told me.

"Do you know what CRISPR is?" she asked.

"Kind of," I replied. "It's some sort of gene-editing technology, right? My biology teacher mentioned something about it last year. Is that what you did to me?"

"Yes and no. The technology we used was similar to CRISPR, but it wasn't as refined. It had never been tried with humans, just mice."

"So, you experimented on me?"

"I saved you! If we hadn't inserted that new sequence into your DNA, you'd be dead."

"Yeah, you saved me, but in the process, you turned me into a freak!" In a fit of sudden rage, I slapped the jar off the table where it shattered against the wall, dropping fingers across the floor. I regretted the action as soon as I had done it, "Sorry," I apologized.

"Why did you do that?" my mother asked, jumping from her seat to run over and collect the fingers. Once she had gathered them, she stood up and turned in a circle, scanning the floor, "Did I get them all?" she asked.

"I think so," I replied.

I didn't know how many fingers were supposed to be in the jar. I assumed she had gotten them all since I didn't see any on the floor.

When she returned to the table, she grabbed one of the fluid-filled jars and shoved the fingers inside of it.

"Why do you keep them?" I looked at the case full of body parts as she placed the jar of fingers back inside of it.

"I need them," she replied, walking over to the sink to wash her hands. "I'm hoping one of them holds the answer to fixing you."

"Is that all of them, or do you have another case hidden somewhere?"

"Yes, that is all of them, now would you please go clean that up?" she pointed at the remains of the jar scattered on the floor.

I got up and grabbed the dustpan from the kitchen cabinet and began sweeping up the bits of broken glass, "This stuff is making my eyes burn, what is it?"

"It's formaldehyde, it's the only preservative that stops them from..." she suddenly stopped speaking.

"Stops them from what?" I asked, looking at her over my shoulder.

"Nothing, forget I said anything."

"Really, mom?" I scoffed, quickly sweeping up the remaining pieces of glass into the dustpan and carrying it over to the trash can. "I don't think now is the time to start hiding things. This is my body we're talking about." I gestured at myself, the dustpan and little broom still in my hands.

She sighed heavily, "Fine. It stops them from regenerating."

"Regenerating?"

"Your eye, your arm," she pointed at the jars they were in as she mentioned them. "After they were disconnected from your body, you regrew new ones within twenty-four hours. That same regenerative ability is possessed by the parts you shed. Look at the arm." She gestured at the long jar. "It fell off just below the shoulder and was able to regrow a completely new shoulder within 3 hours."

"Are you saying what I think you're saying?"

"I am."

"That's insane," I laughed nervously.

"Not really. If you cut a flatworm in half, both parts will regenerate into a whole new worm."

"Any of these could potentially regenerate into a whole new me?"

She nodded, "Now you know why I'm trying so hard to find a way to undo whatever it is I." She pulled out her phone when it started to chirp. "Shit! I've got to get back to the clinic. I've got patients waiting for me." She walked over to the case and shut it. "Please put this back where you found it," she placed her hand on it.

She studied my face for a few moments. "You know I love you, right?" she asked.

I nodded.

"We'll talk about this more when I get home," she said, walking to the garage door.

"Okay."

After she left, I carried the box into the closet and put it back in the crawlspace.

I spent the rest of the afternoon trying to avoid my thoughts. Being alone in the house gave me too much time to think, and that made me think I might be better off not knowing what was happening to me. My mother managed to keep me in the dark for a couple of years. Maybe she could do it for a couple more. I just hope too much time hadn't passed and that she could still do it.

Once I made up my mind about having my memory wiped, I occupied myself by watching television in my room. The events of the day must have taken their toll on my body because I fell asleep at some point.

I don't know how much time passed before I felt the soft tickle of something caressing my cheek. I woke up and immediately started checking my face making sure everything was in place. Thankfully, everything was where it was supposed to be. *What the hell was touching my cheek? Was it just a dream?*

I turned on the light and swung my feet out of bed, rubbing my face as I tried to wipe away the weird sensation that was making my skin crawl. While I was sitting there, trying to clear my head, I heard a slight rustling sound coming from behind me. The comforter on the bed had shifted, but I hadn't moved. *There's something behind me.* I slowly turned, expecting to see some wayward body part making its way across the mattress.

When I saw the half-formed body lying inches away from where I was just sleeping, I screamed and launched myself off the bed.

Both of its legs were missing, as was most of its skin. Its exposed muscles were covered with a thin layer of slime that glistened in the light.

"What the fuck are you doing in my bed?" I yelled, backing away towards the door.

"Your bed?" it asked, the question coming out as a gurgling wheeze from its lipless mouth. "This is MY bed."

HOLIDAY ACRES

"Are you going to get that?" my wife asked.

"Get what?" I didn't know what she was talking about. We had just finished unpacking, and I was taking the last of the moving boxes out to the garage.

"The door," she replied. "Didn't you hear the knocking?"

"I'll get it," my daughter Stephanie called out, running through the kitchen on her way to the front door.

"No, you won't," I said, setting the boxes I was carrying down on the counter before walking towards the front door. "You're going to go upstairs and help your brother put all of the toys away."

"But...," Stephanie began to protest.

"Butts are for sitting. Now get yours upstairs and help your brother." I pointed at the staircase.

"Fine," she pouted, stomping her way up the steps.

When I opened the door, the older woman waiting on the porch smiled at me. "Hi, Mr. Moore, I'm Betty Clark, president of the homeowner's association."

"Hi, Mrs. Clark, how can I help you?"

"I wanted to welcome you to Holiday Acres and see if you had any questions about the association's rules and regulations. I assume you had a chance to read over them before you signed them."

I hadn't read over the rules and regulations before I signed it. I assumed it was similar to the last place we lived and signed it without bothering to read it.

"No questions," I said. "It wasn't much different from any other HOA agreement I've signed," I lied.

"So, you're okay with the holiday clause?" She asked, raising her eyebrows. "With Easter coming next weekend, I figured I should make sure you understood it."

I had no idea what the holiday clause was but made a mental note to check it out once I finished cleaning up.

"Totally fine with it," I lied again. "It seems perfectly reasonable. You don't have to worry about us," I added.

"Okay then." She turned to leave but stopped. "If you have any questions," she held my gaze, while the smile dropped from her face, "Any at all. Please don't hesitate to ask." The smile returned as quickly as it had disappeared. "Have a great day, Mr. Moore, and welcome to Holiday Acres."

As I watched her walk down the driveway and up the street, my wife came up behind me and wrapped her arms around my waist.

"Who was that?" she asked.

"Mrs. Clark, president of the Holiday Acres HOA."

"What did she want?"

"She was just stopping by to welcome us to the neighborhood and see if we had any questions about the subdivision's rules and regulations."

"That was nice of her," my wife said, releasing my waist from her grip so she could return to the kitchen.

"Yeah, it was," I said, but I didn't mean it, I was too busy wondering what was in that holiday clause that was important enough to make the president of the HOA make a house call.

"Where did you put the HOA paperwork?" I asked my wife after I had finished moving all of the empty moving boxes to the garage.

"I think you put it in the lockbox with the mortgage paperwork," she answered. "Why do you need it?"

"I just want to check something real quick. Something Mrs. Clark said struck me as a bit odd."

"Nothing serious, I hope," my wife stopped putting away the dishes so she could look at me and read my face.

"I'm sure it's nothing," I said, waving off her concern as I left the kitchen to go find the paperwork.

The holiday clause was presented in the last section of the rules and regulations, right before the penalties for noncompliance. I was expecting the clause to cover what was and wasn't acceptable in regards to holiday decorations, but it was much stranger than that. This is what it said:

HOLIDAYS AT HOLIDAY ACRES

All homeowners must take part in the holidays listed below. Homeowners may celebrate the listed holiday as they see fit, but they must also celebrate by participating in the listed holiday activity. Every activity must be completed by 5 AM EST of the day the holiday is being observed. Each holiday must be celebrated on the nationally recognized date of observance.

Easter: Each household must place a dozen colored eggs in a wicker basket and leave the basket on the front porch of the home.

Halloween: Each household must carve a traditional jack-o-lantern and leave it on their front porch of the home.

Christmas: Each household must leave a wrapped gift on the front porch of the home. The gift must contain one personal item from every individual living in the house.

Failure to comply with these regulations or to interfere with the holiday activity of any other homeowner may result in loss of property or personal injury. The Holiday Acres Home Owners Association cannot be held liable for any damages or injuries incurred as a result of noncompliance.

"What the fuck?" I said louder than I intended.

"Mom! Daddy said the F word," my son Cole happened to be walking by the bedroom door and heard me.

"Are you done putting your toys away, tattletale?" I asked him.

He stuck his tongue out at me and continued on his way down the hall.

"You little shit," I said.

"Mom! Daddy said the "S" word," I heard him say as he walked down the stairs.

"Problem?" my wife asked, walking into the bedroom.

"Besides my son being a smartass and tattletale?"

"That shouldn't be a surprise considering he is your son," she smiled.

"Ha, ha," I said without a trace of humor.

"What's got you so annoyed that you're resorting to cursing and picking on Cole?" my wife asked as she sat on the end of the bed.

"What do you make of this?" I handed her the page containing the holiday clause.

"Is this for real?" She handed the page back to me.

"Apparently," I replied, putting the page back in place as I got up to return the paperwork to the lockbox in the closet.

"I guess we shouldn't be surprised considering the name of the subdivision is Holiday Acres. Obviously, they take their holidays very seriously. Seems pretty harmless to me," my wife said.

"Did you not read the part about the loss of property or personal injury?" I scoffed.

"I doubt they'd do anything that serious to anyone that didn't participate in their holiday traditions. That part is probably just there to scare you into doing it. What's got me curious is why those holidays? What about the rest of them?"

"I was wondering about that myself."

We didn't discuss the holiday clause any further that day. There was still too much stuff to be done around the house, having just moved in. By the end of the week, I had mostly forgotten about the holiday clause.

"Did you get the eggs and the dye?" my wife asked when I returned home from the store.

"What?" I asked, momentarily confused as I dropped my keys on the counter next to the shopping bags. Then I remembered. "Shit! I forgot."

My wife grabbed the keys and placed them back in my hand. "Hurry back," she said, kissing me on the cheek as she walked by.

As I opened the front door and began to step out, I almost collided with a man standing on my porch. His fist was raised to knock on the door. We both jumped back when we saw each other, managing to avoid bumping into each other.

"Sorry," the stranger apologized. "I'm Michael. I live next door." He extended his free hand to me. Dangling from the fingers of his other hand, was a basket.

"Darren," I introduced myself, shaking the offered hand.

"I didn't mean to startle you. Mrs. Clark asked me to drop this off for you." He held the basket out to me. "She wanted to make sure you had everything you needed for your first holiday with us."

"Uh, thanks," I said, reaching out to take the basket.

"It has everything you need, eggs, dye, and the basket."

"Can I ask you something?"

"Sure," Michael answered warily.

"What's the deal with that holiday clause?"

"What do you mean?" Michael looked over his shoulder at the neighboring houses. He seemed nervous.

"It all seems a bit odd don't you think, especially the penalties for noncompliance. What do they mean by loss of property or personal injury?"

"I'm not the right person to talk to about HOA matters. You should probably ask Mrs. Clark."

"Have you ever skipped one of the holiday activities?" I set the basket on the floor inside the house and stepped out onto the porch so I could shut the door. I didn't want my wife or kids eavesdropping on us.

"No!" he blurted out. "Never," he added, lowering his voice. "That's only happened once since I moved here."

"Who was it?" I asked, looking out all of the houses that lined the street. "Maybe I can talk to them about it."

"You can't," Michael said.

"Why not?"

"Because you're living in their house," Michael whispered.

"What happened to them?" I whispered back. Michael's anxiety seemed to be contagious.

"All I know is that they didn't put their gift out for Christmas. No one has seen or heard from the family since. A couple of us went to check on them when it happened, but the house was completely empty like no one had ever lived there."

"That sounds ridiculous."

"It is what it is." He shrugged. "Look, I've already told you too much. If you're smart, you'll follow the rules. It was nice meeting you, Darren. Welcome to the neighborhood." He sounded anything but welcoming.

"You okay?" my wife asked later that night as I sat watching her and the kids color the eggs Michael had dropped off.

"Just tired, I guess." I didn't bother to tell her what Michael had said about the previous owners of the house. I didn't want to worry her unnecessarily, plus I wasn't sure if I believed it myself. All she knew was that he had dropped off the basket as a housewarming gift.

"You look like you could use a drink." She walked over to the fridge, pulled out a bottle of beer, and popped the cap off before setting it in front of me.

"I won't argue with that," I said, saluting her with the bottle.

If I could go back in time and change one thing about that night, I wouldn't have had that beer. That one beer led to a second beer, then to a third, and before I knew it, I had finished the whole pack.

Somewhere around beer number three, Cole and Stephanie showed me the eggs they had created before heading off to bed. That particular memory is fuzzy. No matter how hard I try, I can't remember what color their eggs were.

After she tucked the kids into bed, my wife came back downstairs and got the kid's Easter baskets ready for the morning. She then placed the leftover grass, those annoying little slivers of plastic, into the basket Michael had given us before placing the colored eggs inside. When she was done, she set the basket in front of me.

"Do you want to put it outside, or should I?" she asked.

"I'll do it," I said, getting up from the chair. "I just have to take a piss first."

"I'm going to bed. If you're not up in five minutes, I'm turning the lights out." She ran her hand along my back as she walked by me on her way to the stairs.

I wasn't drunk, but I did drink enough to make me a little uneasy on my feet. On my way into the bathroom, I hit my shoulder on the door frame and then stopped and stared at the wood molding as if it had attacked me. When I left the bathroom, I stepped away from the frame to avoid hitting it again, but that just made me bump into the door, causing it to slam against the wall.

"Stupid HOA rules," I muttered to myself as I lifted the basket of eggs off of the counter and carried it to the front door.

When I stepped outside, I looked across the street at some of the other houses. All of them already had their basket of eggs sitting on their porches.

"This is stupid," I said, setting the basket down on the ground. At least I thought I was setting it on the ground. Because I was slightly drunk, my depth perception was a bit off. When I released the handle of the basket, it fell about a foot before it landed on the porch.

The basket tipped over, spilling the eggs, sending them rolling towards the street. It took me a moment to process what was happening before I started running after them. I was able to retrieve all of them but one, which I chased down the driveway and into the gutter where it disappeared down a storm drain.

"Eleven is going to have to be good enough. There were twelve. I'm sure the HOA will understand once I tell them what happened." I was trying to convince myself everything would be okay.

I would have replaced the egg with a new one, but we didn't have any more eggs in the house. I briefly considered stealing one from a neighbor's basket, but then I remembered what it said in the holiday clause about interfering with another homeowner's holiday activity. I decided to put it behind me and deal with it in the morning.

***

"Cole! Stephanie!" My wife's frantic voice woke me up.

"What's going on?" my throat was dry, and my voice came out as a croak.

"I can't find the kids!" she said from the doorway.

"What?" I got out of bed and rushed into the hall. When I checked the kids' rooms, I noticed that both of their beds had been made as if they had never slept in them. "Did you make their beds?" I asked my wife.

"No. They were like that when I got up."

Seeing the beds like that was strange since neither of our children had ever made their beds. They were usually just a jumble of sheets and blankets.

"Did you check downstairs?" I asked, running down the steps.

"Yes. I checked everywhere. They haven't even touched their Easter Baskets," my wife replied, following me through the dining room and into the kitchen.

"The Easter basket," I said to myself, remembering what had happened last night when I set the basket of eggs on the front porch.

"What did you say?" my wife asked.

"Nothing, don't worry about it." I walked over to her and placed my hands on her shoulders. "Why don't you make us some coffee while I go outside and see if they might be playing somewhere in the neighborhood."

"Okay," she nodded as she spoke.

I ran back upstairs, threw on some pants and a pair of slippers, and rushed out of the front door. I would have kept on running if it weren't for the Easter Basket sitting on my front porch. It was the same basket I had left out the night before only the eggs were no longer in it. In their place was a folded piece of paper.

I squatted down to retrieve the paper. It was a handwritten note. I didn't bother to stand up as I unfolded and read it. This is what it said:

Dear Mr. and Mrs. Moore,

We regret to inform you that you have failed to complete your holiday activity as is required by the rules and regulations of your home owner's association. Since this is your first holiday with us, and since you did try to complete the activity, we are going to give you a chance to redeem yourself.

We have taken your children and hidden them within the confines of the Holiday Acres subdivision. To redeem yourself, all you have to do is find them before the day is over. Good luck.

Sincerely yours,
The Holiday Acres Easter Bunny

P.S. I'll give you a hint to get you started: What is lost can always be found.

The paper crumbled in my hand as I stood up and clenched my fists. Someone in the neighborhood took my kids, and they were going to pay for it. They could threaten me all they wanted, but I draw the line at my kids. They had nothing to do with what happened. It was entirely my fault.

I cut across my yard and through my neighbor's yard until I came to the home of Mrs. Clark. Using my clenched fist, I pounded on her door until she answered.

"How can I help you, Mr. Moore?" She wasn't intimidated by my threatening posture.

"Where are they?" I thrust the note into her face.

She pulled a pair of reading glasses out of her pocket and used them to read the note. "It says here they are somewhere in the neighborhood." She put the glasses away and handed the note back to me.

"Tell me where they are!" I yelled at her.

"I don't know where they are, Mr. Moore. If I did know, I would tell you." She placed her hand on my shoulder, trying to comfort me. "This may come as a surprise to you, but I am not your enemy here, none of us are. Your neighbors didn't take your children, the subdivision did."

"I don't understand."

"Come inside," she moved to the side as she invited me into her home.

A few minutes later, she set a cup of tea in front of me and then took the seat across the table.

"We don't know what they are how long they've been here," she said, staring into the swirling liquid of her cup as she stirred her tea. "We just know that as long as we follow the rules and regulations, they leave us alone. You should consider yourself lucky that they are giving you a second chance. They aren't normally that forgiving."

"Do you know how insane that sounds?"

"I do, but you know I speak the truth. The proof is in your hands."

I looked down at the crumpled note. "What am I supposed to do?"

"Go find your children, Mr. Moore."

"Can you help me?" the question came out as a whine. "Maybe you could convince some of the neighbors to help me."

"I think you already know that this is something you have to do on your own. I will give you whatever moral support I can, but I can't aide you in any other way."

"I don't even know where to begin," I said, getting up from the chair.

"Start with the clue," she suggested. "Have you recently lost something?"

"I don't know," I said, letting her lead me through the house and out of the front door.

"You'll think of something," she said. "I'm sure of it. Good luck Mr. Moore." With that, she shut her door, leaving me all alone.

Before I started searching for the kids, I ran back to the house.

"Did you find them?" My wife called out before I could shut the door.

"Uh…Yes, I did," I lied.

"Where are they?" she asked, looking behind me, expecting them to walk into the room at any moment.

"I forgot I told them they could go to Easter service with the Carmichaels." The best way to make the lie convincing was to sprinkle it with a little truth. The Carmichael kids had invited Cole and Stephanie to attend the Easter service at their church, but I had originally told them no.

"I thought you told them they couldn't go." My wife narrowed her eyes at me.

"I did, but then I changed my mind. I figured it might do the kids a little good to hang out with their friends, plus I figured we could use a little break from them this morning and sleep in."

"What time are they coming back?"

"Sometime before noon, I'd imagine." That sounded like a reasonable amount of time for them to be gone before my wife started getting worried again. Plus, it gave me plenty of time to search the neighborhood for the kids.

"Where are you going?" my wife asked as I headed back out the front door.

"Michael stopped me and asked if I could help him with something." It was getting way too easy to lie about the situation. "I'll be back soon."

"What about your coffee?"

"Put it back in the pot. I'll drink it when I get back." I quickly shut the door before she could say anything else and so I could go find Cole and Stephanie.

Mrs. Clark was right, I did think of something I had lost, but it took me a good half hour of searching through neighbor's yards and knocking on doors before I remembered the clue. Going back to the house and talking to my wife had distracted me, but I was reminded of it when I saw the storm drain in front of the house. The answer to the clue was the egg, the one that had rolled into the storm drain. That is the only thing I had lost, besides my children. If you wanted to get technical, it wasn't lost, it was just out of sight. If I had crawled down into the drain, it probably would have been easy to find, assuming it hadn't been washed away or carried off by an animal.

They're in the storm drain. They have to be.

I ran back to the drain the egg rolled into and started calling for my children. I yelled until I was hoarse. When I didn't get a response, I went to the next drain and did the same thing. I yelled down every drain in the neighborhood but found no sign of my children. I was starting to give up hope when I remembered there was still one drain left to search, the one in the middle of the retention pond at the back of the neighborhood.

I ran to the back of the neighborhood and threw myself over the fence, all the while calling out my children's names. Thankfully it hadn't rained in weeks, leaving the pond dry and full of weeds.

"Dad!" it sounded like my son's voice, but it was hard to hear over the thumping of my heart. It could just be wishful thinking.

"Dad! Over here!"

That wasn't my imagination. That was my kids. I climbed up to the top of the concrete structure and was able to see them through the narrow slit where the water is allowed to drain once the pond reaches a certain level.

"Hold on! I'm going to get you out of there." I tried to pry the maintenance hole cover off of the top with my fingers, but I couldn't get any leverage. "Dammit," I yelled, pounding my fits on the rusty iron circle. I didn't want to leave them now that I had found them.

"Try this," I heard someone below me say.

I looked over the edge of the structure to see Michael holding out a crowbar.

"I thought you weren't supposed to help me," I said, reaching down to grab the crowbar.

"I wasn't allowed to help you find them," he answered. "But they didn't say I couldn't help you get to them once you had found them."

"Thank you," I said, trying to keep away the tears.

We shared a silent moment before he waved me off, "Go get your children," he said. "If you need me, I'll be in my backyard." He jerked his thumb over his shoulder.

I pried the maintenance hole cover free and flung it onto the ground. Then I used the metal rungs embedded in the concrete structure to descend into the drain and get my children. Before I could step off of the ladder, my daughter threw her arms around my waist and began sobbing uncontrollably.

"It's okay, I've got you," I said to her, hugging her as tightly as I could.

"What happened?" I turned and asked my son. I wasn't going to get anything out of my daughter until she was able to calm down.

"The Easter Bunny said you made a mistake and that to fix it we had to play a game of *Hide and Seek*," he said. I could tell he was doing his best to hold back his tears.

"What did this Easter Bunny look like?"

"He looked like one of those people who wear those costumes, but I don't think he was wearing a costume."

"What makes you think that?"

"I tried to pull his mask off, but I couldn't. Then he started laughing at me, and the way his face moved, it had to be real." The last few words came out between sobs.

"Come here." I motioned for my son to come over to me.

He took a couple of steps towards me, keeping his hands behind his back. When he was a few steps away, he stopped. "He said I had to give this back to you." He pulled his hands out and placed them in front of him, palms up to show me the cracked and dirty egg he was cradling.

"Put that down, son."

"I can't." He shook his head. "You have to take it. He said if he doesn't see this egg in his Easter Basket next year, there will be no seeking, only hiding."

THE SKY IS FALLING

CHAPTER 1

"What's that?" my son Patrick asked, pointing his finger towards the sky.

We were out walking along the beach that served as our front yard when he saw something moving among the clouds.

I looked up and squinted, shielding my eyes with my hand. It was hard to focus on the object my son was pointing at, with the sun shining directly in my face. I couldn't tell what it was. Initially, I thought it was some sort of aircraft flying by, but I quickly discounted that as it got larger and began to cast a shadow over us.

It's coming down right on top of us!

Right as that thought materialized in my mind, a sudden sense of panic took hold of me. *We need to move out of the way!* If we didn't, whatever was falling from the sky was going to land right on top of us.

There was no time to yell a warning to Patrick. I picked him up by his waist and started to run back towards the house, carrying him like a sack of potatoes.

"What are you doing?" my son called out while trying to wriggle into a more comfortable position within my grasp.

I ignored him and kept running. My attention was on the object hurtling down upon us. I prayed the house was far enough away from where the thing was going to land.

My wife came rushing out of the front door when she saw me running with Patrick in my arms. "What happened?" she cried out, fearing Patrick had gotten injured. Then she saw the growing shadow chasing us across the yard. She cast her eyes to the sky and gasped.

I leaped onto the porch, set Patrick down, and turned around just in time to see the object hit the ground a couple of hundred feet from the house. I couldn't believe what I was seeing. I blinked several times and rubbed my eyes to make sure they weren't playing tricks on me. They weren't. A whale had just fallen out of the sky. The dunes my son and I were walking along had been flattened by the impact.

That could have been us.

The whale hit the ground with enough force to shake the house like an earthquake. The shockwave knocked several planters off the porch railing and caused the wind chime to clank angrily. The windows rattled so hard I thought they might break.

I put my hand on Patrick's shoulder, "Go inside with your mother." I nodded towards the door.

He started to protest, but my wife grabbed him by the hand, leading him into the house.

As I stepped off the porch and approached the broken carcass, a couple of neighbors came over to see what had happened.

"Did that goddamn thing just fall out of the sky?" Rory, my closest neighbor, asked as he walked along the driveway. "That happened, right? Please tell me I wasn't the only one who saw that?"

"It happened," I confirmed for him, "It nearly flattened Patty and me."

I walked as close to the carcass as I could get, then started to circle around it. It was impossible to avoid all of the blood and guts that showered across the sand when it hit the ground, so I stopped worrying about it. It wasn't any worse than working on one of the fishing boats. My boots could handle it. It wasn't anything a spray of the hose couldn't fix.

"What kind of whale do you suppose it is?" Rory asked, coming to stand beside me once I had finished walking around it.

"Looks like a humpback." My eyes settled on the fleshy knobs that surrounded the remains of the whale's mouth, the only identifying characteristic I could find.

"I called Sheriff Donovan," Gene, my neighbor from further up the road, said as he walked up to stand next to Rory. I could see his wife talking to Rory's wife at the edge of their driveway.

I glanced over at the house and noticed that my wife and son had come back out to watch what was going on. I lifted my hand to call Patrick over for a closer look, but I was interrupted by a noise emanating from the carcass.

It started as a low bubbling sound that increased in volume and intensity until it ended with a loud pop, signaling the explosion of the whale's bloated intestines. It happened so quickly that I didn't have time to get out of the way. The ruptured bowels continued to sputter as they showered Gene, Rory, and me with a cold viscous liquid that stank like shit and vomit.

"Holy Fuck, that is nasty," Rory took several steps back and started to shake the goo off his arms.

"That's just great," Gene complained, wiping the thick liquid from his brow and flicking it onto the ground.

A few minutes later, while we were still trying to remove the whale gunk from our bodies, the sheriff pulled up.

"What the hell happened to you three?" He smiled and walked across the sand to meet us. When he was close enough to catch a whiff, he added, "Whoa, you smell like you just crawled out of that thing's ass!"

Rory scraped a bit of the sludge off his shirt and flicked it onto the sheriff's jacket.

"I'll add the cost of dry cleaning to the parking fine you're going to get before I leave," Sheriff Donovan pointed to Rory's truck, which was illegally parked on the side of the road.

"In that case...," Rory took off his dirty jacket and tossed it at the sheriff, "You can take mine with you."

We were all part of a small island community off the New England coast. Most of us had grown up together and had been friends since we were kids, the sheriff included. It was typical of Rory to give Sheriff Donovan a hard time and vice versa. They had been doing so since grade school.

Once they finished heckling each other, the sheriff walked over to the whale carcass and started asking us questions about what happened.

"Okay," the Sheriff eyed each one of us, "Let me get this straight." He started tapping his pen against his notebook as he read back over everything we had told him. "That thing," he stopped tapping his pen so he could use it to point at the body of the whale, "Fell out of the sky?"

"I know how ridiculous it sounds, but I watched it fall from the clouds," I said.

"If I hadn't seen it with my own eyes, I wouldn't have believed it," Rory added.

"I didn't see it, but I felt it when it hit," Gene offered. "It shook the whole damn house."

"You're sure it wasn't flung onto the beach?" He nodded towards the coastline, "Maybe by another whale."

I scoffed at his suggestion. "You know as well as I do there isn't an animal alive that can fling a whale that far out of the water."

"You're right, of course. I'm just trying to make sense of this, that's all." He resumed tapping his pen against his notepad, thinking about how he should proceed.

Rory, Gene, and I just stood there looking miserable, wanting to get out of dirty clothing.

"I guess you can go get cleaned up now," he said, putting the pen and notebook back into the pocket of his jacket. "I'm going to head back to the station and make a few calls. I'll let you know if I find anything out." He stood there for a few moments looking at the whale before glancing up at the sky, shaking his head.

Rory and Gene turned and walked back to their respective houses. Gene's wife walked a few steps behind him waving her hand in front of her nose to ward off the smell.

We are never going to hear the end of this.

"Hey Walter," Sheriff Donovan called out to me as I started to turn and walk away. "Would you mind helping me rope this thing off real quick? Once word gets out about this, you're likely to have a bunch of unwanted visitors traipsing through your yard, and I don't want the scene to be disturbed before I can have someone from the mainland come out and take a look at it."

"Sure," I said and waited for him to return from his truck with the stakes and caution tape.

Fifteen minutes later, I was in the shower, trying in vain to get the stink of whale shit out of my hair. When my wife came in to get my clothes, I told her to throw them in the trash outside.

Early the next morning, there was a knock on my door. Patrick rushed to the door and swung it open before I could stop him. That allowed the smell of the decaying whale to waft into the house.

I was hoping the sheriff would permit me to dispose of the body soon. The warm sunny day was making it decompose faster, and that made it stink a whole hell of a lot worse. It had gotten so bad that even with all of the windows and doors closed, we could still smell it.

"Hi," a young blonde woman wearing khaki pants and a grey turtle neck sweater squatted down to greet my son. "I'm Laura," she reached her hand out.

Patrick stared at her hand for several seconds before he realized she wanted him to shake it. "I'm Patty," he smiled and shook her hand vigorously. "I was almost killed by a whale."

"Is that so?" She stood up and offered her hand to me, "Hello, Mr. Ketterman, I'm Laura Thorpe. I'm a research assistant at the oceanography institute. I was asked to come and take a few samples from the Megaptera."

Megaptera? I looked at her puzzled for a moment.

"The Humpback," she clarified. "I just need you to sign this form saying you give the institute permission to come onto your property to collect the samples." She pulled the folded form out of the back pocket of her pants and handed it to me. "Once I'm done, the sheriff said you could have it hauled out to sea."

I glanced over at the whale carcass and the small crowd of locals gawking at it from the edge of the road. I couldn't wait to get rid of it.

"Do you know if that whale has anything to do with the hole they found on the ocean floor?" my wife asked Laura.

I turned and looked at her. I didn't know she had walked up behind me to eavesdrop.

She was referring to a thermal vent that had opened up not far offshore from our island. The research vessel that was tasked with studying it stopped at the marina a week ago to refuel on their way home. That is how we learned about it. News travels fast across the island.

"Hello, Mrs. Ketterman," Laura raised her hand in a wave. "I'm just a research assistant. They don't tell me much about these investigations. I just get stuck doing the grunt work."

While the two of them talked, I walked over to the small table we had in the entryway of the house and signed the form.

"Thank you," she said as I handed the paper back to her. "It shouldn't take me more than an hour." She whirled around and jogged down the steps and back to her jeep. I watched for a moment as she pulled a couple of large duffel bags out of the trunk and walked over to the taped off area.

When I turned back around to face my wife, I glanced at the clock on the wall and realized I was running late. "I've got to run." I kissed her on her forehead and ruffled Patrick's hair as I walked out of the house and headed down to the marina to start my day.

Most of the people on the island made a living through fishing; I made mine by repairing their boats. When I pulled up to my shop, I noticed a small crowd of fishermen had gathered at the end of one of my docks.

I walked down and stood a few feet apart from the group. "What's going on?" I asked Dale, one of my mechanics.

"I came out to scrape the barnacles off the pilings like you asked and found that," he pointed to the carcass of another humpback whale where it bobbed in the water.

Just my luck, I thought. Two dead whales show up on the island, and they both found their way to me.

"Do me a favor and call the sheriff. Ask him if he can get Dirk to come over and pull it away from the dock."

"Sure thing, boss." He headed to the office to make the call.

"Don't you guys have something better to do? Shouldn't you be out checking your traps, Colton?" I tried to shoo the gaggle of men away. "You've all lived here long enough to have seen a dead whale. Come on, get off my dock, I have work to do."

They grumbled and groaned, but eventually dispersed.

About an hour later, I heard the sound of an approaching motor and looked up to see Deputy Dirk, or as Rory liked to call him Deputy Dork, pulling up alongside the dock in the patrol boat. He waved his arm in greeting. I waved back and started to walk down to the pier.

"Do you mind hauling it out of here before it starts to stink up the place?" I asked Dirk as he pulled alongside the carcass.

"That shouldn't be a problem. I just have to tie it off."

I watched as he unraveled the rope and failed to figure out a way to loop it around the whale. I tried to help by giving him suggestions, but eventually gave up when it was apparent he didn't understand what I was trying to say. It was easier to have him pull the boat in closer so I could jump aboard and do it myself.

As I was climbing back up to the dock, I heard the screeching of tires as Laura pulled into the parking lot and slammed on the brakes of her jeep.

"Wait, wait, wait," she cried out, waving her arms to get my attention as she ran down to meet me.

I waited for her to catch her breath and continue.

"I heard you found another carcass."

"Yeah, it washed up sometime last night," I jerked my thumb at it over my shoulder.

"I need to take some samples from it before you have it hauled away."

"Why? Do you think it's connected to the one on my property?"

The whale floating in the water wasn't the first one to wash up against the docks on the island. I just assumed it was a coincidence that it washed up on my dock the day after one landed next to my house.

"Possibly, but I won't know anything until I get the samples back to the institute."

"Hold up, Dirk," I yelled to the deputy as Laura ran back to her jeep to collect her gear.

A few minutes later, as I was watching Laura take her samples, Dale came running up to me from the shop. "You've got to come and see this!"

I walked into the office. In the corner was an old TV that we kept tuned to the local news and weather channel. Dale pointed at the screen.

I watched for a moment and couldn't believe what I was seeing. The video being played showed several large objects falling from the sky, landing in the middle of a crowded city street. The objects looked an awful lot like the whale carcass that had landed on my property. Written on the bottom of the screen in big white letters were these words: IT'S RAINING WHALES.

"I'm done," Laura called out from behind me. When I didn't answer, she called out again, "Mr. Ketterman…I'm done…I told the deputy he could move the carcass…hello…Mr. Ketterman."

When I still didn't answer, she walked into the office to see what was keeping me from acknowledging her.

When I noticed her standing next to me, I turned and pointed at the TV, "Looks like you are going to be taking a lot more samples."

"Holy shit," was her reply.

CHAPTER 2

"I just got confirmation from the institute that all five of the humpback whales that fell out of the sky came from the same pod." Laura set a piece of paper on the table in front of Sheriff Donovan.

It had been two days since the whale landed on my property. The Sheriff was trying to relax after a couple of stressful days dealing with the mainland officials and the press. He glanced across the table, giving Greg, Rory, and I a look of exasperation at being interrupted.

"Two of the whales were tagged." She pointed at something on the sheet after the sheriff put his bottle of beer down and picked the paper up.

"What does this have to do with me?" He leaned back in his chair and waited for her to explain.

She pulled the sheet out of his hand and laid it flat on the table. "This is the island," she pointed to a small white icon, "and this is the last known location of the two tagged whales," she moved her finger across the paper and stopped when she came to the two small red dots about an inch away from the island. Both dots were labeled with a string of numbers.

"And?" the Sheriff asked after picking up his bottle and taking a drink.

"Whatever happened to the whales happened somewhere in this vicinity." She used her finger to draw an imaginary circle about an inch away from the island icon. "There could be something in the water. You have to cordon off that area. Prevent people from fishing there until we know what's going on."

Rory laughed at her suggestion, "He doesn't work for the Coast Guard."

"Even if I could block off a section of the ocean, I wouldn't." He pushed the paper back towards Laura. "Not without being told to by someone with a lot more authority than you. Besides, it wouldn't stop these degenerates from fishing there anyway." He angled the top of his bottle, so it was pointing at Rory when he said those final words.

In response, Rory pretended to turn an imaginary crank next to his fist while slowly raising his middle finger. Then he turned to Laura, "I'll make a deal with you, if you buy the next round, I will stay out of that area when I go out tomorrow."

"You weren't going out tomorrow anyway," Gene never could resist an opportunity to make Rory look bad. "You promised Carol you'd take her shopping on the mainland, and she invited Annette." Carol was Rory's wife, and Annette was Gene's.

"Thanks for reminding me," Rory said, reaching over and grabbing Gene's beer. "This is your contribution to the trip." He lifted the beer bottle and finished it one long swallow.

Gene tried to grab the beer out of Rory's hand before he could take a drink, but Rory was able to lean back and out of his reach.

As Gene began to demand Rory buy him a new beer, Sheriff Donovan's radio came to life, silencing everyone at the table.

"Uh…Sheriff," Deputy Dirk's voice squawked out of the radio.

"Go ahead, Dirk," The sheriff stood up and walked a few feet away from the table, looking for privacy.

Gene got up and went to the bar to get another beer, bumping into the back of Rory's chair along the way. Rory, who was in the process of taking a drink from his bottle, spilled beer all over his shirt.

"Asshole," Rory sputtered, slamming the beer bottle down on the table before reaching for some napkins.

"It's not my fault you can't hold your alcohol," Gene said, walking away.

"This isn't over," he called, wiping off his face.

Once Rory was sure Gene wasn't watching, he picked up his beer bottle and poured a little on Gene's empty seat.

"Did the institute tell you anything else?" I asked Laura, ignoring Rory's childish antics. I was just as eager as everyone else to find out why a group of whales had fallen out of the sky.

"Nothing conclusive," she answered, sitting down in the sheriff's vacant chair. "They think the samples might have been contaminated."

"Contaminated how?"

"The preliminary test results showed high levels of helium in both the blood and tissue samples I collected from the two whales."

The confused look on my face showed her that science wasn't my area of expertise and that I didn't understand the significance of her comment.

"Helium is an inert gas," she explained. "It can't be picked up by blood cells. That means it shouldn't be in the samples I sent them." She began to toy with one of the empty beer bottles on the table. "I have no idea where the gas could have come from. Nothing in my kit has helium in it, and the water sample I took near the dock tested normal."

Before I could ask anything else, Sheriff Donovan came back to the table. "I've got to run. Apparently, a school of dolphins just rained down on the Fish Shack across the island."

Laura stood up, almost knocking her chair over in the process. "This is huge! If dolphins are being affected, that means whatever happened to the whales might be moving through the food chain."

He looked over at her expectant face and sighed, "Come on."

"Really?" She seemed surprised the sheriff had invited her along. "You're not mad about before?" She held up the piece of paper she had shown him when she first arrived.

"I was a little annoyed, but I know you were just looking out for the people that live here. Besides, you're the closest thing we have to an expert on the island, and I'm sure your institute is going to want more samples."

"Let me grab my stuff, and I'll meet you outside." She hurried out of the bar.

After they left, Rory finished the rest of his beer and slammed the empty bottle down next to the one he had stolen from Gene. Then he pushed himself away from the table and got up to leave.

"Where are you going?" Gene asked, having just returned to the table.

"To see the dolphins," Rory replied.

"What?"

"Some dolphins fell on the Fish Shack," I said.

Gene sat down in his chair. His look quickly changed from one of interest to one of annoyance. "God damn it, Rory!" he said, getting up and putting his hand on the bottom of his wet pants.

"What," Rory said, "It's not my fault you've got a tiny bladder."

Gene grabbed the rest of the napkins off the table and tried his best to dry his pants.

"I've got to go see this with my own eyes," Rory answered, turning and heading for the door. "Plus, I hear the press is paying good money for videos and photos."

"Wait," Gene said, "We're going with you." He gestured at himself then at me.

***

Thirty minutes later, Rory, Gene, and I pulled into the parking lot of the Fish Shack. Word had already spread across the island. By the time we arrived, a small crowd of locals had already gathered around the small restaurant, watching as Sheriff Donovan and Deputy Dirk worked to secure the area.

The Sheriff walked over when he noticed us standing on the other side of the police tape. "I was wondering when the three stooges would show up." He glanced down at his watch, "Took you long enough."

"Gene refused to leave until his pants were dry," Rory bumped his shoulder against Gene's.

"They wouldn't have been wet if you hadn't poured beer on my seat," Gene replied, pushing Rory away.

"You started it when you made me spill my beer," Rory said.

"No, you started it when you stole my beer," Gene said, pointing his finger in Rory's face.

"Shut up and take your pictures so we can go," I interrupted. "I told Nadia I wouldn't be out late."

Sheriff Donovan shook his head. "Pictures, huh? What makes you think I'd let you get close enough to take pictures," he said to Rory. "Do you want the media to come swarming back to the island?"

"Depends," Rory said, "If they bring that hot little reporter from channel 3 with them, then yes, I would love for them to come back.

The sheriff stared at Rory. He didn't look amused.

"Fine, no pictures," Rory relented, putting his phone back in the pocket of his jeans.

"How bad is it?" I asked

"It could have been worse. One fell through the roof, a couple damaged some tables on the deck, and the rest landed on the beach. Thankfully, no one got hurt."

I looked past him to where Laura was taking measurements of one of the dolphin carcasses, but my eyes didn't linger on her for long. Something else had caught my attention, something on the horizon.

That's a lot of ships!

It wasn't uncommon to see a variety of boats passing by the island, but never so many at once. And they didn't seem to be passing by. They looked like they were spreading out and dropping anchor just offshore.

"What's going on out there?" I pointed at the line of ships.

The sheriff turned around and surveyed the horizon, "Shit...That isn't good."

"Is that the Coast Guard?" I asked, noticing the red band painted on the bow of several of the larger ships.

"Hey, Dirk," he motioned the deputy over with his hand. "I need you to finish up here." He placed his hand on Dirk's shoulder, "Do you think you can handle that?"

"Sure thing, sheriff," he turned to walk away and stumbled over the parking block behind him. He smiled, embarrassed. "I got this," He assured the sheriff before heading over to try and get Gene and Rory to return to the other side of the police tape.

The two of them had ducked under the tape so they could talk to Laura and take a few pictures while the sheriff was distracted.

"Do me a favor and keep an eye on him," Sheriff Donovan nodded towards the deputy as he lifted the police tape and started to walk to his truck, "I've got to get back to the station."

"What? Why?" I asked as he hurried by me.

"I think they're quarantining the island," he answered without bothering to turn around.

***

They were quarantining the island. I got a call from Sheriff Donovan later that night, explaining the situation.

"The island is under quarantine until they find out what's going on," he told me, "The coast guard has orders to scuttle any boat that tries to leave and escort any survivors back to the island."

"Did they explain why?" I asked

"Not exactly. I was just told that the island may have been exposed to a potential biohazard and that I was to assist the CDC in whatever capacity they deemed necessary. Which brings me to the reason I'm calling, they're sending a team of specialists to come and take a look at that whale in your yard."

"When?"

"Sometime tomorrow morning," I could hear him take a deep breath and let it out. These recent events were taking their toll on him. He sounded exhausted. "They're also requiring all residents to submit to medical testing, and the military is authorized to use force to ensure that everyone complies with the CDC."

"What kinds of tests?" I wasn't concerned about myself. I was worried about Patrick. He didn't do well around needles.

"They didn't tell me," there was a brief pause and then the sound of muffled voices, "Sorry Walter, I have to run, could you do me a favor and let Gene and Rory know."

"Sure," I said, then hung up the phone.

Early the next morning, there was a knock on my door. When I opened it, I expected to see a team of doctors dressed in containment gear. Instead, I found Laura looking over her shoulder as if she were afraid someone was following her.

"Sorry to bother you, Mr. Ketterman, but I didn't know who else to turn to."

I could tell she was nervous about something, but I didn't know what I could do to help. She would have been better off going to see Sheriff Donovan if something was bothering her.

"Come on in," I stepped out of the way and let her inside.

"Hello Laura," My wife greeted her from the kitchen, "Would you like some breakfast or some coffee?"

"Coffee would be great, Mrs. Ketterman. Thank you."

"Hi," my son waved at Laura from where he sat eating his breakfast at the kitchen table. She smiled and waved back.

"Have a seat," I gestured towards the living room and then went and grabbed the cup of coffee my wife had offered her.

I returned to the living room, handed Laura the cup, and then took a seat in the armchair opposite her, "What's on your mind?"

She ran her hands through her hair, "I don't know where to begin...it all sounds so crazy."

She sipped her coffee, collecting her thoughts. I waited for her to continue. I didn't have anywhere else to be. The quarantine had pretty much shut down the island.

"Have you seen the news...about the whales?" she asked.

I nodded in response.

"You don't actually believe it was some sort of freak waterspout, do you?"

There are a lot of things I don't understand, but even I knew the odds of a waterspout lifting a single humpback whale and flinging it out of the water were practically nonexistent. Having that happen to an entire pod of whales had to be impossible. Waterspouts didn't get that big.

"No," I answered, "I just figured that is what they told the media to keep people from panicking while they try and figure out what really happened."

"That's exactly what they are doing." She leaned towards me and started to whisper, "Except they already know what happened and don't want anyone to find out."

"What gives you that idea?"

"I have a friend at the institute that let slip a few things before they cut off communication with the mainland."

I pulled my cellphone out of my pocket and noticed I had no bars. When I turned on the TV, the only thing that appeared on the screen where those bands of color accompanied by that obnoxious high pitched sound.

"Why would they cut us off like that?"

"Because they don't want the truth to get out," she continued to whisper.

"Which is what?"

She looked towards the kitchen where my wife was cleaning up, and Patrick was playing a game on his tablet, then back towards me.

"Remember when your wife asked me if the whale in your yard had anything to do with that vent they found off the coast?"

"Yeah," I vaguely remembered.

"Well, it has everything to do with that, except it wasn't a vent they found, it was a," she paused as she searched her mind to find the appropriate word, "it was a fissure or a fracture."

"What's the difference?" I cut her off before she could continue. She seemed to keep forgetting that I am just a mechanic, and things that were obvious to her weren't that obvious to me. "Aren't they all just different types of holes in the ground?"

"I'm not talking about those kinds of holes. I'm talking about a break in reality. A door to another dimension." When she saw the look on my face, she sighed in frustration, "I told you it was crazy."

"What does that have to do with the whales?"

"When the research team from the institute was examining the samples they collected from the supposed vent, they discovered an unidentified microorganism, some sort of extremophile."

"Extreme file?" *That was an odd name*, I thought.

"Extreme-o-file," She corrected me, "It's the label given to creatures that can live in harsh environments. Environments that scientists once thought were incapable of supporting life."

She paused and waited to make sure I didn't have any more questions. I was going to ask her to elaborate more on what an extremophile was but decided to wait and let her continue.

"You're aware of how bacteria and viruses work, right?"

"I think so." That didn't sound very convincing, so I elaborated, "they infect cells and make bad things happen, right?"

"That's good enough," she smiled. "The samples I collected from the two whales were infected with the extremophile. That was the reason the blood and tissue samples contained high levels of Helium. Once the organism invaded a cell, it was somehow able to change it, make it lighter, and fill it with Helium."

"Wait. Are you seriously suggesting that…"

She cut me off, "I'm not suggesting it. That organism turned those whales and those dolphins into helium-filled body-balloons. They would have kept on floating to God knows where if they didn't freeze in the upper atmosphere and come crashing down."

"If this is affecting them, why have they quarantined the island? Why aren't they out there quarantining that…fissure or fracture?" It took me a second to remember the words she had used.

"Because it isn't just affecting sea life. Yesterday afternoon, two of the researches that discovered the fissure floated off as they were leaving the lab."

CHAPTER 3

"Does that mean we are infected?" I asked Laura. I assumed I was since I had been showered with whale shit, but I had to ask.

"More than likely," she answered. "Anyone who has come into contact with the whales probably is, myself included."

"How do we stop it? Can't we take antibiotics or something?" I was grasping at straws. I wasn't a doctor. I didn't know how they dealt with things like this.

"I don't know," she shrugged. "The last thing I heard was that they quarantined the institute and the city block where those whales landed on the mainland."

"That's a good thing, right?"

"I guess...If they can find a cure."

Both of us turned and faced the front door when we heard the sound of approaching vehicles outside. The noise also drew the attention of my son. He ran over to the window and pulled the curtains back. Laura and I joined him, the three of us watching as several Humvees pulled into the driveway.

Once they parked, several people filed out and gathered together in my front yard. The small crowd was comprised of soldiers and doctors. The two groups were easily distinguished from each other by the gear they were wearing. The soldiers were dressed in standard green MOPP gear while the doctors wore light blue hazmat suits.

"They've got flamethrowers!" Patrick said in awe as he watched a pair of soldiers walk over and ignite the corpse of the whale.

"Did he just say flamethrowers," my wife asked as she left the kitchen to join us. "Why are they burning it?"

"They think the whale was infected...and that we might be infected too," I told her.

"What! When were you going to tell me?"

I held my hands up to ward off her anger, "Laura just told me a few minutes ago. I was going to tell you, but with them showing up the way they did," I nodded towards the group assembled outside, "I didn't have a chance."

"What are they going to do?" A look of concern came over my wife's face as she saw a couple of doctors break away from the gathering and step up onto our porch. The rest broke into two groups and headed across the street to Gene's and Rory's houses. A few soldiers followed closely behind them.

"They look like astronauts," I heard Patrick say while my wife and I talked.

"They are probably just going to take some blood samples and maybe a few mouth swabs," Laura said when she heard my wife's question. I'm glad she answered because I had no idea what they were going to do.

I opened the door before they knocked.

"Mr. Ketterman?" The doctor asked.

"Yes," I took a step to the side, "Come on in."

"I apologize for the inconvenience, but we are going to have to ask you to step outside. It's safer if we limit contact with any contaminated surfaces."

"Of course," I placed my hand on my wife's shoulder and followed her and my son outside. Laura was a few steps behind us.

"Ah, Ms. Thorpe, we have been looking for you," the other doctor said when Laura stepped out onto the porch. The doctor motioned to one of the soldiers to come over, "Could you please take Ms. Thorpe to the command center, Dr. Calloway would like to speak with her."

"Thank you, Laura," I said as they led her away. She just smiled and gave me a quick wave of her hand.

"If you would, please come and have a seat. We will try to get this done as quickly and painlessly as possible." The doctor motioned to a collapsible table that had been set up next to a folding chair.

I sat down and did everything they asked, as did my wife. It took a little bit of coaxing and a lot of reassurance from the doctors and us to get Patrick to cooperate.

"That didn't hurt," Patrick said as he stood up. I know he was lying. I saw the look on his face when they inserted the needle. He just wanted us to acknowledge how brave he was.

I smiled at him and patted him on the shoulder, "You did great."

As the rest of the doctor's packed up to leave, the doctor that had taken our samples walked up to us carrying a large duffel bag. "I'm going to have to ask you to put these on," The doctor reached into the canvas sack and pulled out three weighted dive belts.

When I saw the belts, I knew then that everything Laura had told me was true. Why else would they provide us with something to weigh us down if we weren't at risk of floating away.

"Don't take them off under any circumstance," the doctor fixed me with her eyes to let me know she was serious. "I don't know how much Ms. Thorpe told you, but I get the feeling you understand how important your weight will be in the coming days."

I took the belts without saying a word.

"Oh…and don't leave your house. There will be several soldiers assigned to the area. If you need anything, let them know, and someone will be in touch."

"Come on, let's go inside." I placed one arm around Patrick's shoulder and the other around my wife's and led them back into the house.

"Why do we have to wear those?" my wife asked.

"I'll tell you when we get inside."

The rest of the day was uneventful. I took the time to work on a few repairs around the house while my wife occupied herself by cleaning. Patrick had his tablet and Nintendo, so he was set for the day.

As promised, a few armed soldiers were stationed at various points along the road and beach. Their assigned posts gave them an open field of view of all three of the houses on our street and the long stretch of beach that ran behind them.

I didn't risk going outside. I didn't have a reason to, but I knew the soldiers took their job very seriously. Rory discovered first hand just how serious when he tried to go outside and talk to one of them. I watched the whole incident through the kitchen window. The best part was when he was escorted back to his house at gunpoint.

With nothing else to do but wait, we called it an early night and went to bed.

***

"Help! Daddy! Help!" the pleas from my son jolted me awake.

I jumped out of bed and ran to his room, but he wasn't there.

"Help!" he cried out again.

I walked out into the hall and heard the shower running.

I opened the door to the bathroom and was frozen in place by the absurd scene before me.

Lord, please tell me this is a dream, but I knew it wasn't.

This craziness was our new reality.

My son was pressed against the ceiling, dripping wet and completely naked. He was desperately trying to reach out and grab hold of the shower rod, but he couldn't pull himself down far enough to reach it.

I looked down to see his dive belt sitting on the floor on top of his clothing. He started to cry when he saw me.

I pulled the shower curtain back and turned off the water. Being as gentle as I could, I pulled Patrick away from the ceiling by his legs, then wrapped a towel around his shivering shoulders. He was so incredibly light. I had to keep a firm hold of him as I dried him off. Otherwise, he'd start to float back up.

Once he calmed down, I helped him get dressed and put his dive belt back on. "You have to keep this on," I told him, "You can't take it off, even when you take a shower, understand?"

He nodded his head.

"Was I flying?" he asked excitedly.

I couldn't help but laugh at his question.

"Yes, you were, but not like a superhero, more like a balloon. You can fly, but you can't control it. That is why you need to wear this." I tugged on the straps of the dive belt.

"Will I be able to control it if I practice?" he sounded so hopeful. I'm sure he was already daydreaming about flying around the house.

"No, Patty. I'm sorry, you won't be able to control it." I looked up to see my wife turn from the doorway and walk away, tears in her eyes.

As I ushered Patrick back to his room, someone began banging on my front door. I walked downstairs and slowly approached the door, not knowing what to expect. I started to worry that the soldiers had heard Patrick yelling for help and were coming to investigate. I didn't want them to take him away from me.

"Open up, Walter!" It was Rory calling out from the other side of the door. I exhaled in relief, not realizing I had been holding my breath.

"Give me a second," I said, trying to get him to stop pounding his hand against the door. Once I unlocked the door, Rory didn't wait for me to open it. He grabbed the knob and let himself in.

"They're gone!" he said, brushing past me.

"Who's gone?" I turned and asked. He could be talking about anyone.

"The soldiers, the doctors, all of them, they packed up and left in the middle of the night. The quarantine is over, at least for our little island it is."

"What…Why?"

"Turn on your TV. It's on all of the news channels. The shit has hit the fan on the mainland."

I walked over and turned the television on, happy to hear the voices of the reporters. Not being able to watch the news during the quarantine was annoying, I was glad to have it back. But my joy was short-lived as I listened to the somber tone of the reporter.

Rory wasn't lying. Things had gone from bad to worse in the short time we were cut off from the outside world.

Whales and other sea mammals had begun raining down on various towns along the entire eastern seaboard, with reports as far inland as Atlanta and Pittsburg.

There is no way they are going to be able to stop this. I shook my head as I watched the alarming reports.

"The CDC has much bigger problems than a few infected people on a small island," Rory pointed to the newscast.

I started to flip through the channels to see what the other stations were reporting. I stopped when I saw the words BREAKING NEWS filling the screen.

"That's new," Rory said after reading the headline stretched across the bottom of the television screen.

It read, WHALES FALL ON EUROPE

The reporter that appeared on the screen began to give details about the first whales to fall on Greenland and Portugal.

"It's only a matter of time now," Rory smiled.

I couldn't understand how he could smile at a time like this. "Only a matter of time before what?" I shouldn't have asked.

"Before it starts raining men, hallelujah," he sang the last word.

I groaned at Rory's lame attempt at a joke. What's worse is that I wound up having that song stuck in my head for the rest of the day

CHAPTER 4

"Do you have to go with them?" My wife asked from the doorway.

I was standing on the porch, getting ready to join Sheriff Donovan, Gene, Rory, and Laura on a trip to the mainland to find supplies for our families.

"I don't think it's fair to let them take the risk on their own. Not when we stand to benefit as much as they do." I reached out and took her hands in mine. "We'll be fine," I gently squeezed her hands before letting them go.

"And you," I squatted down so that I was eye level with Patrick. "No flying until I get back got it. Keep your belt on at all times. You listen to your mother and behave around Mrs. Poole and Mrs. Baker."

Gene and Rory's wives were going to be staying with my wife while we were gone.

"Okay, daddy," he replied as I stood up and ruffled his hair. "Can you bring me back some candy? I don't care what kind as long as it doesn't have nuts in it."

"I'll see what I can find," I smiled down at him.

"Deputy Dirk and Dale are going to be staying over at Rory's to keep an eye on things while we are gone." I gestured across the yard at Rory's house. If you need anything, call them on the radio. I left it on the kitchen counter." I placed my hands on her shoulders and kissed the top of her head. "I love you."

"You better come back," she said. That was her way of saying she loved me, too, while letting me know she wasn't happy about me going.

I leaned down, picked up my bag, and walked over to the Sheriff's truck. I tossed my stuff into the back with everyone else's then joined Gene and Laura in the back seat.

As we pulled away, I waved to my wife and Patrick until they were out of sight.

"Jesus Christ, that took long enough Walter. Watching that was worse than being forced to sit through one of those cheesy romantic comedies," Rory complained from the front seat.

"Is he always this pleasant?" Laura asked.

"Only when he hasn't gotten laid," Gene answered. "Our wives aren't happy that we are leaving, and that means no loving for Rory."

"Doesn't matter, I still get laid more often than you do," Rory responded.

"Sure, if you consider your hand a sexual partner."

Rory responded by lifting his hand over his shoulder so that Gene could see his middle finger.

"Alright children," Sheriff Donovan chided the two men, as they continued to insult each other's sexual exploits

Rory turned his upraised middle finger towards the sheriff.

"You are seriously pent up," the sheriff turned towards Rory. "If this is how you are going to be the entire trip, maybe we need to pull over so you can go jerk off."

That got Rory going again.

The fifteen minutes it took to get to the docks were the longest of my life. Having to sit there and listen to Gene, Rory, and the sheriff insult each other like children was torture. Laura and I weren't even involved, and we were the ones that had to suffer.

After pulling into the parking lot, the two of us couldn't get out of the truck fast enough. I was so eager to get away from them that I opened the door and started to step out before the sheriff had even come to a complete stop.

Thankfully, the bickering stopped once everyone got out and started gathering their belongings from the back of the truck. The mood suddenly darkened as the uncertainty of what we were going to find on the mainland began to set in.

We planned to take the island's harbor patrol boat to the mainland, load up as many supplies as we could find, then head back as soon as possible.

"How bad is it out there?" I asked Sheriff Donovan as we walked down the dock to the boat.

"Bad," he replied, "Last I heard, the president had called for the evacuation of the entire Eastern Seaboard. Everyone was encouraged to get as far inland as possible. That was just over a week ago."

"That's ridiculous," I tossed the bags I was carrying onto the boat.

"I agree, but what do you expect from a president who thinks global warming is the answer to the unseasonably cold winters we've been having?"

I just shook my head then returned to the truck to help gather the rest of our stuff.

An hour later, I was leaning on the railing that ran along the back of the patrol boat, watching the island fade in the distance.

We were making good time until we reached the halfway point. The weather was clear, and the sea was calm, but we had to slow down considerably when we started to encounter an increasing number of whale and dolphin corpses floating on the surface.

"Can one of you grab the gaff pole and see if you can help push some of those bigger bastards out of the way," Sheriff Donovan called out from the wheelhouse. "We aren't going to have enough fuel for the return trip if I have to keep weaving our way through this graveyard."

"Not it," Rory called out. "I'm not going to risk one of those things exploding in my face again."

I got up and started to walk to the front of the boat.

"I can do it, Walter," Gene offered.

"I got it," I waved him off. "It gives me something better to do than sit here and worry about Nadia and Patrick."

The boat radio was our only means of contact with the rest of the world, but the Sheriff hadn't been able to get ahold of anyone yet, and that was making me feel isolated.

I grabbed the pole from the rack on the side of the boat and walked to the bow. A few minutes later, Laura walked over, stopping a few feet away. She leaned her arms on the railing and looked out at all of the death that surrounded us.

"The ocean is never going to recover from this?"

"What do you mean?" I asked, using the pole to push a whale carcass to the side. I then pointed to the left to let the sheriff know he should alter his course a bit.

"Without them," she gestured out at the bodies bobbing in the water, "And the other affected sea mammals to help balance the ecosystem, things are going to get chaotic."

"Won't the other fish just take their place?" I asked. I didn't know what I was talking about. I could tell she wanted someone to talk to, and I just said the first thing that came to mind.

"Yes, they will. And that is part of the problem." She turned around, folded her arms over her chest, and leaned back against the railing. "All of the animals of the ocean live together in a delicate balance. If you remove too many predators, the prey will multiply too rapidly and cause overcrowding, which can quickly drain an environment of important resources. That is what is going to start happening here."

"I've got a question for you," Rory said as he came over and joined us. "If these things inside us cause us to fill up with helium like party balloons, how come they don't keep floating back up into the air?" He pointed at the closest whale carcass.

She eyed him for a second, wondering if he was setting her up for one of his jokes or if he was being serious for once. She decided to answer either way. "Their bodies can't hold the gas any longer. Look at how badly mangled they are." She pointed to a dolphin whose belly had ruptured. "Too much of the gas is escaping from holes in their bodies to lift them back up."

"So…what you are saying…is that they can't float because they are passing too much gas?" Rory looked over at me then back to Laura, a big smile on his face.

Laura rolled her eyes and shook her head, "I should have known. You can't take anything seriously, can you?"

Rory just smiled, taking her comment as a compliment.

"Hey Walter, you need to hurry it up out there," Sheriff Donovan called out. "The sonar shows something big passing beneath us."

Gene and Rory walked into the wheelhouse to have a look at the digital sonar display.

"It's got to be a whale," Gene suggested, "It's too big to be anything else."

"Hurry up, Walter!" Sheriff Donovan yelled, fearing that Gene was right.

"I'm trying!" The bodies were not easy to move. The waves kept bouncing them off each other, sending some of them back towards the boat.

"It's rising!" Gene called out while pointing to the sonar display.

I felt the deck vibrate as the engine roared to life. The sheriff had increased our speed. The boat lurched forward but quickly got hung up on the fluke of a whale, causing us to slow down and drift to the side.

I tried to push the carcass out of the way, but the keel of the boat was making it difficult to wedge the gaff pole into place. Laura, noticing how hard I was struggling to free us, ran over and tried to offer her assistance, but it wasn't enough.

"Hang on to something!" The sheriff called out as a giant sperm whale rose out of the water catching onto the rear of the boat in the process. The impact lifted the stern of the craft several feet out of the water. A few seconds later, it slammed it back down after the whale rolled free and continued its ascent into the sky.

While everyone's eyes were on the whale, I watched in horror as Laura got thrown overboard. When the bow of the boat fell back into the water, it sent us listing from side to side. The sudden movement knocked her over the railing and into the sea.

She struggled to stay afloat, but the helium in her body made her too light. She quickly disappeared below the surface, the dive belt quickly dragging her under the water. The thing that was supposed to keep her from floating away was now causing her sink.

I frantically scanned the deck of the boat for something I could use to help her. All I saw were the life ring and the coil of rope hanging beneath it and the gaff pole I had let fall from my grip. Laura was sinking too fast for the life ring or gaff pole to be any help.

The rope!

An idea started to take shape in my mind.

"Gene!" I called out, "Give me a hand." I pulled my pocket knife out and cut the rope free from the life ring.

"What's going on?" He ran over to meet me. "Where's Laura?" He asked when he noticed she was missing.

"She fell in," I explained, tying the rope around my waist. I handed the other end of the line to Gene. "Tie this off," I said. Then I jumped in after Laura.

I entered the water moments after she did. I used my hands and legs to propel myself towards her as quickly as I could.

She fought to slow her descent, trying to claw her way back to the surface while kicking her legs behind her. Her struggle to survive allowed me to catch up and grab hold of her outstretched hand.

I pulled her close as I worked to unlatch the dive belt I was wearing, letting it drop to the ocean floor once I was free of it. That slowed our descent, but we continued to drift towards the bottom. I reached over and unlatched her dive belt and let it drop. The moment I let go of it, the two of us began to rise.

We were ascending much faster than I anticipated. Right before we broke through the surface, I wrapped my arms around Laura in a bear hug. I was afraid she might slip from my grasp when the rope reached its end and was pulled taut.

I could see Gene, Rory, and Sheriff Donovan watching us from the bow of the ship as we floated up into the air. I prayed the rope would hold.

"Mary Fucking Poppins to the rescue," Rory yelled out as the three of them worked to reel us in.

CHAPTER 5

"It's better than nothing," Sheriff Donovan said as he unceremoniously dropped the pair of boots on the deck in front of me.

Gene and Rory held onto me and kept me from floating away while I tugged the oversized weighted boots on. I had to pull them on over my tennis shoes before I began to lace them up. We only had one spare dive belt, and I told them to give it to Laura.

"Where did you find these?" I asked the sheriff.

"I took them from the display in the visitor center," he answered.

That was why they looked so familiar. Our island has a small visitor's center with a few displays about the history of the island. The boots he gave me were part of the deep-sea diver suit that stood in the center of the room. It was Patrick's favorite piece. I remember when he first saw it. He thought it was an astronaut. Thinking about that made me miss him and Nadia even more. I hoped they were okay.

"Watch where you're walking, Sasquatch." Rory jumped back to avoid having his foot crushed by my boot as I got used to walking in them

"Sorry," I apologized, giving him a wide berth as I passed by. "It's going to take me a bit to get used to these." I was heading back to the bow of the boat, so I could continue to clear a path for us. As I walked by the wheelhouse, I gave Laura a brief smile and a nod of my head.

She hadn't left the wheelhouse since they got us back on board. I don't blame her. The prospect of drowning at the bottom of the sea or floating off into the clouds was not one I wanted to experience again anytime soon.

"Looks like we are getting close," I said to Gene when I saw a cloud of smoke on the horizon. The two of us had spent the past hour taking turns keeping watch for carcasses.

"There's another," he pointed.

By the time the coastline came into full view, there were several plumes of smoke visible. It wasn't long before the smell of whatever was burning reached us.

"We should probably head north a little," Sheriff Donovan called out. "Get upwind from all of that," he gestured towards the smoke on the horizon.

"Do you think there is anyone out there," Gene walked over and asked the sheriff.

"I'm sure of it," he responded. "There's always going to be people too stupid to leave, or too greedy to let an opportunity like this pass them by. Which reminds me," he turned and looked at Rory, "We are only here for supplies, nothing else. Don't get any stupid ideas."

"Me?" Rory looked offended.

The sheriff didn't bother to elaborate. He didn't need to.

"I suspect most of the warehouses and stores have already been cleared out of anything useful. Our best bet is to try one of the shipping ports and start popping open containers until we find something useful," The Sheriff said as he throttled the engine and turned the boat north.

A short time later, we found a place to tie off the boat and gathered on the dock of one of the smaller shipping ports on the coast.

"We should split up and meet back here in an hour." Sheriff Donovan said. "Laura and I will check the containers on this side of the row, while you two," he pointed at Gene and Rory, "Check the other side."

"Sorry, Walter," he apologized for not including me. "With those boots on, you won't be able to cover much ground without exhausting yourself. It's probably best if you stay with the boat." He reached into the canvas bag he was holding and pulled out a pistol. "You should hold onto this," he said, handing it to me. "That boat is our only way home, don't let anyone near it."

Sheriff Donovan reached into the bag again and pulled out two pairs of bolt cutters. He kept one pair and handed the other to Gene.

"One hour," he reminded them, and then they went off to see what they could find.

I stood there for a few minutes, feeling useless.

There has to be something I can do.

I surveyed my surroundings. Other than the towering stacks of containers that lined the various docks, the only thing in the area was a few abandoned cars parked in front of one of the offices and a few container trucks.

As I looked at the trucks, I remembered that there were a couple of gas cans on the boat. That was when I realized I had found a way I could be useful and contribute to our stockpile of supplies. I was going to top-up those cans with gas. Fuel was something that was going to be harder and harder to come by. Stocking up now seemed like a good idea.

I stuffed the pistol the sheriff had given me into the waistband of my jeans and covered it with my shirt. I then went and grabbed the empty gas cans and the portable bilge pump. I was hoping to use the latter to siphon the gas out of the trucks, so I didn't have to use my mouth.

By the time I had gotten everything off of the boat and chosen a truck, I was exhausted. Walking around in those dive boots was like walking around with full cans of paint strapped to my feet. My calves were on fire from the exertion.

Thankfully, the truck I had chosen had gas in it, and the bilge pump worked beautifully at getting it out. I was able to feed the tube from the pump into the tank of the truck and draw the gas out with ease.

After resting for a bit, I was able to drain the remaining trucks of their fuel, which allowed me to top off one of the cans and fill the other one about halfway.

As I was gathering everything up to take back to the boat, I was feeling pretty good about my contribution. I was so proud of myself that while I was patting myself on the back, I let my guard down. That brief lapse was the opportunity someone was waiting for so they could sneak up on me.

"That looks really useful," I didn't recognize the voice of the speaker behind me. "I think I'm going to have to take that from you…and those fancy boots you're wearing."

I assumed he was talking about the pump. I stopped and slowly set everything back down upon the ground and turned around. Standing before me was a young man who I'd guess was in his mid to late twenties, pointing a small revolver at me.

He was dressed in baggie jeans and a t-shirt and was wearing several articles of jewelry. He must have had at least a dozen thick chained gold necklaces around his neck, a few of which had large medallions attached to them. On each wrist were several gold watches, and on every finger was an oversized gaudy gold ring.

I had never seen someone adorned with so much gold. It was comical, even under the circumstances. I knew he was using the jewelry to weigh himself down, but it was still ridiculous looking. I thought I looked ridiculous in the deep sea diver boots I was wearing, but this guy had me beat.

"Kick the pump over here and then take off your boots," He used the gun to point at the objects as he mentioned them.

"I don't think kicking anything with these boots is a good idea." The guy didn't seem very bright. There was a good chance I'd break the pump if I tried to kick it.

"Then pick it up and toss it over here."

I took my time leaning down and picking up the pump. I didn't want to make any sudden moves. The guy seemed jumpy. He kept darting his eyes all over the place. Once I stood back up, I tossed the pump so that it landed a couple of feet in front of him.

"You can have the pump, but I'm not taking off these boots." I could feel the sheriff's gun pressing against my stomach, where it sat in the waistband of my pants. I'm glad I had concealed it with my shirt. There's no telling how he would have reacted if he knew I was armed.

"I'm the one with the gun. If I tell you to take your boots off, you are going to. Take. Your. Fucking. Boots. Off." He emphasized the last four words with a jab of the gun as he spoke them.

"You know I can't do that. If I do, I'll float away."

"Not my problem."

As I stood there and thought about my predicament, I got the crazy idea that this guy wasn't going to shoot me. If he was, I think he would have already done it while I was busy siphoning the gas. It would have been much less of a hassle for him. That meant he didn't have any bullets left, or he didn't have the stomach to shoot me.

"Hurry up," he yelled.

"If you want them, you are just going to have to shoot me," I gestured at myself. "I'm dead either way. If you want the boots, you're going to have to come and take them off my feet yourself."

"I'll do it," he threatened me.

I was about to take a step towards him when I caught sight of something falling from the sky. *Not again*, I thought to myself as I watched the object fall.

"I will shoot you. I've done it before and have no problem doing it again." He adjusted his grip on the pistol.

I continued to watch the object as it fell, trying to identify it. The man noticed that my attention had wandered and began to glance to the left and right as he became paranoid that someone might be sneaking up on him.

"What are you looking at?" He asked.

I didn't answer. I just stared at the body that was falling from the sky. It was the body of some unfortunate person unable to weigh themselves down before floating away like a balloon. I watched it descend until it slammed into the roof of one of the abandoned cars. It hit with enough force to crush the top of the car and bust out all of the windows.

The man jumped and instinctively turned around when he heard the thud and the resulting explosion of glass. I took that opportunity to pull the gun out of my waistband and point it at him.

"Drop it," I commanded him.

His mouth dropped open in surprise when he realized the tables had turned on him.

"You drop yours," he said, regaining his composure and trying to act like a tough guy again.

I turned the gun to the side and fired it. "I've still got a full clip. How many shots do you have left?"

He jumped and covered his ears.

I fired the gun for two reasons. The first was to scare the guy. The second was to let the others know that I was having some trouble.

"Okay...you win," he said, slowly laying his gun on the ground.

"You're lucky I don't make you take off all of that...," I searched my mind for the word the kids use, "...all of that bling. Now get out of here before I change my mind."

"You're lucky I was out of bullets." He turned and stalked off.

Once he was out of sight, I picked up his gun and the pump, then went and loaded the gas cans onto the boat.

Sheriff Donovan and Laura were the first to return. They had a flat cart loaded down with cartons of various food products.

"Was that a gunshot we heard?" Laura asked as she stopped her cart alongside the boat.

"Yeah," I said, climbing back up to the dock to help them.

As we unloaded the cart, I told them everything that had happened since they left. Once we finished loading everything, I handed the two pistols to Sheriff Donovan.

"Do you think I should go look for them?" The sheriff was referring to Gene and Rory, who hadn't returned yet.

I pointed behind him at the forklift coming down the road. "Here they come now."

Rory was driving while Gene stood on one of the steps holding onto the bars that surrounded the cab. There were a couple of pallets stacked on the forks.

As they reached the dock, something made a large splash not that far from the boat. We all turned and looked out at the water.

"Is that what I think it is?" Gene asked.

"It is," I confirmed. "That one fell earlier," I pointed at the body lying on the roof of the car.

"Are we ready to go?" Sheriff Donovan asked after everything was loaded onto the boat. Once we indicated we were all set, he started the boat.

As we pulled away from the dock, I happened to glance up into the sky as a shadow fell across me. "I think you might want to speed up," I said, noticing the source of the shadow.

There were so many of them. I didn't understand why there were so many falling at once. *Something terrible must have happened near here.* I walked into the wheelhouse and averted my gaze, so I didn't have to watch.

As the bodies began to rain down around us, Rory walked over and slapped his hand against my back. "Didn't I tell you, Walter?" He pointed at me with his other hand, "I told you it was going to happen, and now it is finally happening." He had a massive grin on his face.

"Please don't say it," I said.

"For the first time in history, come on sing it with me, Walter, its going start raining men!"

"You're sick. You know that, right?" I said, pushing past him, singing the chorus to that damn song in my head.

EPILOGUE

The trip back to the island was uneventful. We returned home a few hours later and started to divide up what we had found so that we could deliver it to the residents who decided to remain on the island. When the quarantine was lifted, many residents fled to the mainland, thinking it would be safer. Less than half of the islanders remained.

The island was my home. I wasn't going to leave it. I was born there and expected to die there, just like my father and grandfather before him.

Things never returned to normal, but people were eventually allowed to return to the coast and resume their lives as best they could under the circumstances. Last I heard the global death toll was suspected to be around 100 million. More devastating than that was the loss of over 75% of the ocean's sea mammals.

Scientists are still trying to find a cure and think the answer lies somewhere in the link between cetaceans and primates. They were the only animals the extremophile was able to infect at first. Laura tells me they are close to a breakthrough. I hope they find it soon before the microbe mutates again.

"That shark is back," Patrick said as he looked out the window and watched the shark float by the front of the house.

"Again," My wife said from the kitchen, "Can't you do something about it, Walter?"

"It's harmless," I said, "It's just exploring its new surroundings."

The extremophile that had infected us and the whales had mutated over the past few months and began affecting fish. But, they were able to regulate their buoyancy, allowing them to float through the air and return to the water when they wanted. Laura tried to explain it to me, but lost me when she started getting into the technical aspects of a fish's physiology and how their swim bladders work.

I don't need to understand the why of it. It doesn't change the fact that fish can now fly. I've accepted it and moved on.

FIND YOUR NEXT CREEPY READ FROM VELOX BOOKS!

Where Darkness Dares To Tread by Connor Phillips

How to Exit Your Body by Christopher Maxim

Printed in Great Britain
by Amazon